THE END
OF
SUMMER

IRVING MUNRO

Acknowledgments

This book would not have been possible without the help and support of many people in Austin, Texas, and Pagosa Springs, Colorado.

To all of my dear friends in the northwest Austin neighborhood where I live, you know who you are. Thanks for your patience, help and understanding as I transitioned into my new career as a writer.

Thanks to Bill Tucker for your help in editing and structuring. Thanks also to Roger Wade of the Travis County Sheriff's Office, Detective Sergeant Jacob Beach of the Archuleta County Sheriff's Office and to Pastor Tim Clayton of the 1st Baptist Church in Giddings, Texas.

Last and by no means least, thanks to my son, Mark, for his help and advice and for his service to our country in the Marine Corps and to my wife, Aileen, for her love, patience, and support.

Internal formatting and cover design by ebooklaunch.com
Editing by Bill Tucker

Disclaimer

This is a work of fiction. Names, characters, businesses, places, events and incidents are either the products of the author's imagination or used in a fictitious manner. Any resemblance to actual persons, living or dead, or actual events is purely coincidental.

Chapter 1 - Texas fireflies

2005 - The Initial Investigation

"I'M TELLING YOU, Ethel, there is someone in Jim's backyard!" slurred Bill Andersen, as he sat on his back deck, enjoying his customary after-dinner cocktail. Bill and Ethel Andersen lived in Riverside, an upscale suburb of northwest Austin. Their neighbors, Jim and Mary McCord, had a vacation home in Pagosa Springs, Colorado where they went after every Memorial Day to escape the intense heat of the central Texas summer. Their home was left empty each year while they were gone.

"You're imagining things again, Bill," shouted Ethel, irritated that he had interrupted her favorite PBS show. "I'm watching *Masterpiece Theater.* Stop shouting at me! If something is so important that you want to talk to me, come inside. Don't just sit out there and yell at me."

Exasperated, Ethel got up from the couch and marched out onto the deck. "Okay, I'm here now. What did you see?" she demanded, looking in the direction of Jim and Mary McCord's home.

"I saw the flicker of a flashlight or something. One minute it was there and then it was gone," said Bill.

Ethel turned on Bill, her anger and frustration with his rude, self-centered behavior at boiling point. "Bill, I'm sick and tired of this. It has to stop. You think the entire world revolves around you and everyone has to stop what they are doing at the drop of a hat to come running to you. There is nothing to be seen over there. You know we always get fireflies at this time of year, you old goat. You sit there with a couple of shots of Jack after dinner and the next thing you know, you're imagining Osama Bin Laden coming through the woods."

"I tell you, Ethel, I saw something," said Bill.

"Rubbish. You're out of your mind!" With that, Ethel stormed back inside. Bill was left to stare into the blackness of the night with Jack Daniels for company.

~

Like most of the homes in the area, the Andersen estate sat on a five-acre lot. Being a neighbor meant that you saw each other occasionally while working in the yard or driving to the store. Privacy was important and everyone in the neighborhood respected that.

Still, this was Texas, a place where people watched out for one another. Woe betide the stranger who might wander into this quiet part of God's country or, worse still, try to break into a home. The typical owner was someone who took the second amendment seriously and would likely shoot first and ask questions later.

The following morning, Bill awoke to a feeling of uneasiness. He was still thinking about the night before and what he thought he had seen. Bill and Ethel had been married for almost forty years and, as Ethel constantly reminded him, he did have "one too many" after dinner some evenings and had "seen things" in the past. But this time, it felt different; he was sure that he'd seen something.

As he walked downstairs to the kitchen, each downward step sent a shudder that vibrated through his body and up through his head as the Jack Daniels hangover kicked into maximum overdrive. He ran over the events of the previous night in his mind and was sure he wasn't mistaken.

When he arrived in the kitchen, he saw that Ethel had a fresh pot of coffee already made. *I'll have my coffee first and think about it some more,* he thought to himself. *Maybe Ethel was right again.* He sighed as he poured the steaming hot coffee into his burnt orange University of Texas mug.

The coffee didn't help. His head still hurt and his mouth felt like he had eaten cat litter for breakfast. This health kick that Ethel had him on was a complete waste of time. There was no way he was going to get by with grapefruit and oat bran for breakfast. He snuck out the backdoor.

"Mickey Dee's, here I come," he muttered to himself. He could taste the Egg McMuffin as he backed the Lexus out of the driveway. "Just the ticket when you have a little hangover in the morning," he said to himself. "Hope John Harkins is there and I can talk to him about what I saw last night."

~

"Not like you to listen to what Ethel ever says!" laughed John Harkins as he shoveled another mouthful of eggs and hash browns into his mouth. John was a retired oilman and didn't give a crap about anything or anyone. He had been divorced three times;his last wife, Emily, had left him for her tennis instructor and they now lived together in Florida.

"Good riddance!" John had said to Bill at the time, "I always thought the tennis guy was a faggot. Shows you never can tell with people. Don't trust them, never will." That was John's comprehensive assessment of the human race. Bill loved the guy.

"Why the hell didn't you just grab your Smith & Wesson and get over there?" barked John. "To hell with what Ethel thought; you should have gone over."

"I know, I know, but I did have a few pops in me, Johnny. Alcohol and guns don't mix," said Bill.

"Let's finish up here and get on over there now," replied John. Bill could see the excitement in his friend's eyes. John was now in his full Clint Eastwood/Dirty Harry mode and was itching for someone to "make his day."

"Nah, don't think so, Johnny," said Bill, "but I do think we should go ask the cops to check the place out."

~

It was almost noon when Bill and John reached the Travis County Police Office at Hudson Bend. The main Travis County Police HQ was on 34th Street in Austin. The Hudson Bend office was a small gray single-story building with the U.S. and Texas flags hanging from huge flagpoles on either side of the glass-fronted entryway.

John Harkins led the way across the parking lot with a swagger that said he was ready to knock some heads to get things done. He had a wad of chewing tobacco stuck in his cheek and paused outside the entry to the office so he could propel a mouthful of dark brown spit in the general direction of a white trash can with Travis County PD stenciled on the side.

John barged through the doors, sauntered up to the front and announced, "We need to see someone about a house invasion in Riverside."

"It's not a house invasion, John," snapped Bill. "We need to get real here; we don't know if it's anything yet."

The African-American woman behind the desk looked up and said, "Do you two want to go out and come back in once you get your story straight?" She chuckled and turned her attention back to the current edition of *People* magazine.

"Sorry, miss, but we'd like to speak to a detective about a disturbance out at Riverside last night, if that's possible,," said Bill. John rolled his eyes in disgust at his buddy's lack of assertiveness.

"It's Mrs. Celia Brown, not Miss. Take this form, sit over there and fill it out. I'll see that it gets to the right person." Celia went back to the more important issues of the day, namely, Oprah Winfrey on the cover of the magazine.

John stormed away from Celia and shouted, "This is a complete waste of time!" He was livid that Bill had not demanded to see someone in authority. "They'll just take the form and throw it with all the others. It will never see the light of day!"

Bill glared at his friend. Maybe it was bad idea to bring him along after all. "Shut it, Johnny, this is just the way things are done down here. Being rowdy and belligerent won't help! Let's just get this form done and we can then see if we can talk with someone. And get rid of the chew. Clint Eastwood never had brown drool seeping from the corner of his mouth in any of his Dirty Harry films!"

As Bill filled out the form, the door next to Celia's desk opened and a guy who looked like he belonged in a Texas rodeo burst on the scene. He reminded John of the actor in the *Longmire* TV series with his boots, blue jeans, belt and Longhorn buckle. When he saw Bill, his eyes lit up.

"Hi, Billy! How the hell are you? What are you doing down in this neck of the woods?"

"I'm good, Garrison, haven't seen you in a while," replied Bill.

Garrison McMullen should have been a lawman or a steer wrangler. Instead, he was one of the most successful real estate developers in Austin. He owned a huge ranch on the shores of Lake Travis and had built most of the homes in Riverside. He knew Bill Andersen well and had built the home of Jim and Mary McCord, the very house Bill was in to report.

Bill shook Garry's hand and said, "Hi, Garry. Good to see you. You know John Harkins? He and I are down here to try to get the cops to take a look at the McCord place. I was sure I saw someone in their backyard last night and, as you know, Garrison, they are gone for the summer in Colorado."

Garry's brow wrinkled. "Someone in their backyard, you say? Are you sure their son isn't in from Oklahoma and staying at the place?"

"I just want to see if an officer can drive over there and check it out. It may be nothing," said Bill. "Celia here was good enough to give us the necessary paperwork to get the ball rolling." This little side compliment was completely lost on Celia as the admiration for Oprah in her red dress was getting the better of her and she had gone off to powder her nose.

Garry nodded. "I just finished up with Detective Stan Hardwick. He recently bought a piece of land over by Lake Buchanan and wants me to build him a retirement home on it. Let's go see him right now and see if he can just get on the radio to one of the officers in the area and ask them to swing by and check it out."

Garry turned on his heels, went back inside, and when he returned had Stan Hardwick in tow.

"Hi, guys, Stan Hardwick. It's good to meet you both. Come on back to my office. Garry here says that you want us to check out some goings-on out by Riverside?" bellowed Stan.

"They are filling out the necessary paperwork, Detective Hardwick," interjected Celia with a hint of desperation in her voice.

"No worries, Celia. We can get that done later," replied Stan.

This deviation from standard procedure resulted in Celia being on the verge of a nervous breakdown. Her mouth fell open and she stared in amazement at Stan Hardwick. She had just returned from a weeklong training course at 34th Street on new procedures in effective policing and here she was, less than a day back on the job, being asked to violate standard practice. This would need to be written down in the violation notebook and sent in with her weekly report.

Celia was busily checking the date and time of the violation as the three men disappeared back to Stan's office at the rear of the building.

Chapter 2 - Jedi knight

2005 - The Initial Investigation

IT WAS GETTING LATE IN the day when Officer Tommy Ross rolled up in his police cruiser at the McCord home in Riverside. Stan Hardwick had called and asked him to make sure everything was kosher at the residence as a favor for a friend of his.

A graduate of the Travis County police-training program, Tommy had recently been approved to be out on his own for routine neighborhood duties. He lived in an apartment in Cedar Park, a working class section of Austin. When compared to the upscale Riverside neighborhood, Cedar Park was at the other end of the Austin real estate market.

His apartment was on the second floor with two bedrooms and was about the max Tommy could afford. He didn't really need a two-bedroom but the second room gave him a little more space for his big screen TV and his PlayStation. Every night, he would settle down after a long day of law enforcement and become Count Dooku, Imperial Commander and Jedi knight in Star Wars Battlefront II. His Jedi accomplishments had been proclaimed across the galaxy and Princess Leia had honored him with the sacred cross of Revered Knights. A battle-hardened universal soldier was Tommy.

"Impressive pad," muttered Tommy to himself as he walked up the driveway.

Nothing seemed out of the ordinary. It was a two-story home with five bedrooms, four baths, a pool and a large backyard that backed on to Lake Austin. There was a separate building off to the right that had a living room, kitchen, two bedrooms and bathroom that could be used for in-laws or for guests who needed to be kept at arm's length. A large swimming pool and BBQ pit took up a major portion of the yard.

Tommy walked up, rang the bell and, for good measure, knocked on the huge metal door. It was a custom, wrought-iron door, typical to this type of home with frosted glass panels. He could see light shining through from the back of the house. There was no response and there appeared to be no movement. It was as quiet as a grave.

He walked around the side of the house to see if the owners were perhaps working in their yard. Being a seasoned Jedi knight, he knew you should never make assumptions and always be on your guard. The enemies of the Republic can be lurking around any corner. He moved cautiously, inching closer to the rear of the home, step by step, diligently looking for any signs of abnormal activity.

He never saw it coming; it struck him with full force on the side of the head. The automatic sprinkler system engaged and, in an instant, he was soaked from head to foot.

"Fuck!" he roared, "this is bullshit!" A Jedi warrior would never have been caught so unaware. "Fuck!" he roared again.

Tommy ran back to the cruiser, grabbed a towel that he kept in a sports bag in the trunk and dried himself off as best he could. He had a strange feeling that all was not right at this house. He couldn't put a finger on it, but his sixth sense was kicking in.

"Detective Hardwick? Officer Ross here. I'm over at the McCord place and everything seems fine, but I have a funny feeling," said Tommy.

"A funny feeling? What the heck is a funny feeling, Tommy? I just asked you to check the place out, not do a mind meld with it!"

Stan Hardwick knew about Tommy's exploits in other galaxies and, being a Star Trek aficionado himself, was pleased with his Mr. Spock reference. He knew Tommy was a good deputy and had potential but he could turn a case of simple traffic congestion on FM620 into the precursor of a Dark Star invasion.

"Have you checked every point of access into the property and ensured everything is secure?" asked Jim.

"I'll do another three-sixty, Detective Hardwick, and give you an update *ASAP*," replied Tommy. He climbed out of the cruiser and went back down the driveway to the house.

What if there is an alarm system? thought Tommy. *I better get that checked out before I go further.*

He called Celia Brown on his radio. "Hey, Celia, I'm out at Riverside at 2016 Braker Lane. Do we have any record with the alarm companies on this property?"

Celia had recovered from her earlier meltdown and recognized the location based on what she had overheard when Bill Andersen had been in the office earlier. "I don't have any paperwork on this, Tommy!" announced Celia, feeling that wonderful tingle of administrative power course through her veins.

"Come on, Celia. Stan asked me to check it out on the QT. Be an angel and check the security records, *please*."

The *please* did it.

"OK, Tommy. Just for you and since you asked so nice, let me check. Yes, there is a security service on the property. It's a division of Time Warner and I have the number here. Let me call them."

Tommy could hear Celia on the other line with the security service.

"This is Celia Brown for the Travis County Police Department. I can see from our records that you provide security services for the home at 2016 Breaker Lane in northwest Austin. Yes, that's the one. A violation last night, you say? And it will be OK for the officer to proceed ahead? OK, thank you. I'll tell him."

Celia came back on the line with Tommy to update him on the call.

"It seems that there was a systems failure on this property last night and they've been trying to reach the owner, Jim McCord, on his cell phone with no success. So they said that there is no risk that you will trigger an alarm as it's already down."

"Thanks Celia," said Tommy, and ended the call.

"The security system went down yesterday?" muttered Tommy. "Now that's a strange coincidence." Tommy suspected intergalactic interference and immediately looked to the sky. He decided that proceeding with caution would be the best approach.

Tommy went down the right side of the house and then circled around to the guesthouse. The gate between the guesthouse and the main house was locked securely, so there were no problems there. He walked around the guesthouse to the path leading to the boathouse. He could see a Malibu Wakesetter ski boat up on the powerlift by the dock.

These people have real money, thought Tommy. *One day, I'll be able to have a boat on Lake Austin, invite my buddies and their girlfriends, have a few beers and go wakeboarding on the lake.* For a moment, he was lost in the dream and could taste the beer and tequila shots. A smile of anticipation crossed his face.

Tommy continued around to the other side of the house, where he had a great view of the pool, deck area, and BBQ station. And that's when he saw her. She was stretched out on a recliner under the awning. She wore a brilliant white cotton dress that reflected the light of the setting sun. A large-brimmed sun hat was down over her face and Tommy could barely pick out that she was wearing a pair of large round designer sunglasses like movie stars wore. By her side, resting on the terracotta deck and just beyond the reach of her right hand as it dropped down lazily from the recliner, was a bottle of wine and a wine glass.

"Ma'am! Travis County Police! Is everything okay?" yelled Tommy.

No response. It was eerily silent. No music, nothing to disturb the serenity of the moment. Tommy thought that a little odd given the idyllic setting as she watched the sunset over the hills beyond the lake. If it had been him, he would have had some *smooth soul* playing in the background. He knew, however, that many people just preferred silence.

"Ma'am, are you okay? I was just passing on my route and your neighbor asked that I check on you."

Still no response.

The gates were locked and Tommy was unsure about hopping over the fence. He didn't want to scare her and there could be a guy around somewhere and weapons in the house, so no need to take any chances.

It was a big pool, and she was perhaps 150 feet away. Tommy tried to get a better look and inched himself up on to the railing that surrounded the pool to prevent kids from accidently falling in.

"Hey, lady!"

Still no response.

Suddenly, Tommy had a moment of genius. Relying on the skills that he learned as a pitcher in high school, he picked up a rock, went into his windup and sent a fastball into the pool. It landed perfectly and sent a spray of chlorine water all over her.

Nothing.

At that, Tommy thought it best to run back to the cruiser and update Stan Hardwick.

"Get over that fence and go check it out!" yelled Stan after Tommy updated him.

Tommy ran back around the house, jumped the fence and drew his weapon. He slid along the wall of the main house, his eyes darting from side to side looking for any possible threat. He couldn't see her from where he was but he knew that she would be around the next corner under the awning, between the pool and the BBQ.

He rounded the corner and there she was. "Ma'am, Travis County Police!"

Still no response.

He inched his way toward the awning. His heart was pounding now as he suspected that all wasn't right. Step by step, he moved slowly toward her, his eyes darting from side to side looking for any sudden movement.

Inside a minute, he was by her side. Tommy gently lifted the wide-brimmed sun hat from her head and her beautiful blonde hair cascaded over her shoulders and down over the sides of the recliner like molten gold. She was spectacularly beautiful. The only blemishes on an otherwise perfect face were her dead milky white eyes that stared unflinchingly at the setting sun. Looking but not seeing. Eyes that would never see anything ever again.

Chapter 3 - Reese

2005 - The Initial Investigation

TOMMY KNELT DOWN NEXT TO the body and called Stan on the radio. "Detective Hardwick, we have a dead Reese Witherspoon look-alike out here! The place is locked up tight and there's no one home. She's just laying here like she walked down from her bedroom, grabbed a bottle of Chardonnay and lay down to watch the sun go down. What now?"

"Okay, I'll call EMS and I'll be there as soon as I can," said Stan. "You hold down the fort, Tommy. We'll need to secure the area, but wait to do that until I get there. We can work the scene together."

The radio went silent as the sun sank below the horizon, prompting the cicadas to begin their evening chorus. Tommy went and sat by "Reese."

~

Bill Andersen had been running constant surveillance on the McCord place since he returned from the police station at Hudson Bend. Bill had his binoculars and was standing on his back deck like German Panzer Commander Erwin Rommel searching for any sign of General Patton coming over the horizon. He had seen Tommy arrive in the cruiser. His view had been partially obscured by the cedar trees that grew in the greenbelt between his property and the McCords', but he had seen most of Tommy's investigative efforts.

"Damn it, Ethel, I told you there was something going on over there!" snorted Bill.

"So? What were you going to do? Stagger over there and attack whoever was there with your empty bottle of Jack? Sometimes, Bill Andersen, I despair!" said Ethel as she went back into the house to continue preparing their supper.

Fifteen minutes later, the EMS arrived in their distinctive blue and yellow truck. Their sirens and flashing lights alerted everyone in the neighborhood that something unusual was going on. Everyone came out onto their front yards or walked the street to try to get more information. By this time, Bill Andersen had joined his neighbors and was explaining to anyone who would listen the vital role that he had played in the day's events.

Stan Hardwick arrived in his unmarked, standard issue, Ford Crown Victoria cruiser.

"Keep these people back!" barked Stan.

Tommy took the roll of crime scene tape, tied it to a large oak tree to the left of the McCord residence and around the mailbox to the right in an attempt to keep the driveway clear. He took another length of tape and strung it around several trees and onto the gate at the side of the pool entrance. After all this was done, some neighbors still needed to be politely pushed behind the line so EMS could get on with their work.

Marla Edwards, the head paramedic on the EMS team, stepped forward, placed her equipment bag by the side of the recliner and began her examination of the body, recording everything as she went. Later in the day, this first-responder record would be delivered with the body to the medical examiner. There were no obvious signs of any trauma. There was no blood or any other body fluids that had stained the white cotton dress. Marla confirmed what they all already knew: the beautiful lady lying on the recliner was dead. Other than that, there was nothing obvious to suggest how she died. That would be the job of the medical examiner to figure out. She did note, however, that there was substantial bruising on both arms and that on the right arm there appeared to be needle marks.

Stan looked down at "Reese" and said, "What a beautiful woman! Why would anyone want to do this?"

Stan got on the radio and asked for more resources to get out to Riverside to help. Dispatch confirmed that Detectives Marie Mason and George Turner were on their way.

One of the EMS team was trying to adjust the recliner so that the body was horizontal.

"Don't do that!" yelled Stan, "We need to take photographs of the crime scene before anything is touched. Marla, if you are done with your initial examination, please take your team back to your truck. We will call you back down here when we are done with our work and you can then take the body to the ME."

Stan Hardwick hated to use the term *Jane Doe*.

"Tommy, this woman is far too beautiful to be called Jane Doe. I hate that term anyway. What was the name you used earlier when you discovered the body and called me?" said Stan.

"Reese Witherspoon. Last weekend, I had a date with a girl from Cedar Park and we went to the movies and saw *Just Like Heaven*. Reese Witherspoon played the lead. The minute I took the sun hat from the dead woman's head and saw how beautiful she was, I thought of Reese Witherspoon," replied Tommy.

"Then *Reese* it is. We'll call her *Reese* until we know her true identity," said Stan.

Reese had a French manicure on her fingers and toes and her makeup was perfect apart from a pair of water blotches on her cheeks caused by Tommy's pitch hitting the pool. Her white cotton dress had been recently laundered and her hair looked like she had just come from a salon. A bottle of wine and a wine glass were adjacent the recliner. They were in the perfect location by her right hand and the glass contained a small quantity of wine and red lipstick on the rim. It was as if she had poured a glass, drank a mouthful, put the bottle and glass down on the tile and lay back to enjoy the sunset. Someone had gone to a lot of trouble and effort to ensure that she looked radiant, and it had worked. What they were to discover later about *Reese* would not align with this degree of care and concern.

Another unmarked Crown Victoria pulled up alongside the EMS truck. Marie Mason and George Turner made their way past the truck and down the driveway. They met up with Stan and Tommy in the backyard.

"Fabulous home," said Marie as she scanned the backyard.

"A little more than you can afford, Marie," replied Stan. "Glad you guys could join us. Let's get to work."

They measured, sketched, and photographed everything that seemed to be relevant.

Marie checked out the main house and the guesthouse. They were both locked. They would get permission from the owners later to gain access and check the inside of each building.

George Turner was assigned the remainder of the yard down to the lakeshore, including the boat dock. Nothing looked out of place. He searched the walkway from the dock to the pool, including the immediate surrounding area, and nothing seemed out of place there either.

Stan and Tommy concentrated on *Reese* and the recliner. They speculated that the killer must have prepared her somewhere else and brought her there. It looked like she had been dressed just prior to being placed on the recliner. How could the killer have done that?

George Turner was the forensics expert on the team. After all measurements and photographs had been taken, he went over the recliner for any sign of fingerprints. The dead woman's body would be fingerprinted at the ME's office later.

There were no fingerprints found on the recliner. This suggested that it had been cleaned, as it would have been unreasonable not to find any prints on this piece of poolside furniture that was in regular use. George then asked that everyone leave the backyard area and he walked it off, looking for any evidence that seemed unusual and may have been left by the killer. Nothing was found.

With their investigation complete, Stan and George Turner gave clearance to the EMS team to remove the body. With the body gone, George went over the recliner one more time. Still no fingerprints were found.

Chapter 4 - Jim McCord

2005 - The Initial Investigation

THE NEXT DAY, *REESE* was laid out on a cold, steel table in the Travis County forensics lab. Stan Hardwick looked on as Sven Stevenson, the Travis County medical examiner, stood over her and began his work.

Reese's clothes had been removed. Her body was a patchwork quilt of bruises and contusions from head to toe; only her face had been left undamaged. Stan had seen many dead bodies over the course of his career, but seeing *Reese* lying there, her body a testimony to the depravity of another human being, tore at his soul.

Sven Stevenson spoke into his handheld recorder as he walked around the body.

"The body is that of a young woman, natural blond hair, five foot ten inches tall and weighing one hundred and thirty-two pounds. There is a strong odor of chlorine mixed with perfume. We should run tests on the skin to determine the cause of the smell, but my initial conclusion is that she may have been in the pool before death. Another possibility is that the body may have been washed in a bleach solution and then the perfume applied."

Sven bent over her torso and spoke into the recorder's mouthpiece. "We can be more specific later, but my assessment at this time is that she is in her early twenties and quite physically fit. She has well-developed muscles in her arms and shoulders, which would suggest that she might have done manual labor or worked out regularly. "

Sven picked up *Reese's* hand and said, "Her fingernails have been manicured. This is strange based on the condition of the rest of the body, and the pristine condition of the manicure would suggest that it was done postmortem."

"The bruising around her wrists and ankles suggests that she has been restrained. The type of bruising suggests a shackle of some sort, not rope. She has needle marks on her right arm. They do not look like those caused by a habitual drug user and therefore I would conclude that she was injected to disable her. I will be able to tell more after I run toxicology."

Stan fought the urge to turn away as Sven flipped *Reese* over and continued.

"There are areas of intense bruising on the buttocks, the thighs and lower abdomen. The bruising on the remainder of the body looks like it is caused by punching or pounding by a flat object. There are no cuts visible."

"There is significant tearing of the tissue of the vagina and anus that would suggest violent penetration. I have seen similar injuries in other sexually abused bodies and would speculate, at this stage, that the killer carried out this penetration using solid objects of some type. I will know more when I open her up."

"Open her up!" Stan mumbled to himself. He hated that phrase. You open up a Christmas present. This is a human being, for God's sake! He wished that Sven could find a better expression, but for now, he didn't have an alternative.

"I'll have something more definitive in the morning," stated Sven.

Stan left the ME's facility trying to contain his emotions. *This one is getting to me*, he thought as he got into his Crown Victoria and headed back to Hudson Bend to meet with the team.

~

Stan barged into the conference room of the station and bellowed, "Marie and George, you two get started on interviewing all the neighbors starting first thing in the morning.

"We need to find out if anyone saw anything last night. We know that Bill Andersen was a witness, but given that he was two sheets to the wind who knows what he saw. Tommy, you get hold of Jim and Mary McCord at their place in Colorado. The security company tried to reach Jim a day or so ago without any luck. Find them, talk to them and see what they know. They'll be out of their wits when we break the news to them, so, Tommy, go softly please."

The office phone rang right in the middle of the briefing. "Hello, Stan Hardwick here."

"What the fuck is going on there!" screamed Jim McCord. "Why wasn't I called immediately before you entered my property? I want to speak to Police Chief Dunwoody and I want to speak to him now!"

"I would ask that you calm down please, Mr. McCord," said Stan.

It was like trying to extinguish a forest fire with a garden hose. There was no way Jim McCord was calming down.

"Am I right in guessing Bill Andersen called you, Mr. McCord?" continued Stan.

"So what if he has? He's a good neighbor and his only interest was to let me know that some arrogant police department assholes were walking all over my property and scaring the crap out of everyone!"

Jim McCord was running off at the mouth and Stan knew instinctively why.

"There is no need for that language, Mr. McCord and may I ask you, sir, have you been drinking? If so, perhaps we leave this until morning. I'll call you first thing. What is the best number to reach you on, Mr. McCord?"

"Call me on my cell," said McCord. It took him three attempts to give Stan the correct cell number.

"Call me at 7:30, no, better make it 8:00," slurred McCord. "You better have a good explanation for all of this or Bill

Dunwoody will have your balls mounted on his wall!" Jim McCord hung up the phone.

"Yep, McCord has been drinking," muttered Stan Hardwick. "My balls are safe for another night."

~

The following morning on his way to the Hudson Bend office, Tommy stopped off at Rudy's on FM620 for breakfast tacos. It was 6:30 and they had just opened for the morning rush. Rudy's was Tommy's favorite BBQ joint and, although it was a chain, they had great food.

The temperature was already seventy-nine and it would be close to one hundred by midday, typical late summer weather in Austin. By the end of September, it would be back down to the eighties.

"Good morning, my Jedi knight!" quipped Marie as Tommy walked into the office.

"I guess you don't want a breakfast taco then?" responded Tommy with a little smirk and twinkle in his eye.

"You come bearing gifts, o' great Jedi!" responded Marie as she knelt, adopting a groveling pose.

"I have to ensure that my fellow warriors are well fed," said Tommy and threw her a sausage, egg and cheese.

"Thank you, o' great knight!"

Suddenly, Darth Vader aka Stan Hardwick burst into the room, "Cut the crap; let's get to work," he bellowed.

He obviously didn't get any last night, thought Marie.

"Change of plan, Tommy," said Stan. "I'll take Jim and Mary McCord, you check out their son, Bobby. He lives in Oklahoma and played for the Sooners as a kid. Didn't make it to the NFL but a pretty reasonable tight end, I understand. George, you and Marie canvas the neighbors as we discussed last night and let's all get together back here at 6:30 tonight for a review of the day."

Chapter 5 - Neighborly love

2005 - The Initial Investigation

"GOOD MORNING, MR. McCORD," said Stan. It was 8:00 a.m. on the dot when Stan called Jim McCord on his cell as he had requested.

"Good morning, Mr. Hardwick," said McCord, feeling decidedly shaky from a night of carousing in the Marriott Hotel bar in San Antonio.

"You can call me Stan,"

"And you can call me Jim. Sorry about last night, Stan, I had had a couple of cocktails as you had guessed and my mouth got away from me. It won't happen again."

"So, Jim, what exactly did Bill Andersen tell you when he called?" asked Stan.

"He told me that there had been a woman's body discovered laying by my pool and that you guys were all over the place like flies on shit. Oh, sorry, Stan, there goes my mouth again."

Stan was beginning to lose patience with Jim McCord.

"Look, Jim. We're just trying to get as much information gathered as we can on this. The faster we gather the data, the faster we can try to understand who this woman was and how she got into your backyard. Given that you are in Colorado, it's unlikely that *you* put her there," said Stan.

"Oh, I'm not in Colorado, Stan. I'm down here in San Antonio attending a cyber-security conference at the Lockheed Martin facility."

Jim McCord's words hit Stan in the chest like one of Lockheed Martin's surface-to-air missiles. "You're not in Colorado?" he asked. "You need to get up here to Austin. How quickly can you make that happen?"

~

While Stan was having his call with Jim McCord, in the adjoining office Tommy made the call to his son in Oklahoma.

"Hi, is this Bobby McCord? This is Deputy Tommy Ross from the Travis County Police Department in Austin."

"Yes, I'm Bobby McCord. What's happened? Is my mom and dad okay?"

"Your parents are fine, sir, but there has been a situation. We have found a body on your parents' property and we are trying to identify her," responded Tommy.

"A woman's body?" asked Bobby.

"Yes, she appears to be in her early twenties. About your age, Mr. McCord."

"Are you trying to suggest that I had something to do with this?"

"No, sorry, Mr. McCord, I didn't mean to suggest that at all. Simply that she is a young woman about your age and discovered on your parents' property."

Tommy realized that he had made a rookie mistake. There had been no reason to mention that the body was a woman and it had been wrong to draw the age comparison.

"Okay," said Bobby, calming down. "Has my dad been contacted? My mom will be a basket case when she finds out. I better get on a plane and get down there."

Bobby McCord was now engaged and trying to help. Tommy sensed it was about supporting his parents, not about trying to protect his ass. Tommy thought he might like to meet Bobby McCord sometime. He seemed like a standup guy.

"I don't think that will be necessary, Mr. McCord. My supervisor, Detective Stan Hardwick, is talking with your mom and dad as we speak. Tell me, when were you last down here in Austin?"

"My wife, Crystal, and I were down there over Labor Day weekend with some of our friends. The six of us stayed at Dad's place for the week and hung out on the lake."

"I see. Exactly when did you leave and return to Oklahoma?" replied Tommy.

"We left on Friday morning to fly back. I had a cleaning company come in after we left and they finished their job on Monday night," said Bobby.

"That would be Monday of this week. The 12th, is that right?" asked Tommy.

"Yes, that's right," said Bobby.

"Don't worry, Bobby, we will get this sorted out. I suggest that you wait a couple of hours before calling your mom and dad. Detective Hardwick will have briefed them by then," suggested Tommy.

"They will be beside themselves, Oh my God, what a mess," said Bobby as he hung up the phone.

~

Detectives George Turner and Marie Mason were doing the door-to-door. They were an odd couple. George was well over six feet tall and skinny as a beanpole and Marie was five-four when standing on a rock.

They got the normal responses. Didn't see anything. Didn't hear anything. Don't really know the McCords that well. There was the occasional ghoul who tried to get more information. Was the woman shot? Had she been assaulted? They had done the rounds of the neighborhood in a systematic manner, starting with Bill and Ethel Andersen and going around counterclockwise. The last call of the day was to the home of Harvey and Dawn Cohen, the neighbors on the adjoining property to the McCords.

They rang the bell, and immediately they could hear the barking of what sounded like one of those small toy dogs that young ladies seem to favor. A few minutes later, a woman appeared in the doorway. She was dressed in a shimmering translucent pool wrap. The light coming through the house backlit her profile and provided the complete outline of her stunning figure. She was a hair under six feet tall with long black hair. She cradled a shih tzu with a pink bow on top of its head in one hand and a glass of wine in the other.

"Can I help you?" slurred the woman.

George Turner was doing his best impression of a fairground clown's face like the one you throw balls into to win a stuffed koala. Marie Mason, confident as ever, took charge.

"Mrs. Dawn Cohen, is it? I am Detective Marie Mason of the Travis County Police Department and this is my colleague, Detective George Turner. May we come in for a few minutes to talk to you about what happened last night at the McCord residence?"

"Of course, anything I can do to help officers. Come on in," said Dawn as she staggered slightly, allowing them to enter her home.

Marie was not convinced that the mutt with the pink bow was in agreement with her owner that they should enter. Marie didn't like toy dogs and she hated shih tzus the most.

Dawn laid back on the pure-white overstuffed sectional as Marie and George sat in a pair of fake Louis the Fourteenth chairs.

"Is your husband home, Mrs. Cohen?" asked Marie.

"No, he is gone in Vegas at some orthodontist convention. He left Sunday night and will be back on Friday. It's just Rita and me, I'm afraid. We've been left all on our own, haven't we, snookums." She kissed the mutt right on its nose.

Marie almost sent the morning's egg and sausage taco all over the white sectional but caught it in the nick of time.

"Did you hear anything or see anything last night?" said George, seeing that Marie was not quite ready to lead the questioning again.

"No, nothing, officer. Rita and I had gone to bed about eight and I heard nothing. The first time I heard about the commotion was this morning when I went to get my nails done and Miss Loo told me all about it," said Dawn, already bored with the conversation and thinking about refilling her glass of Riesling.

The commotion, thought Marie. She wanted to slap Dawn, but resisted the temptation.

For the next ten minutes, the interview of Dawn Cohen followed along the same path as the others in the neighborhood. She hadn't seen or heard anything and didn't know the McCords that well.

"Harvey and I have our own lives and our own circle of friends. We do not have much in common with the McCords and their group," continued Dawn.

There was something about the way that Dawn Cohen talked about Jim and Mary McCord that both George and Marie picked up on. As they walked back to the car, George was the first to bring it up.

"It was like she was over-stressing that they had absolutely no contact with the McCords'. Like they were a different social class or something," said George.

"She has something to hide, that one. I can feel it. I can taste it. She knows something, for sure. She also makes my skin crawl but that might be just me. I hate trophy wives, and Dawn Cohen is a prime example," said Marie as George drove the car back to Hudson Bend.

Chapter 6 - San Antonio

2005 - The Initial Investigation

IT WAS RAINING WHEN JIM McCord arrived at the Hudson Bend office a quarter before noon. Celia showed McCord into the conference room and offered him a cup of coffee that he declined. He took off his leather jacket, draped it over a chair, and as it began to drip water on the floor, he took off his glasses and used a Kleenex to dry them off. Jim McCord hated the rain. He loved the snow and cold of Colorado but wet days in Austin were not his favorite.

Stan had Celia bring in some sandwiches, and as they sat across from one another in the small conference room, the sound of the traffic on 620 reverberated around the room.

"So what do you do for a living, Jim, and why were you in San Antonio?" asked Stan.

"I am an expert in cyber security," replied McCord, pumping out his chest, full of his own importance. "I work for the federal government investigating military contractors to ensure that they are compliant with current standards."

Stan Hardwick watched as Jim McCord ran his hand over his beard. *He's doing this for effect, like some kind of visiting professor,* thought Stan. *Or else he has some mayo from his sandwich stuck in the beard and is trying to wipe it off.* Stan chuckled a little at the sight as Jim McCord continued.

"I flew into San Antonio from Durango on Sunday night for the compliance review and I fly back tomorrow. Mary and I will set out next Saturday morning to drive back to Austin. We are generally back in Austin by now; however' the conference in San Antonio changed our plans somewhat."

"So how the heck did a woman's body get on my property?" asked McCord, trying to move the conversation forward.

"If we knew that, we might be able to find out who killed her," retorted Stan. What did McCord think they were, the fucking A-Team?

"When was the last time you were in your home on Braker Lane, Jim?" asked Stan.

"We left the evening of Memorial Day and drove to Pagosa," replied McCord.

"So, that would have been May 26th. And you haven't been back since?"

"That's right, Stan. Bill and Ethel keep a watch on the place and my son uses it for vacation once a year," replied Jim.

"So do Bill and Ethel have a key to your home? I would like to take a look around the inside of the house if I can. I don't think that the killer went inside, but I would like to check it out and make sure."

"Not a problem, Stan. I could come with you right now if you would like and let you look around. No need to trouble Bill and Ethel."

Stan pulled in closer to the table, lowered his voice and made sure that Jim McCord knew that this was a murder investigation and that the two of them were not going to saunter off to his home for a couple of cold ones.

"That won't be possible, I'm afraid. Your property is now a crime scene. I will let you know when we can let you gain access again but it might be several days.

Jim's eyes narrowed as Stan leaned back in his chair and said, "I think that will do it for today, Jim. Thanks a lot for coming up from San Antonio. I'll be back in touch with you as we continue the investigation. It's still raining cats and dogs out there, so be safe on your drive back."

After Jim McCord had left to drive back to San Antonio, Stan felt that there was more going on with McCord than met the eye, but felt it unlikely that he had anything to do with the murder. Why would he go to such elaborate effort to stage a body in his own backyard?

Stan was convinced Jim McCord had nothing to do with the murder but was equally convinced he was hiding something. He was sure of it. Stan pushed the thought to the back of his mind and headed off to the evening briefing.

~

Jim McCord was not a happy man as he made the drive back to San Antonio. "Shit, shit, shit. A fucking body in my yard! Either someone is trying to fuck with me, or worse still, frame me for murder! That bitch Dawn Cohen better keep her mouth shut!"

Chapter 7 - Rohypnol

The Initial Investigation

THEY WERE ALL TOGETHER AGAIN in the conference room. Stan kicked off the evening briefing. "Okay, team. What do we know?"

Tommy was first up. He cleared his throat, took out his notes and began.

"I talked with Bobby McCord and he seemed like an honest guy. He, his wife and two other couples stayed at the house a couple of weeks ago. They must've had a great time, as he paid for a cleaning crew to come in for a couple of days and clean the place from top to bottom. A week later, we find the body. So, if anyone had been in the house, we might be able to see where they walked on the carpet if the cleaners vacuumed it thoroughly."

"Good job, Tommy," responded Stan. "I'll go over and get the house key from the Andersens and take a look inside tomorrow. Marie, did the house-to-house reveal anything?"

"Nothing." replied Marie. "No one saw anything, no one heard anything. That said, I want to do a follow-up with Dawn Cohen. She was being a little shifty with me. There might be something there, maybe not, but I want to give it another go."

"Okay, Marie. Take George with you," replied Stan.

Feeling somewhat disappointed, Marie agreed to take George. She would have loved to give that bitch Cohen a going over on her own. "Calm down, Marie," she said to herself as she walked out of the briefing room with the rest of the team.

~

Sven Stevenson had delivered his written autopsy results late Thursday night and Stan had read them in bed before dozing off. Stan's wife, Doreen, was used to this nightly ritual. She had an eye mask and earplugs so that she could sleep while Stan did what he needed to do.

It was confirmed that *Reese* had been suffocated, and the toxicology showed there had been drugs in her system. There was evidence of several different varieties including Rohypnol. Rohypnol is usually dissolved in drinks but it can also be injected. Stan thought it was likely that the killer had sedated the girl by injecting her with the drug, based on examination of her arm.

Sven had concluded that she had been injected several times over an extended period. The killer could have had her in his control for many days. What was also disturbing were the internal injuries. She had been brutally raped and sodomized. In addition to external tearing, there was internal tearing in both the vagina and anus. Sven was of the opinion that "various items" might have been used to penetrate her. He also noted that she would have been in considerable pain, as the internal injuries were horrendous.

She had also been completely cleaned. Not just washed, *cleaned.* The killer had used some sort of bleach mixture before applying significant quantities of Chloe perfume.

Sven also noted that her facial makeup looked like it had been professionally applied. The final comment in the report significantly added to the mystery. Sven speculated that her facial features were almost certainly Eastern European.

~

The following morning, Stan picked up the keys for the McCord place from Ethel Andersen. He arrived at the house, took a deep breath and opened the front door. He put on a set of blue medical shoe covers along with a pair of latex gloves and stepped inside.

There was a tiled hallway leading to the main living room, which had a deep-tufted beige carpet. It was obvious that the place had been thoroughly cleaned. The telltale marks left by the vacuum cleaner on the tufted carpet were still clearly visible.

As Tommy had said in the briefing, if someone had been in the house, these vacuum cleaner marks would have been disturbed and they would have seen the footprints on the carpet. Unless, of course, they also vacuumed before they left. The place was pristine: no water droplets in sinks, no evidence of anyone having been in the house post cleaning. Stan was sure the killer had not come into the house.

When he was finished with the internal inspection of the McCord home, Stan sat back in his police cruiser and let out a long sigh. "We are nowhere on this! Who was this woman? How did she meet her killer? How did she get into the McCord backyard? Why was she staged?"

The team had been at it for several days and they had made little progress on any aspect of this killing. They needed a breakthrough and they needed it fast.

Chapter 8 - Galina Alkaev

2005 - A Great Adventure

THE SUN'S WARMING RAYS WOKE Galina Alkaev as they penetrated through a one-inch crack in the thick red curtains covering her bedroom window. She lay there for a few seconds, allowing some time to clear the sleep and to focus. Her heart started pounding with excitement. She was going to do it.

She threw back the covers, jumped out of bed and stepped across the hallway to the bathroom. As she sat on the commode, tears began to slowly roll down her cheeks. She felt sad for her parents, Alexi and Lyudmila, who had already left to handle the breakfast rush at the Alkaev Family Restaurant, a Russian ethnic restaurant they owned on Reisterstown Road. Local workers from the Pikesville Ford engine plant and medical staff from the night shift at Johns Hopkins Hospital in central Baltimore would be streaming in with big appetites. Galina could almost smell the grenki cooking on the grill.

As she pulled off her nightgown and stepped into the shower, soothing jets of hot water caressed her long golden hair and washed away her tears. She had to do this. Had to get away and make a new life.

"This is the right thing to do," she whispered to herself, trying to force the last remnants of doubt from her mind.

She dried herself and then stared at her reflection in the bathroom mirror. She had to pull herself together. The face looking back at her had bloodshot eyes from crying and looked drawn and tired, as the past few weeks of sleepless nights had taken their toll.

"You're going to do this!" she said as the image in the mirror repeated back word for word. She opened the bathroom cabinet and began filling her overnight bag with all of her shampoos and toiletries. She grabbed a set of dry towels from the airing cupboard and stuck them in her bag.

Before returning to her bedroom to pack her clothes, she walked down the hallway to her parents' bedroom. She could smell the Novaya Zarya, her mother's favorite perfume, lingering in the air. She walked into her parents' closet and, driven by some hidden force, ran her fingers gently over the garments like a maestro pianist at the Tchaikovsky Concert Hall in Moscow. She landed on her mother's favorite dress, grabbed it in both hands, pressed it against her face and slowly inhaled.

As she turned from the closet to leave, she looked at her mother's dressing table. Everything was in its normal place. "This room hasn't changed in twenty years," she thought to herself.

Her parents loved each other deeply and they had raised two children who loved and respected them. She felt a twinge of regret that she was now betraying that respect. She and Pavel were eloping and she knew her parents would be devastated. Before leaving her parents' bedroom, she whispered a prayer of hope asking God to guide them on their journey to find a new life together.

Galina ran to her bedroom and packed her things. She stood in the center of the room and slowly looked around to say goodbye. She had had a good and happy childhood growing up in this house. The bedroom had witnessed her tears of joy after Pavel told her he loved her for the first time. She also remembered the night she cried herself to sleep when she heard her grandmother had died.

Galina thought of her parents again. The restaurant would be full and food orders would be backing up. They relied on her and she was letting them down. Suddenly, she realized that she had to leave soon. Her mother would be on the phone at any minute demanding that she get to work.

Galina had worked in the family restaurant in Pikesville, Maryland for as long as she could remember. She had swept floors, washed dishes and peeled potatoes on her way to becoming a combination maître d' and waitress. She hated it. Galina wanted to go to college, but her parents couldn't afford to help. They had offered to pay her to work in the restaurant so she could save money before going off to school, but Galina knew their hidden agenda. They hoped she would stay permanently. Galina knew that there was no future in this and that when her parents retired, if they ever did, that the restaurant would go to Nikolay. He was their son and that's how it worked in Eastern European families.

With her bag in hand, Galina crept past her brother's room and gently pushed open his door. She blew a goodbye kiss to the snoring Nikolay and crept downstairs. She placed the letter she had written on the worktop by the cookie jar and looked around her childhood home before creeping out the back door. Galina Alkaev was gone, off on her great adventure, never to return.

Chapter 9 - Bill Ross

2014 - The Cold Case Investigation

THE KILLER LAY IN WAIT. There were several viable targets. He just needed to be patient and the right one would show. The killer had chosen the perfect spot, lying in the dense undergrowth just off the main path alongside a chain-link fence. It was just after midday and many had flown in to enjoy the sumptuous buffet. He struck! It was over in an instant. It was now all about enjoying the kill and he would do it leisurely over the days ahead. His dark eyes blinked rapidly in anticipation while his tongue flicked back and forth, salivating at the thought.

William Ross, Bill to most of his friends, had never witnessed a Texas rattlesnake kill in the wild. Many years ago, back in his native Scotland, he had gone on a school trip to the Edinburgh Zoo and had watched the zookeeper feed the snakes in the reptile exhibit, but this was his first experience seeing it in the wild.

Bill scanned the greenbelt at the rear of his home in the Balcones neighborhood of northwest Austin with a pair of vintage binoculars. His father-in-law had given them to him, so he guessed they were made before the Second World War. His deck ran the total length of his home and was some fifteen feet above his yard. He could scan the entire greenbelt and could also see the high-rise apartment buildings in the distance in downtown Austin. Every couple of months it seemed that a new one appeared on the horizon. Austin was booming and every part of the city infrastructure was being stretched to maximum capacity.

The maker of the binoculars was Barr & Stroud, a Scottish engineering company that was initially formed in 1913 and was recognized for its pioneering work in optical engineering. They made rangefinders for the Royal Navy. This morning, Bill was not aboard a naval destroyer and was not about to lob fifty-pounders over the sea at the German navy. Moments before witnessing the rattlesnake strike, he had finished filling the two bird feeders that hung over the greenbelt and the birds were flying around enjoying the feast. The rattlesnake knew to lie directly below the feeders as eventually a bird or a small rodent would walk by looking for the seeds that the birds had shaken loose and discarded from the feeders dangling overhead.

Bill thought about the rattlesnake lying in wait for new prey and smiled. He remembered reading about their hunting style. Texas rattlesnakes are creatures of habit; they find a good spot and return to it each morning before it gets too hot. Then, in the heat of the day, they go back to their underground nest, and return in the evening when the sun goes down. They do this every day.

Snakes also have incredible patience as they lie in wait for an unsuspecting creature to walk past. When the victim is near, they can sense it through cavities in their head that pick up both scent and vibration. The snake will then shoot forward from its hiding place, like a spring being released from its coiled retention, and sink its fangs into the prey, convulsing its body to drive the venom into the poor victim, immobilizing it. It can then take its time to devour it whole.

In this case, it had been a gray mourning dove, about the same size as the common pigeon. It didn't seem possible that the rattler could devour something that large, but it did. It was able to disconnect the neck bones at the back of its jaws and extend its mouth over the victim and, with a pulsating, hypnotic, rhythmic motion, slowly suck the bird down its throat.

"Fascinating," mumbled Bill to himself. "Time for a coffee!"

~

Bill Ross was born in Scotland in 1950 in the town of Kilmarnock, located twenty-one miles south of Glasgow, in the county of Ayrshire. Ayrshire is the heart of Robert Burns country, the world-famous Scottish poet. The first published works of Burns were printed in Kilmarnock and aptly called "The Kilmarnock Edition." If you were to find a copy today, it would be priceless.

For most of the year, Ayrshire is bleak; cold and dark as the winter storms blow in from the North Atlantic and pass over the River Clyde estuary, bringing with them wind and freezing rain. Ayrshire is one of the main agricultural regions of Scotland. The heavy black soil and rolling hills of grassland form a patchwork quilt of green, home to herds of brown and white Ayrshire dairy cows that produce the finest milk in the world.

It takes tough, hard-working people to work the land. The county town is Ayr and, as Burns wrote in his poetry, Ayr is the place for "honest men and bonny lassies!" Where Ayr is the agricultural center of Ayrshire, Kilmarnock in the 1960s was the industrial center of the county. Bill Ross was Kilmarnock to the core. There, he met and married his first and only love, Elaine, and they were blessed with two children, Tommy and Jenny.

Bill had a long and successful career in law enforcement and was now retired, living in Austin. His son, Tommy, following in his father's footsteps, was a detective in the Travis County Police Department.

Bill's police career started straight out of school. He did his time as a cop on the beat, walking the streets of Kilmarnock. On any given night, the pubs and bars of this industrial town were packed to overflowing. On the weekends, after a long week of working in the heavy engineering works dotted around town, it was like the men had just been let out of jail. They would party like there was no tomorrow. There were bar and streets fights over disagreements about girlfriends or which local football team was best. Bill never started a brawl but he never walked away from one either. He earned a Ph.D. from the "University of Hard Knocks" on the streets of "Auld Killie."

After transferring to the Glasgow police force, a promotion to detective quickly followed his officer training at Tulliallan Police College in Fife. He worked major crimes in the west of Scotland for several years before being offered a transfer to the Homicide and Serious Crimes Command of the London Metropolitan Police (the Met).

In 1990, he left the Met and took a position with a major security firm in the U.S. Bill, Elaine, and the family settled in Thousand Oaks, a city north of Los Angeles where Tommy and Jenny attended Thousand Oaks High School.

Tommy joined the Marine Corps straight out of high school, did basic training at Camp Pendleton and MCRD in San Diego, and then joined the Marine Corps 26th Expeditionary Unit. He did two tours of duty during the Balkan conflict and was part of the peacekeeping force in Kosovo. His sister, Jenny, went into nursing school, married, and settled in Huntington Beach, California. Bill and Elaine missed Jenny and her family and made frequent visits back to California whenever they could.

After Tommy left the Corps in 2003, he wanted to pursue a police career and was hired on by the Travis County Police Department. It took Tommy several years to make detective and then, in January of 2013, he was finally promoted to the major crimes unit. His dad could not have been more proud of his son. Not only did he serve his country in the Marine Corps, he was now serving the good people of Travis County in their police department.

~

Bill sat in his den relaxing with his coffee after watching the assassination of the dove in his backyard. Elaine came in to use the computer to get the bills paid.

"Stressful day?" quipped Elaine as she sat down at the computer. From the day they were married, Elaine took care of the family and the family finances, allowing Bill to "do his thing" and find the baddies. She was a feisty five-two brunette with a smile that would turn heads whenever she walked into a room.

"Are Tommy and Claire coming over for barbecue on Sunday?" asked Bill.

"As far as I know, that is still the plan," replied Elaine as she got on with the bill paying.

Tommy was a single parent with a four-year-old daughter, Claire. Tommy met his wife, Jill, at a Round Rock Express baseball game at the Dell Diamond. Round Rock is home to Dell Computer Corporation and the company bought the naming rights to the stadium after the city built the facility in 2000. They married in 2008 and bought a house in the Brushy Creek neighborhood of Cedar Park. They were very much in love and it had always been Tommy's plan to own his own home, raise a family and live the American dream.

This dream was shattered when Jill died in a tragic car accident when Claire was only a year old. She had been driving to work one morning in heavy rain after dropping Claire off at daycare, and a pickup truck driving in the opposite direction lost control and slammed into her Toyota Camry. She died instantly.

Tommy was a fantastic father but could not have done it without the support of Elaine and Bill. Being a single parent was already incredibly hard. Having a very stressful job with long hours made it even tougher. Tommy dropped Claire off at daycare every morning but Elaine picked her up most evenings and made sure that she was bathed and fed. Her daddy would then pick her up after he finished work and tuck her into her own bed each night. This ritual was repeated each weekday morning starting at 6:30. The weekends were the best of times when father and daughter could hang out together and enjoy life in Austin.

Bill stared blankly out the window of his den, took a sip of coffee and said, "I want to talk to Tommy about something, so I just wanted to make sure that the plan was still the same."

~

When Sunday rolled around, Bill and Elaine played golf with their friends in the morning, and then when they got home, Bill made sure that the Green Egg (the greatest outdoor grill ever invented, in Bill's opinion) was cleaned out and ready for the Sunday night ritual of steak, chicken, and burgers. He loaded the oak charcoal into the Green Egg about five o'clock and fired it up. The coals took about an hour to be perfect for grilling.

As the aroma of the sizzling meats on the grill wafted across the backyard, Bill sat on his deck, cold beer in hand and thought about the discussion he planned to have with Tommy later in the day. He needed to be a bit tactful and not just dump it on him without any context. He needed his son's help and Bill was not accustomed to asking for it.

"Hi, Dad. Hi, Mom!" called Tommy as he opened the front door. Claire ran ahead of him with her mass of long golden hair blowing in the wind, yelling, "Mimi, Papa, where are you?"

When Elaine came out of the kitchen, Claire almost bowled her over.

Two long hours of meat, beer and conversation followed. When the BBQ was over, Mimi and Claire watched an episode of "Peppa Pig" (Claire's favorite) in the family room. Tommy and Bill sat on the back deck overlooking the greenbelt. Bill poured a glass of Glenmorangie single malt for himself, popped a bottle of Corona for Tommy and launched into the subject he wanted to talk about.

"I always dreamed about retirement, but it's not what I imagined, Tommy. Is there any way that I might get involved and help out at the Travis County Police Department?" asked Bill.

"What? Do you want to be like a Wal-Mart greeter? Welcome to the Travis County Police Department and have a nice day," laughed Tommy.

"That's not quite what I meant," said Bill, taking another mouthful of the single malt. "Is there a cold case team where I could help out looking over old files and stuff?"

"Look, Dad, I just made it to major crimes and I don't want to be seen as trying to create a job for you. Detective Sargent Jack Johnson heads up the cold case unit. Let me ask him on the quiet and see what he says," said Tommy.

"Great, that's all I ask, son. I am bored out of my skull. God Almighty, I sat watching a rattler in the greenbelt today for two hours. How lame is that?"

"You know, the way things are done today in the U.S. and in the Travis County Police Department might be totally different from what you did in the Met, Dad," said Tommy with a hint of concern in his voice.

"Police work is police work the world over, Tommy. There is certainly more technology available today than back in my day, but the process of finding the baddy is basically the same. It's hard work. I'm sure that your Detective Johnson would agree."

Tommy's face held concern as he said, "You're also going to have to be careful with the British police thing, Dad. Most people know about the London Met and we don't need anyone thinking that a big-city detective has come to teach Texas rednecks how to do their job."

"You need to give me a little more credit than that, Tommy. I understand. If you would prefer that I didn't stick my nose in, then let's just forget about it," said Bill, now more than a little pissed off with his son's reaction.

"Sorry Dad. I didn't mean it that way. It just came out bad. I'll talk with Jack Johnson in the morning. I need to get Claire home and get her clothes ready for daycare tomorrow."

Tommy and Claire left and Bill sat on the deck looking at the lights of Austin in the distance. *That didn't go too badly*, he thought.

"Hmm, soon be dark," mulled Bill as he poured himself another two fingers of the nectar of the gods.

Chapter 10- The Scottish cavalry

2014 - The Cold Case Investigation

THE FOLLOWING MORNING, JACK Johnson was pouring himself his third cup of coffee. The clock on his desk read 9:30 but it felt much earlier than that. Earlier in the morning he had popped a Zantac, but his acid reflux was still bubbling. Being the good detective he was, he thought, *There's something wrong with this picture*, With coffee in hand, he went back to the files spilling over on his desk.

"Got a minute?" said Tommy Ross as he stuck his head around the door of Jack's office.

"Sure, Tommy. Take the weight off," responded Jack.

Tommy tried to find a space on Jack's desk to put his coffee cup down.

"Sorry, buddy, the cleaners come in tomorrow," joked Jack. "What can I do for you, son?"

Jack Johnson was a local hero. Overworked and underpaid, he'd been with the Travis County Police Department almost thirty years. He had held every job other than the top spot and knew where all the skeletons were buried.

"Do you need any help, Jack?" asked Tommy with a hint of a smile forming on his lips.

"You auditioning for a stand-up comedian spot, Tommy?"

Tommy chuckled and got down to why he was there. "Did you ever meet my dad?"

"Not sure I ever did, why?"

"He worked as a cold case detective back in the day in the UK. He's retired now, lives here in Austin and is looking for something to do with his time so he can feel productive. And judging by the state of your desk, it looks like you could do with another pair of hands. Is there any role where he might be able to help? He's sharp as a tack, but he is my dad, so I'm biased," said Tommy.

Jack stopped and thought for a second. "Hmm, not a bad idea. There would be no compensation as I don't have any budget for that, but if he wanted to volunteer his time, I'm sure that his years of experience in police work could be really helpful to us.

"A few years ago we had a woman volunteer to help us and we gave her a job on the front desk. So, there is a precedent here. Give me a couple of days to get the paperwork to you so your dad can apply for a volunteer officer role," said Jack, now fully bought into the idea of getting some additional help.

"Perfect!" Tommy responded, and left Jack to his troubles, confident that soon, the Scottish cavalry would arrive and all would be well with the world.

Chapter 11 - You're hired

2014 - The Cold Case Investigation

"YOU LOOK FINE, Willie!" yelled Elaine from the kitchen as Bill Ross went back to the bathroom for the fourth time to check that his tie was straight.

Jack Johnson had given Bill the necessary paperwork to apply for a role with the cold case unit. There were two types of jobs available: a reserve officer and a special reserve officer. Bill had read the qualification criteria for both, and after the third reading still couldn't understand the difference between the two, so he applied for both.

Today was the big day. Bill was up, out of bed, showered and shaved well before six. He was now back in the bedroom closet and rummaging through his clothes.

"What the heck are you doing, Willie? Most people are still in bed and it sounds like you're building a new set of shelves in there—like that'll be the day," yelled Elaine as she angrily drew the covers over herself and rolled over, trying to get a few more minutes of sleep.

It had been years since Bill had last been on an interview. He remembered the process he had gone through to apply for the Met job in London. It took four interviews, extensive background checks and three references to testify to his moral character and standing in the community.

I hope I don't have to go through all of that again, thought Bill as he paced back and forth in front of the bedroom mirror. His heart was pounding in his chest just like it had the first time he had taken Elaine out on a date.

Bill had chosen the dark suit. It wasn't a tough choice as he only had one suit that he kept for weddings and funerals. White shirt, dark tie, and his shoes shined to perfection. He had nipped down to Walgreens the previous night and managed to locate the only jar of Brylcreem they had in the store. Now his hair was perfect, parting on the left, combed back on the right. His mother called it a "cow's lick" and he always made sure that this was the style he adopted for the more important occasions.

He grabbed the manila folder from the top of the dresser and headed to the garage, giving Elaine a peck on the cheek on the way. She returned that moment of intimacy with a hug as she had always done before Bill went off to get the baddies.

An hour later, Bill arrived at the Hudson Bend office, thirty-five minutes before the time for his interview. Planning was always important, as there could always be an accident or incident that would have caused him to be late. While Bill waited in his car, he nervously checked e-mail on his iPhone to make sure Jack Johnson had not rescheduled the time for the meeting. After confirming the meeting was still on, he surfed the net to pass the time, checking the British football scores via the BBC Sports app. Milton Keynes Dons had beaten Manchester United 4-0 in the League Cup.

"Shit!" he mumbled, "that's a bad omen." The last time Manchester United had been beaten like that, Harold McMillan had been British prime minister.

"9:59. Okay, time to get this done." He pushed open the door of his BMW, checked four times that it was locked and then headed across the parking lot to the police office. He opened the glass doors leading to the reception area. He looked around and saw the African-American lady behind the desk.

"Can I help you, sir?" asked the receptionist, staring up at the apparition in front of her. "You did see the sign on the door—No Solicitation!" she exclaimed, taking charge in her normal efficient manner.

"No, ma'am, I am not here to sell anything. I have an appointment with Detective Jack Johnson at 10:00 a.m.," said Bill, checking his watch to see that it was indeed 10:00 a.m. on the dot.

"Jack, some guy's here to see you!" yelled the receptionist, utilizing the most effective method of communication available to her. "Take a seat, Mr.?"

"Oh, my apologies, ma'am. I didn't give you my card. William Ross is the name," said Bill, sitting down awkwardly on the one available chair. There was a copy of *Guns & Ammo* on the table, so Bill picked it up and stared blankly at the pages.

"Have him come back to my office, will you, Celia!" shouted Jack from down the hall.

"Go through that door, down the hall, second door on your left. That's Jack's office," said Celia with a smirk.

The door of Jack Johnson's office was open. He had just lifted his white Styrofoam cup to his lips and was blowing on the scalding hot coffee when Bill appeared at his door.

"Holy crap!" yelled Jack. The coffee splatted everywhere. Jack jumped up, howled and threw the now empty cup in the general direction of what seemed to be a trash can, but it may have been what was referred to as file 13.

"You caught me a little by surprise there, buddy!" exclaimed Jack as he used a sheet of paper towel to mop up his mess. "You know, Sanderson's Funeral Home is two blocks down the street. You're not here for a job driving a hearse, Bill."

"Sorry, Mr. Johnson, I was not sure how formal the interview process might be," said Bill, feeling a little embarrassed. "I have brought my CV for your review," he said, trying to recover the situation as best he could.

"CV!" exclaimed Jack, "I know all about you from Tommy and it sounds like you are the right guy for the job. You're hired!"

Bill Ross was both totally confused and elated. He was hired! He was going to be back doing what he loved. It was like being picked to play for the first team and he couldn't wait to get on the field.

I need to break out the twenty-one-year-old when I get home tonight, Bill thought with resolve. *Yep, it's a twenty-one-year-old kind of day!*

"Can't give you an office, Bill, but you can sit yourself down in the breakroom. No files leave this office without my approval, clear?"

"Absolutely, Mr. Johnson!"

"Less of the mister. You can call me Detective Johnson or Jack. Most times, its just Jack, but if there are other people around, it's Detective Johnson. There may be times when you want to call me asshole, but you do that when I'm not in earshot and at your own risk," said Jack with a smirk. "Celia, can you get Bill a cup of coffee and bring it to my office, please? We have work to do."

The piles of files on the desk had recovered sufficiently from the dousing with coffee. Jack took them one by one and began to explain to Bill the organization of a cold case file and the content of each section.

"Bill, these are all major crimes. Serious assaults, shootings, rapes, child molestation and, of course, murders. I suggested that you take a look at the murders first. There are twenty-six of them going back fifteen years. These are four murder files I pulled out last night and are ready for you to take a look at as a first step.

"There's more where this came from in the file room at the rear of the building. All of these are summary files that we keep here in this office. The main files are at the 34th Street location in downtown Austin. I have talked with the desk sargeant at 34th Street and he will give you a tour of the main file room down there whenever you ready."

Bill shuffled the pages and said, "Nice to see you still do things the old-fashioned way. I was afraid I'd have to learn a bunch of computer programs."

Jack laughed and said, "Wait five years. There is an ongoing program of converting these files to electronic format. All we care about is that you're thorough in your research to ensure that all available information on a specific cold case has been reviewed and that you didn't jump to any early conclusions."

"I don't jump to early conclusions," said Bill with a serious tone that made Jack feel like he was being put back in his place for making such a foolish statement.

"Don't be a smartass, Bill. No one like a smartass." snarled Jack.

Jack left and Bill got to work.

Bill decided that the best approach was to study the contents of each file in reverse order, oldest first. He would do a cursory review of each and see if anything jumped out alerting him to engage in a further, more detailed review.

He took the four files from Jack's desk and settled down in the breakroom. Throughout the day, other officers would come and go and they would extend a hand and introduce themselves. Bill was sure that he could hear them snigger as they left the room. He also caught sight of a couple of admin staff sticking their heads around the corner and then disappearing, giggling as they went. He was on display and no one could remember ever seeing anything like it. He was the talk of the sheriff's office. Bill never felt prouder.

~

The following morning, Bill arrived in the office bright and early. "Morning, Celia!"

Celia almost choked on her blueberry muffin as she stared at Special Reserve Officer Bill Ross. Black snakeskin cowboy boots, blue jeans, belt, buckle (not too big), and western shirt. Bill Ross had metamorphosed into a slightly older version of Luke Duke, from *The Dukes of Hazzard* Overcome, Celia felt her face blush and ran off to the bathroom.

Bill settled in the breakroom and was once again the center of attention, but for different reasons this time. The giggling from the admin girls took on a different form that made Bill feel twenty years younger.

After reviewing the first few files, nothing jumped out at him as out of the ordinary. They were a mosaic of life's garbage, especially the sexual assaults on children. Over the years and through all he had seen, child molestations affected him the most and made the bile rise up in his gut. Now up to 2005, Bill walked back to the file room and returned with three files from that year.

When he opened up the first 2005 file, the name on the folder jumped out and hit him square in the face: "Deputy Tommy Ross." Almost ten years ago, Tommy was involved as part of the investigating team on a murder in Riverside. He was a young officer, just out of training, and had found himself in the middle of a murder investigation.

"Wow, I need to take a closer look at this one," said Bill.

Chapter 12 - Pavel Orlov

2005 - A Great Adventure

WHEN GALINA FIRST MET PAVEL Orlov in high school, she didn't like him. She thought he was always trying to be the center of attention.

"Do you know that my family name means son of Oryol and that Oryol means eagle?" he would boast to those who would listen.

As the years went by she became attracted to him. His eyes were deep ocean pools of blue she could dive into and get lost in. He was dark haired, almost black in contrast to her long blond locks. They made a handsome couple and began to spend more time together after school. Every morning, Pavel would be waiting for her at the end of the street to walk with her to school, and every evening he would walk her home again.

For Pavel, Galina was the love of his life. He would lie in bed at night and plan out their future together. They both loved American history and he imagined them traveling west, as the original settlers had done, and finding a place by a river with tall pines and rolling hills where they could settle down and build a home together.

The one thing Pavel wasn't was an athlete, but the jocks left him alone, especially after an ugly incident after school one day. A linebacker from the football team tried to demonstrate how tough he was and picked a fight with Pavel in the schoolyard. Pavel tried his best to talk his way out of it but the jock would have none of it and threw the first punch. Galina saw it all happen from a distance. As if in slow motion, Pavel sidestepped the punch, came around and hit the jock in the kidneys with a right hook. When the guy bent over gasping for air, Pavel hit him square on the chin and he went down like a sack of potatoes.

"Son of eagle!" Pavel whispered in the jock's ear as he walked away.

As it happened, an eagle had very little to do with it. Pavel's father had been a heavyweight boxing champion in the Ukraine before coming to the U.S. He had taught Pavel how to look after himself from the time he was old enough to hold up a pair of boxing gloves.

Their joint love of U.S. history brought Galina and Pavel together. They eagerly read about the early explorers who traveled west, and how they documented their journey so that those who followed after them could learn from their experiences. These were the real pioneers.

The exploits of Lewis and Clark held particular intrigue for them. In May 1804, Lewis and Clark had set out on their expedition heading west across the country, taking a northern route and making the Pacific Ocean by November of 1805.

Galina would lean against Pavel and sigh. "How exciting. They forged a trail not knowing what risks lay ahead. They just did it. Swallowed hard and did it."

Pavel kissed her and held her close, "I love you, Galina."

She leaned into him and said, "And I love you, Pavel. The world is out there for us to explore together, and maybe someday we'll be like those early settlers. Swallow hard and just do it."

In May of 2005, Galina and Pavel were finally ready to do exactly that.

~

In his final year of high school, Pavel had saved enough to buy a motorcycle, a 2003 Triumph Bonneville T100. His dad had known an old British guy in Baltimore who knew a lot about bikes, as he called them, and he reckoned that the Triumph was the best there ever was (it was a British bike, of course, so the old guy was a little biased).

Pavel paid cash for the bike, and as he drove it back home to Pikesville he could feel the power of the 790cc engine course through his body like an electrical charge. As each mile went by it was like the wind was blowing away the boy and a man was emerging. He was on fire. "This is my time!" he yelled. He was going to do something big. He was going to be someone.

As a kid, Pavel had heard his father play the music of country singer Tim O'Brien, and the words of one of his songs had struck a chord. The song was called "Turn the Page Again" and the words he remembered rang in his ears as the Bonneville ate up the miles between Baltimore and Pikesville.

> *I'm soaring like an eagle.*
> *I'll find a place to land.*
> *I'll let the west wind take me.*
> *See what it has planned.*

~

It was 6:30 a.m. when Pavel walked into the empty living room. Galina was due to arrive in about an hour and Pavel need to write his father a note. His father was a truck driver and was off on one of his overnights. Pavel's mother had died when he was young and his father had raised him on his own. His father never remarried. and worked hard to give Pavel the best and teach him all he could. He was an uneducated man, but a good man.

Pavel walked to his father's den, pulled out a piece of paper and began writing.

> *"I love you. Tato. I know that you will be angry and disappointed when you read this. I have to make my own way in the world, stand on my own two feet. You have been a good father and you have taught me well. Mama, I know, is looking down from heaven with a smile on her face for the job you have done raising me. Do pobachennya. Tato."*

The tears hit the paper as he wrote the words. He left the note on his father's chair by the fireplace.

Galina arrived at 7:30 in the morning as they had agreed. They kissed and hugged each other for what seemed like an eternity before going upstairs to Pavel's room. He had everything laid out on the bed: his clothes, two sets of brand new leathers and his and her motorcycle helmets. He had bought them three weeks earlier and hid them in the loft so his father wouldn't find them. They opened their packs, shook their money out on the bed and counted it up. Together they had $2,132 in cash.

They went over the plan. They would ride west to St. Louis and pick up the beginnings of Route 66. Pavel couldn't resist and started doing his best impersonation of Elvis singing about the famous highway. Galina sat on the edge of the bed and laughed hysterically.

It would be two days to St. Louis, stopping overnight at Columbus, Ohio, which was roughly halfway. After St. Louis, they would cruise through Tulsa, Albuquerque and past the Grand Canyon on route to Las Vegas. There they would get married, and then on to California, where they planned to work in restaurants and bars, save all they could and then find a permanent place to live. After that, they would see what opportunities life would reveal.

It was a well-constructed plan. As Pavel straddled the Bonneville and gunned the engine, a famous scene from *The Blues Brothers* popped into his head. "There's one hundred six miles to Chicago; we've got a full tank of gas, half a pack of cigarettes, it's dark out, and we're wearing sunglasses! Hit it!"

~

Less than an hour later, they were on I-70 headed for Columbus. Galina had her arms wrapped tightly around Pavel. The air was crisp and clear and she enjoyed the rhythm of the Bonneville between her legs. Galina reached around and stroked Pavel's thigh. They would have to stop soon; she wanted something else between her legs and it wasn't a Triumph motorcycle.

Two hours later, they pulled in to the Buckeye Lake campground just a few miles east of Columbus. It was late in the afternoon and they had already stopped a couple of times for food, gas, potty breaks and to satisfy Galina's "needs." She knew that by now her parents would be hysterical. As she thought about her abandoned cell phone sitting on the nightstand with a panicked voicemail waiting, she cringed. They had both deliberately left their phones behind and had purchased new ones. Neither of them wanted to be tempted into listening to voice mail. They were committed to their plan.

They pitched their small two-man tent close by the RVs and used the washroom and shower facilities at the site. A few hours later, they lay together in the tent and held each other tight as they both thought about what they had left behind. They kissed deeply and made love until sleep engulfed them. They hoped that the pain they had caused would be short-lived and that their parents and friends would eventually understand and forgive them.

~

The next morning, they were back on I-70 headed to St. Louis. It was raining heavily and it was cold. The euphoria of the day before had worn off, only to be replaced by the harsh realities of riding a motorcycle in the driving rain on a cold May morning. They stopped several times, not to deal with Galina's needs, but to get coffee to warm up and get some respite from the weather. It took several hours for them to reach the St. Louis West Route 66 campground. When they arrived, they were wet, felt like shit and had to pitch a two-man tent in the driving rain.

"I can't do this," pleaded Galina. "There are log cabins here for rent, and they have their own shower and fireplace. Can we just stay in one of them tonight, Pavel, *please?*"

"There may be none available," replied Pavel.

"Please go check. I can't stand being wet anymore!" said a distraught Galina.

Pavel sighed and headed to the campsite office. He returned a few minutes later with a smile on his face.

"There's one available. It is normally $59.75 plus tax but he gave it to me for $50 cash," announced Pavel, adopting a triumphant pose. "Jump on, Galina, it's just over here."

After a shower and a burger and fries in the restaurant, they both felt much better. Pavel had secretly wanted to pay for a cabin rather than stay the night in the tent but couldn't admit it to Galina. It was a trait learned from his father to never show weakness. That night, they slept well in a warm bed and rose early to continue their journey along Route 66.

Chapter 13 - My birthday

2014 - The Cold Case Investigation

BILL ROSS WATCHED JACK JOHNSON pass by the breakroom, with coffee in hand, on the way to his office. Bill quickly followed Jack and cornered him before he got wrapped up in other work.

"Jack, can I take this file home with me tonight?" asked Bill.

"Which one is it, Bill?"

"It's the body of a young woman that was discovered in Riverside in 2005. My son, Tommy, was part of the crime scene team. It was soon after he was officially out on his own as a young officer," replied Bill.

"I remember that case well. It was a real conundrum. Stan Hardwick was the lead detective, I believe. Didn't know that Tommy was part of the team," said Jack.

"He had been asked by Stan Hardwick to swing by the house to just check it out. It was purely by accident that he was involved at all," replied Bill.

Jack smiled and said, "Stan is retired now and living out by Lake Buchanan, lucky sod. Spending his days fishing, I understand. Good guy, Stan Hardwick."

Jack thought back to some of the cases he and Stan had worked back in the day and smiled. "Not a problem, Bill. Take the file home, but keep it intact and don't copy anything, Okay?"

"Got it, boss." Bill headed out the office with the file tucked under his arm.

~

Bill crossed the dark parking lot, found his BMW and put the Riverside file on the passenger seat. He then headed into the Austin commuter traffic for the journey home. Bill called Tommy from the car.

"Tommy, do you remember a murder case where a body was discovered in the backyard of a house in Riverside? Sometime in 2005?"

"I sure do, Dad. Is that one of the cold cases you have been assigned to take a look at?" asked Tommy.

"Not assigned per se. I was just going through the files, opened that one and spotted that your name was front and center," quipped Bill.

"I wouldn't say front and center, Dad. That was Stan Hardwick's case and I was a rookie member of the team. Just happened to be in the right place at the right time, I guess."

"I'll give it a good going over the next couple of days and if there are any questions, I'll run them by you first, if that's okay."

"It's okay with me, Dad, if it's okay with Jack Johnson. He needs to authorize my involvement as it's his case now."

"Yes, Tommy, that was dumb of me. Of course, I need to clear it with Jack. Have a good night and give Claire a kiss from Papa."

"Will do, Dad," Tommy hung up.

~

"Reese!"

The name pounded in Tommy's brain. Reese, like the mention of the name of a long lost lover. Reese, a beautiful flower.

Tommy thought about a father yearning for his daughter who had left home never to return. He thought about her last thoughts as the selfish killer extinguished her life for his own diabolical pleasure. He imagined her pleading and begging, wishing that her father were there to save her. Tommy wanted to be there. Tommy wanted to save her.

He could hear Reese screaming in the back of his mind. "Daddy, Daddy!" The plea was deafening, "Daddy, Daddy!" it continued pounding in his brain and he wanted it to stop.

"Daddy, Daddy!"

Tommy snapped out of his trance. He was at home and had just hung up the phone with Bill. Claire was looking up at him.

"Daddy, Daddy. I love you!" said Claire.

"I love you too, my love," said Tommy, and he picked up his daughter and hugged her tight.

Claire kissed him back and then ran to her bedroom to find her doll.

"We're going to find out who killed you, Reese," said Tommy, whispering to himself so Claire wouldn't hear. "An old Scottish cop and a Marine *are* going to find you, you son of a bitch! There will be no hiding place, no rock you can crawl under, and if it is you and me one on one, I'm going to rip your fucking head off!"

~

After dinner that night, Bill walked out onto his deck with the Riverside file in one hand and a glass of single malt in the other. Elaine never appreciated the magical properties of single malt Scotch whisky and how it allowed Bill to see things others had missed when reading a file. "I'll make you see things," she used to say, as she smacked the back of his head playfully with her hand. As he remembered it, sometimes that slap was not all that playful, as Elaine worried about what his alcohol intake was doing to his liver.

"Ah, well, we all have to die sometime." mused Bill, "If I have to drown myself in single malt, so be it. Someone has to step up and take the punishment, so it might as well be me!" he chuckled as he opened the Riverside file.

Bill had a very specific method for reviewing a case file. He always tried to read it cover to cover in one sitting if he could, scribbling notes as he went. He would then go back and reread each section where he had made his notations, studying each piece more carefully, allowing the details to sink in. It was like a mental jigsaw puzzle, looking for pieces that didn't fit properly or missing pieces that resulted in an incomplete picture.

So it was that night on the deck with the Riverside file. By the time he got to the end of it, it was 10:30 and he had been at it from just after seven. He looked at his scribbles. They were extensive and, in his mind, the neurons and electrons were firing like a twenty-one-gun salute on Queen Elizabeth's birthday. Jack Johnson told him that Stan Hardwick had been a good detective but there were more holes in his analysis of the Riverside case than on a target on an East Texas shooting range.

Bill decided he needed some rest and time to let what he had read further sink in. He took himself to bed. One of the other little-known properties of single malt is that it allows you to get to sleep pretty fast. The downside is you tend to dream some weird shit.

Bill sat upright in bed fully awake and just in the nick of time as his dream killer was about to pump him full of Rohypnol and leave him comatose in the green belt at the rear of his house for the rattlesnakes to enjoy. It was just before 3:00 a.m., so he grabbed a cup of coffee in the kitchen and took it, along with the Riverside file, back out on to the deck.

He began to make a list:

1. Marie Mason - Good cop, like her, is she still with the police department?
2. Dark Ford Explorer with Alabama plates?
3. Harvey Cohen - Was the orthodontist really at a conference in Vegas?
4. Dawn Cohen - Body language!
5. Jim McCord - San Antonio
6. Body - killed elsewhere - transportation? - Staging of body?

7. Body - Why the backyard of the McCord house?
8. McCord - Is he being set up? Does he know something? Who has a grudge?
9. Where are the dirty little secrets?
10. We need to go talk with Stan Hardwick!

It was 5:30 and he needed to shower, freshen up, and prepare for the day ahead. He also needed to brief Jack Johnson *ASAP*. How would Jack react to him suggesting that Stan did a less than thorough job? Would Jack support him or tell him to back off?

The possibilities whirled in Bill's mind. There was something there, just under the surface. He could sense it, smell it and taste it. If he could just find the one piece that didn't quite fit, he was convinced the rest of the puzzle would fall into place. He was sure that Stan Hardwick could help if he was inclined but it might damage his reputation and he might tell him to go take a hike. He needed to try and he needed some help.

Bill made a mental note to talk with Marie Mason and then Tommy. He needed to get Jack's approval to do that and then gather enough ammunition to go back to Jack to request that he reopen the case.

A few days ago, Bill had been watching another killer in his backyard and the methods employed by the little assassin were not all the different from those used to kill "Reese." He had noted in the file that this was the name given to the Jane Doe by the scene-of-crime team. "Well, Reese, I'm going to find out who killed you and I'm going to nail the bastard. You have my word on that!"

~

The next morning Jack Johnson gave the green light for Bill to talk with Tommy and Marie. He informed Bill that George Turner, the forensics detective on the original investigation, had left the police force and was living somewhere on the east coast. He agreed that Bill should meet with Stan Hardwick if Stan was agreeable to a meeting. Jack would make the call to Stan and set it up. Marie Mason was still a detective and a meeting with her was arranged for the following morning.

Tommy and Bill were in the conference room going over the file contents when Marie Mason arrived.

"Morning," said Marie as she strode into the room, her black suit and white blouse immaculate and not a hair out of place. She was five-four, one-thirty and all business. There was no preamble. She was there to help.

"Marie Mason," said Marie as she thrust out her hand to Bill. "Good to see you again, Tommy. So, we're going to take another look at the Riverside case. I'm happy about that. Never like to have one get away. So, over to you, Bill. Whatever I can do to help, I'm all in."

Bill ran through the contents of the file with Marie and shared his observations, including the loose ends he had found.

"How the fuck did we miss all of this and not connect some of the dots?" said Marie in her normal forthright manner. "We must have had our heads up our asses."

Bill Ross knew when he read the file last night that he would like Marie Mason, and he was not disappointed.

Bill hid a smile and said, "Let's go through the evidence you and the team collected initially, Marie, rather than beat yourself up about what should have been done and what was missed."

"Agreed. Bill. The popping sound you hear is my head exiting my ass! Now, let's focus on finding the son of a bitch. I sure hope he's not dead. I'd hate to think that he went off to meet his maker without being held to account for this."

Bill said, "You and George did the house-to-house and there was a woman by the name of Billy Jo McWilliams. She lived at the entrance to Riverside, almost a mile away from the McCord house. She told you that she had seen a dark Ford Explorer with Alabama plates in the neighborhood the night before the body was discovered."

"Yes, I remember her," said Marie. "She was very sure about it."

"In that case, let's check out if she still lives there and, if so, let's visit her again and see if she remembers any additional details," said Bill. "We need to find out if she saw the driver's face. It's a long shot, I know, but let's try."

"It's a place to start," agreed Marie.

~

Billy Jo McWilliams lived in the same house in the Riverside neighborhood. Her husband, Tom McWilliams, had passed away in 2008 and the house had been paid off by the insurance settlement. She never remarried and by all accounts didn't have a new love in her life.

Tommy, Bill, and Marie had scheduled the meeting for 9:00 a.m., and they picked up some doughnuts on the way. After they arrived and were shown into the spacious living room, they all enjoyed breakfast with Billy Jo. A photograph of Billy Jo and her late husband, Tom, had a place of pride on the coffee table. It was a minute after Marie explained why they were there that Billy Jo finally spoke.

"Gee, that's almost ten years ago."

"You must miss him terribly," said Marie as she gently touched the photograph on the table.

"Yes, I do. He was the love of my life," said Billy Jo, trying to hold back the tears.

"Are you sure you remember the dark Ford Explorer?" said Bill, getting the conversation back on track. "As you said, it's a long time ago, so how can you be so sure after all these years?"

"I am absolutely sure because September 14th is my birthday and we had a party. It lasted until sundown and then our friends began to leave. Tom and I were saying goodbye to Al and Sheila Simpson and their two kids. They had parked their Suburban right out front. The two kids were messing around and Sheila was yelling at them to get in the car. Their younger boy, Steven, ran straight out into the road and this dark Ford Explorer almost hit him! The driver slammed on the brakes and came to a screeching stop. I remember Sheila running up to the side of the Explorer yelling, 'Sorry! Sorry!' The driver didn't even roll down his window. He just waved as if to say, 'It's okay', and he drove on into the neighborhood."

"Did you get a good look at his face?" asked Marie.

"Yes, he wore glasses and had a full beard. It was getting pretty dark, so I couldn't say what color of hair. That was pretty much it."

The team thanked Billy Jo and left. Marie was convinced that Billy Jo would have headed straight back into the living room and picked up the photograph from the table, which is exactly what she did.

"Now, there's a love that will never die," remarked Marie.

As they walked to the car, Tommy turned to Marie. "Didn't Jim McCord have glasses and a beard, Marie?"

"Thinking the same thing, buddy. Thinking the same thing," replied Marie.

Chapter 14 - The LSU crew

2005 - A Great Adventure

TWO DAYS LATER GALINA AND Pavel arrived in Tulsa. The weather had improved along the way, so when they arrived at the Tulsa RV Ranch in Beggs, Oklahoma, they pitched the tent. The RV Ranch was huge and the restroom and shower facilities were again outstanding. They showered, changed into fresh clothes and felt recharged.

The RV Ranch was located in Green Valley, and this area of Oklahoma is cowboy country. The restaurant was filled with dudes with cowboy hats, blue jeans and "shit kicker" boots. There was a saloon with spittoons on the floor and the restaurant served steak. Galina and Pavel were wide eyed at the sight that greeted them when they walked in. They had never seen real cowboys.

"How exciting!" said Galina.

The hostess found them a corner booth. "Y'all might want to split the 24-ounce sirloin if you're hungry. I think it's the best deal on the menu," said the hostess as she went off to deal with the line of hungry travelers waiting to be seated.

The temptation was too great, and although $26 was a little expensive for dinner, they ordered the monster with all the fixings.

An older couple sat in the booth opposite. "Where are you headed?" asked the old man, trying to make polite conversation.

"California," replied Pavel.

The lady's eyes widened as she said, "Oh, we spend most of the year on the road, honey. Archie and I love to meet new people at each stop along the way. We make sure that we get back to Connecticut for Christmas each year so we can spend the festive season with our son and his family and see the grandkids open their presents. Then we're off on the road again."

"We plan to be married in Las Vegas and then we'll see where life takes us. It's such a huge country with so much to explore and experience. The world is our oyster!" replied Pavel,

The old lady turned to Archie and said, "How exciting! Two young lovers off to explore the world. Just like you and me, Archie. We're just young lovers, aren't we?" Archie managed a smirk as he continued the demolition work on the behemoth steak that lay in front of him.

As they returned to their steaks, Galina's mind, for the first time on the trip, felt a sting of doubt. *The world is our oyster? Where did that come from?* thought Galina. *What happened to settling down and raising a family in California?*

~

They rose early the next morning, made good time along the I-70, and arrived at the American RV Park just outside Albuquerque at 4:30 in the afternoon. They decided that they would stay there a couple of nights to recharge their batteries for the next leg of the trip to Vegas. They didn't want to reach Vegas so exhausted that they couldn't enjoy their wedding day to the fullest. A good spot was found for the tent and they got it secured.

The city of Albuquerque is five thousand feet above sea level. On a chilly night in May, they were both glad for the warmth of the restaurant. They found a small corner booth and sat down below a huge painting of a hot air balloon. The waitress arrived to take their order, and when Galina asked about the painting, she explained that every year in October, the city plays host to the largest hot air balloon festival in the world.

The restaurant was quite small, so they couldn't help but hear the group in the opposite corner of the restaurant kicking up a storm. There were five of them, two guys and three gals, and they were whooping and hollering and chugging beers like there was no tomorrow.

A petite brunette with an LSU tee shirt looked up at them and yelled, "Come join us!"

Pavel and Galina looked at each other and, after a brief pause, walked over to the party. The group made some space for them around the huge corner table.

The brunette grabbed a pair of nearby chairs, set them down and moved over. "We're so glad you decided to join us. We saw y'all sitting there together like runaway lovers, staring into each other's eyes, and we thought you'd like some company."

"Well, yes, we are runaways," said a somewhat embarrassed Pavel. Galina was furious that he had told them but bit her tongue.

The brunette squealed, "I knew it! I just knew it! We need introductions! Attention, everybody!" The group looked over and smirked at her antics. She had done this before.

"I am Fran Taylor, this is Rocky Redmond and Gail Anderson, and over the other side of the table are Lani Boudreau and Adelaide Leblanc. We're all seniors now at LSU down in Baton Rouge. We're on our way to Vail to work in the restaurants and bars there to make some extra cash. Afterwards, we're headed back to school for our final year. We'll be back the first week in August."

Galina made their introductions while trying to hide her anger at Pavel for admitting that they were Romeo and Juliet.

Galina was also a little confused about the dynamics of this group of five. She assumed, correctly as it was later to be revealed, that Fran was the odd one out and that the other four were in relationships, given the way that Fran had done the introductions.

Adelaide Leblanc ordered a round of drinks for the new friends. Pavel and Galina knocked back a tequila shot. It tasted weird, and as at shot slid down they screwed up their faces. Growing up in Russian households where vodka was the norm, the tequila tasted like dish soap. They wouldn't be doing any more shots of that. Beers accompanied the shots and the party rolled along.

"Where are you headed?" asked Gail.

Galina had a good feeling about Gail. She was a little five-foot-four bundle of energy with red hair and freckles. She seemed more levelheaded and down-to-earth than the others but she, like everyone else, was now drunk and was having difficulty focusing her beautiful green eyes. The daughter of a third-generation Irish-American, Gail had to work to pay her way through college. The others all had rich parents.

"We're headed to Vegas," replied Galina. "We plan to get married there and then travel on to California, get work, and find a place to live. Pavel worked for his uncle in construction in Maryland, so he's confident that he will get a construction job quite easily in California."

"It's hotter than Hades in Vegas this time of year. Well over a hundred degrees," said Fran, overhearing the conversation between Galina and Gail.

"You can't go outside and you'll spend a fortune in the casinos just to keep cool. Been there, done that!" continued Fran. "You both should tag along with us, find work in Vail and then head on to California at the end of the summer season." Galina felt instantly threatened at Fran's attempt to control their lives.

Fran's voice became higher as she continued, "You could even stay on for the winter. Even more money can be made when the skiing jet set hit town! Heck, we could all be in your wedding; Rocky could be best man, and we three girls could be your maids of honor!"

"You know, sometimes, Fran, you can be a real pain in the ass!" yelled Gail, taking Fran by surprise and taking Galina's breath away. She didn't expect that from the little Irish girl, but she giggled just the same.

An hour later, they all staggered out of the restaurant and headed to the campsite. They were all a bit drunk, some more than others. Rocky Redmond went head over heals in the parking lot.

"I'm going to sue!" slurred Rocky. A law student, he was trying hard to demonstrate that his unfortunate trip was the fault of the owners of the establishment's failure to maintain the parking lot and had nothing to do with the fact that he was drunk as a skunk, They all hugged as eventually one by one they found their tents and said their good-nights.

The following morning, they all met for breakfast slightly the worse for wear from the night of partying. As usual, Fran was the master of ceremonies and got the conversation started.

"So what do y'all think? Want to join the party for a couple of months and come with us to Vail?"

"It's very tempting, but I don't know. We had our heart set on a wedding in Vegas," replied Galina. Her cautious side needed time to weigh up folks she met until she got to know them better. She was a little undecided about the LSU crew, in particular Fran, who didn't sit well with her at all.

Pavel's eyes were wide with excitement. He leaned over and said, "Come on, Galina. Remember what we talked about with Lewis and Clark. Sometimes, you just have to swallow hard and go for it."

Fran leaned in on Galina's other side and said, "You can still head to Vegas after Vail. It will be cooler by then, and you'll have more money in your pocket."

"What's your plan to get to Vail?" asked Galina, softening her position.

Rocky, still nursing his hangover and rubbing the significant contusion on his forehead from last night's festivities, spoke up from across the table. "We're taking North I-25, branching off on Highway 84 toward Pagosa Springs and then north on Highway 160 to River Bend Resort campground.

"If we drove straight to Vail, it would take almost nine hours, so staying the night at River Bend is a better plan. We did it last summer and it's a scenic drive. The campsites at River

Bend are great, with showers and all the amenities," continued Rocky.

"Let's do it," said Pavel, and his excitement to make the change in their plans made Galina feel more than a little nervous.

"Yes!" yelled Fran.

Galina thought she saw Fran look at Pavel as she screamed. She couldn't be sure, but as she turned back to look at Pavel, she could see he was smiling broadly in the direction of Fran. *What is going on here?* she thought, and then dismissed it from her mind as the rest of the LSU crew demanded a group hug.

~

Later that morning, with bags packed and loaded on the bike, the Triumph followed Adelaide's white Cadillac Escalade out onto North I-25.

Chapter 15 - The Three Musketeers

2014 - The Cold Case Investigation

JUST AFTER LUNCH, TOMMY and Marie strode into Jack Johnson's office with Bill in tow. "We would like to give you an update on our meeting this morning with Billy Jo McWilliams," announced Tommy.

"Let's go to the conference room. Not a lot of room in here. The cleaners didn't show up yesterday," joked Jack,

They sat down at the long table and Jack started without any preamble. "So, what's the scoop, team?"

"Billy Jo reconfirmed what she said to Marie and George in 2005," said Tommy. "The reason it's so clear in her mind is that it was her birthday that day and there was an incident in the street where a kid was almost run over by a Ford Explorer. And you'll never guess what else: she saw the driver!" Tommy sat back triumphantly to allow the news to have the desired effect.

"Well then?" asked Jack, his eyes staring Tommy down like a relief pitcher facing a full count. "What did she see?"

"It was a man with glasses and a beard," responded Tommy.

"Would she be able to pick him out of a lineup?" asked Jack.

"Unlikely and, at any rate, it would be difficult to have an ID stick as it was getting dark and she only saw him for an instant," responded Tommy.

"Jim McCord has a beard and glasses," Marie chimed in, excited to get that fact out on the table.

"My brother has a beard and glasses, Marie, and I'm pretty sure he didn't do it," quipped Jack with a note of sarcasm in his voice.

Marie's face deflated until Jack continued.

"But Jim McCord *is* front and center in this whole thing, so we should try to run the traps on this. Any ideas, Bill? Anything else in the file where we might be able to connect some dots with this new piece of info?"

"I would recommend that we keep this new information to the four of us for now," suggested Bill. "We sure as heck should not let Jim McCord know that there has been a new development. Based on the other info in the file, we should also be very careful with any additional inquiries, as I would guess that Bill Andersen would hear about it on the grapevine and Jim McCord would know about it instantly. Thick as thieves, those two,"

"So what do you suggest?" said Jack, wondering where Bill was going with this.

"I suggest we take a look at Dawn and Harvey Cohen first," said Bill.

Marie's eyes lit up as she imagined herself waterboarding Dawn Cohen. Dawn was the type of person Marie disliked the most. To Marie, it was more than obvious that she wallowed in her husband's money, drinking wine all day and looking down her nose at any other woman who hadn't managed to land the "big catch." It was Marie's opinion that she probably had never put in an honest day's work in her life.

After Jack nodded his approval, Bill said, "Okay, let's find out if they still live in the neighborhood. Not sure how we might go about talking to them if they are still around but let's check and get back together here tomorrow morning to discuss what we know and where we go."

Jack opened the conference room door and yelled down the hall, "Celia, can you reserve this conference room for us at 9:00 a.m. tomorrow?"

"Will do, Detective Johnson," replied Celia.

~

The following morning in the conference room, with coffee and doughnuts in hand, the atmosphere was one of subdued excitement. They had discovered Dawn and Harvey Cohen had divorced in 2009 after Harvey found his wife giving the pool boy a lesson in the art of rodeo riding. He had come home early from the office and heard the screams coming from his recreation room. Harvey had burst open the door and found the pool boy lying naked flat on his back on the pool table. Dawn Cohen was astride him, giving her best impression of Clint Cannon, the bareback rodeo champion. The little tassels on her tits swayed rhythmically as she grinded on her "pony." She had been wearing Harvey's black Stetson that he bought at the State Fair. That was the final straw.

"No one fucks with my pool table," Harvey is reputed to have said. It was unlikely he had actually said that, but the pool table did have new felt fitted the following day.

Jack took a bite from his glazed donut and said; "I suggest we keep our powder dry on the two of them for now. I was reading through the notes you made on the file, Bill. I would guess that Riverside has a homeowner's association, an HOA. I wonder if they give out warnings to owners who park cars in their driveways overnight. Some associations insist that you clear it ahead of time if you are expecting out-of-state guests. There have been some reported cases in Austin over the years where out-of-state vehicles were parked in driveways while the owners weren't home. When the owners came back, their home had been robbed. These events had been missed by the HOA patrols, so now each out-of-state visitor has to be cleared in advance."

Jack took another bite along with a sip of coffee and continued.

"Can you do some research on that, Bill? See if Riverside has an HOA and what their rules are regarding out-of-state vehicles. I'm sure that Tommy and Marie have other things that they need to be working on.

"And one more thing," Jack continued. "I haven't decided whether to get approval to reopen this case yet but I am getting pretty darn close. If I get that approval, I will want you three amigos working on it with me."

"There would be four of us," chimed in Tommy, as he had always been good at arithmetic in school. "It should really be the four musketeers!"

"Get back to work!" blared Jack, ending the meeting and going off to see if the cleaners had been in his office yet.

~

The following morning, Bill sat with Jack Johnson in his office. "Riverside does have a homeowners association and they do give out warnings regarding overnight parking of out-of-state vehicles," said Bill.

"Outstanding!" barked Jack.

"I went a step further and called the current president on the pretext that I was conducting a survey for the police department on various neighborhood traffic policies. Apparently, we already have an officer scheduled to drive through Riverside at some frequency looking for people breaking the speed limit, and the HOA president, Bill Larkin, was very complimentary on how effective the program has been. He said he'd be happy to help with any survey and to call him anytime to set up a meeting."

"That was probably a little bit hasty, Bill, but good to know that we have his cooperation if and when we need it," said Jack.

Later that day, the word came down. "Jack wants y'all in the conference room *ASAP*," said Celia, sticking her head around the corner breakroom.

It was almost 6:30 when they walked into the conference room. Jack sat at the top of the table, and standing beside him was Travis County Police Chief Bill Dunwoody with a serious look on his face. Bill Dunwoody was a huge man, well over six feet and weighed two-sixty. He had two sons in college, both linebackers and younger versions of Bill. He was powerful and intimidating. No one messed with Bill Dunwoody.

They all sat down with a feeling of trepidation. Jack cleared his throat and read from prepared text.

"After giving due consideration to the extensive additional information provided by Special Reserve Officer Bill Ross on the Riverside murder case of 2005, plus the latest developments regarding the possible identity of the driver of the dark Ford Expedition thought to be involved, Chief Bill Dunwoody has given his approval to reopen the case. Congratulations, everyone!"

It was like they had won the lottery. Marie turned and gave Tommy a hug and Bill, with a beaming smile, looked like the cat that got the cream.

Bill Dunwoody quickly ended the festivities and said, "I want a thorough job done this time, people. And when you talk with Stan Hardwick, which I'm sure you will, I want y'all to show him the respect he deserves. He was a good detective and served the people of Travis County well. Good luck and Jack, you'll give me regular updates on progress as we agreed. That is all."

After Dunwoody left the room, Jack said, "Beers are on me at the Oasis! And none of that single malt shit, Ross."

"You got it, boss," said Bill, and off they went for a few beers and to watch the sun set over Lake Travis.

Chapter 16 - The Oasis

2014 - The Cold Case Investigation

THE OASIS ON LAKE TRAVIS is a popular restaurant on the western edge of Austin. The restaurant promotes itself as the "Sunset Capital of Texas" with its terraced views looking west over the lake. The thirty-thousand-square-foot restaurant sits on a bluff 450 feet above the lake and is the largest outdoor restaurant in Texas.

The restaurant was first built in 1982 by Houston entrepreneur Beau Theriot, who had purchased the 500-acre ranch overlooking the lake a few years earlier. He still lives on the property in a huge mansion, half a mile down the road from the restaurant.

Many people think that the line from the Garth Brooks song "I've Got Friends in Low Places" when he sings, "...Think I'll slip on down to the Oasis" refers to the Lake Travis hilltop restaurant. In fact, it refers to a seedy nightclub in Nashville.

Marie put her glass down on the table and said, "This place burned down the same year we found the woman's body in Riverside," said Marie.

"Looks pretty good now," responded Bill as he shared the pitcher of Bud Lite and tried to look like he was enjoying it. Bud Lite would not have been Bill's first choice but Jack got the beers, so Bud Lite it was.

Marie continued, "Beau Theriot had the entire place rebuilt after the fire. The apartments, the huge multi-story car park and the other retail outlets were added. None of this was here when the original restaurant burned. Beau is a real entrepreneur and sees great potential in building his empire.".

They were an interesting group brought together by the murder of a young woman less than five miles away from where they sat that night. The sun set over the lake as they drank a few beers, exchanged stories and learned a little bit more about each other.

Jack Johnson was the quintessential Texan and most who knew him were convinced that he had been born with the police officer's patch on his arm. He owned a ranch outside Giddings, a few miles east of Austin, that he had inherited from his father. There he raised a few head of cattle and made significant money from oil extracted from the property. Jack owned all the mineral rights as well as the land. His word was his bond, and if he shook your hand his commitment was absolute.

Marie Mason was born in Tyler, Texas, the only daughter of a cattleman. Before taking a job in the Travis County police department, she had worked as a detective with the Smith County Sheriff in Tyler and cared for her very sick mother, who eventually passed away from breast cancer. Her life partner, Shelly, would tell you that she could chug a beer faster than any man and would arm-wrestle you at the drop of a hat. She was smart as a tack and could sense when the pieces of the jigsaw puzzle didn't quite fit. That's what Bill Ross liked about her, being an old jigsaw man himself.

Father and son Bill and Tommy Ross were more alike than either of them had ever thought. Tommy, once a Marine, always a Marine, had arms like a mixed martial arts fighter and owned a selection of guns that he kept under lock and key to ensure that nothing bad could happen accidently. The stash was sufficient to defend a small town from the zombie invasion, which Tommy was convinced could happen at any time. Tommy had moved on from his Jedi days to a protector of the innocents from the undead. Like millions of others, he was addicted to *The Walking Dead* TV series. Watching it was his

Sunday ritual. Across his shoulders he had a tattoo, *Made in Scotland,* and was intensely proud of his Scottish heritage.

His father was a fanatical Kilmarnock FC supporter while Tommy loved his Oakland Raiders. Even in sports, they had a lot in common; both their teams were crap, losing more games than they won.

Tommy's father was a cross between William Wallace, the Scottish freedom fighter, and Sherlock Homes. He hated guns. Growing up in the UK in the '60s, he had seen what guns could do in the hands of the baddies, like the brothers Ronnie and Reggie Kray. The brothers enjoyed killing and they controlled the East End of London, inflicting the maximum pain on their adversaries while innocent bystanders were often caught in the crossfire.

Tommy was of the belief that guns never killed anyone. It was bad people who killed good people. Bill's opinion was that guns helped the bad guys kill a lot of people,some good and some bad, but most of the time the perpetrator couldn't care less. Guns reinforced the power of evil and increased the probability that the use of said power would result in bloodshed. They certainly differed on the gun subject but their other underlying personalities made them two peas from the same pod.

An interesting team, united in a common purpose: the unrelenting pursuit of justice. If you were a baddy and these four musketeers were on your tail, you should be terrified, no question about that. The bastard who had killed a beautiful twenty-something and left her in the backyard of a Riverside home was going down. All of them agreed that they would be present when the needle went in, the life drained, and the killer's eyes went dark in their skull.

~

The following morning they were back at it. "Okay, team. Divide and conquer and let's be thorough," said Jack as they wrote out their action plan on the whiteboard in the conference room. They had designated it as the "war room" following the approval of Chief Dunwoody to reopen the case.

"Firstly, we need to go visit with Stan Hardwick at Lake Buchanan. Bill and I will do that. Next, we should arrange a meeting with the HOA president, Bill Larkin. Tommy, I suggest you take that one."

Tommy looked up from his notes and nodded. Jack erased a mistake on the board and continued.

"We should also talk with Dawn and Harvey Cohen again, separately. We need to know Harvey's movements and if he really was at the convention in Vegas. We also need to track down Dawn and re-interview her. There was something in the file about her body language when the topic of Jim McCord was raised. You take this, Marie, and please leave Dawn in one piece or at least with no visible bodily injuries," joked Jack.

"Will do, boss," said Marie with a huge smile across her face, not able to contain her excitement at the prospect of grilling Dawn Cohen again.

"Last butanot least, there is Jim McCord. Bill and I will interview him again. We'll give him a few days to stew after we tell him that we have reopened the case."

Jack turned from the whiteboard and faced the team. Everyone looked eager to launch back into the investigation.

"Team, today is Friday, August 29. The next full briefing and update on progress will be one week from today at 10:00 a.m. I'll have Celia put it in the calendar and tell her that this room is now off limits to everyone other than members of the Riverside murder team. From now on, it is under lockdown, with the four of us the only people with access. Also, Marie, can you get these windows blacked out? I don't want people walking down the hallway staring at us like goldfish in a jar or taking notes that end up on the front page of the *Statesman*."

The cold case team was now fully engaged. As they all left the room with their assignments, Bill thought, *Unleash the hounds.* It was time to find the scent and follow it to their prey.

Chapter 17- Stan Hardwick

2014 - The Cold Case Investigation

IT TOOK JACK JOHNSON AND Bill Ross ninety minutes to drive to Stan Hardwick's place. They had gone east on Highway 620 to Highway 183 north and then Highway 29 west to Lake Buchanan. When they drove up the driveway, Stan was sitting on his front porch in his shorts and favorite fishing shirt, tying flies and other lures, readying for his next excursion on the lake.

"How are you, Stan?" bellowed Jack as he got out of the car.

Looking up from his fly tying, Stan replied, "Good to see you, Jack. You look in fine shape for an old curmudgeon."

"This is Special Reserve Detective Bill Ross," said Jack as he and Bill climbed the stairs. "He came on board a couple of weeks ago to help me with the cold case I talked to you about on the phone."

Stan shook Bill's hand and said, "Very pleased to meet you, Bill. Why don't you fellas come on around to the back deck? Y'all want some iced tea? I've been off the booze for some time now, so no beer in the place, if you had had an inclination for a brew," said Stan.

"Iced tea would be just the ticket. Thanks, Stan," said Jack.

Stan went to get the tea as Bill and Jack admired the view out over the lake.

"Quite the Shangri-La he has here," said Bill as he took in the view over the lake. "What an idyllic spot."

Stan overheard Bill's comment as he walked back with the tea. "We liked it the first time we saw it. Doreen and I bought the land back in '95 and we got Garrison McMullen to build us a dream home for our retirement. Unfortunately, Doreen only got to enjoy a couple of years in the place as she passed away from breast cancer in 2009," said Stan, putting the tea down on a wicker table by the matching wicker chairs. "So, you're opening up the case again?".

"Yup, we got the approval from Bill Dunwoody yesterday," replied Jack. "What are your memories of the case, Stan? Why did it stall?"

"In all honesty, we couldn't connect the dots," replied Stan. "No one in the neighborhood saw anything other than the woman who thought she saw a Ford Explorer. No one else saw the vehicle and we couldn't make any connections to trace it. There was the Cohen woman, who was drunk most of the day, so she was of no help. Why would Jim McCord kill a girl and then leave her in his own backyard? Then there was Jim McCord's son and his friends who had the house cleaned after they returned to Oklahoma. Unlikely that they were going to forget one of their friends and leave her dead at the side of the pool with a bottle of wine."

Stan paused, took a sip of tea and continued. "We couldn't even ID the girl. We ran fingerprints through the databank, we had a sketch made up and circulated it to other police departments and sheriff's offices in Texas, with no response. Even the *Austin Statesman* ran an artist impression sketch with an editorial piece, "The Lady by the Lake." All we got was a sea of crap responses that we had to wade through. One guy who lived on the hillside overlooking Riverside swore on a stack of Bibles that he saw a spacecraft hover over the neighborhood that night. According to him, a beam of light shone down from it and deposited the body on a lawn chair. His account was the only one that made any sense and matched the evidence."

Jack laughed and took a sip of tea. "Yes, it sure is a strange one, Stan." Jack felt the need to put his friend at ease. He didn't want Stan to think they were there to beat up on him.

"Are there any other things of any significance that you felt at the time didn't quite fit? Anything stick in your craw? Maybe people that you suspected were not being straight with you?" prodded Jack.

Stan stared into the distance and mumbled something that Jack and Bill could not quite understand.

"What was that, Stan? What did you say?"

After a long pause, Stan sighed and said, "Not my finest hour, fellas. I think I may have missed a lot of things."

Stan stared over the calm waters of Lake Buchanan and the tears began to well up in his eyes.

"Doreen's illness took its toll on us both physically and financially. It was a very aggressive form of cancer and she had to have both breasts removed. The combination of the mental stress and the chemo treatments transformed a beautiful, vibrant woman into a shadow of her former self. Depression set in and she lost the will to continue the fight. A year after the initial diagnoses, she passed away."

Stan paused and reached out his hand, trying to control the shaking, and took a sip of tea to steady himself. Jack got up from his chair and put an arm around his old partner.

Stan continued on, "I may have fucked up and not been as thorough as I should have been. To be honest, there is a lot of it I can't remember because of the booze. Tommy did the best he could but he was just a rookie, and Marie tried hard. I don't think I gave her all the support she needed. As you know, Jack, sometimes the breakthrough in a case comes when you just sit and talk together. I failed to live up to my side of the bargain on that with Tommy and Marie. I just wanted to get home to the bottle."

"Tommy is my son, Stan," said Bill, interrupting the monologue, trying to stop Stan's downward depressive spiral.

"Good guy, Tommy, and a good officer. He'll go far one day," said Stan, almost as a side comment, not fully realizing what Bill had said.

They stayed with Stan for another hour until he regained some composure. Jack was genuinely concerned about Stan's mental state as he stepped outside to call Bill Dunwoody.

After Jack explained Stan's mental state, Dunwoody said, "I know some groups that provide help to retiring police officers as they try to make the transition from being a cop. I'll reach out to some folks I know who are involved with these support groups. It can be really tough for these officers, especially those who have spent their entire life in law enforcement. They can have difficulty adjusting and many experience deep depression. I will ask them to reach out to Stan," said the Chief.

Jack and Bill said their goodbyes to Stan and made their way back to Austin, no further forward on the Riverside murder case.

~

While Bill drove, Jack Johnson called Jim McCord on his cell phone. It rang twice before Jim answered.

"Mr. McCord, this is Detective Jack Johnson of the Travis County Police Department. Would it be possible for us to come visit you at your earliest convenience?"

"What is this about?" Jim McCord asked with an irritated tone.

"We are reopening a murder case, Mr. McCord. The one concerning a young woman who was found deceased in your backyard in 2005," continued Jack.

There was a long pause before Jim McCord responded.

"That terrible event was very disturbing for my wife, Mary, and me, Detective Johnson. It took us a long time to recover from the shock and get our lives back together again. Mary went through almost two years of therapy and still has emotional issues. Why has the case been reopened, has there been a new development?"

"We will explain everything to you when we meet, Mr. McCord," continued Jack.

"Do you need to involve Mary?" asked McCord.

"Not at this time. If we could meet with you as soon as possible, sir, that would be great. Where are you, Mr. McCord?" pressed Jack.

"We're back in Austin. We came home from Colorado a couple of weeks earlier than normal this year. Would it be okay to meet at your office, Detective Johnson, rather than here at our home? Again, I'd like to do whatever we can to not disturb Mary."

"Of course, and please call me Jack. When would be a good day and time for you?"

"I am available now and could meet later today, Jack, if that would work for you," said McCord,

"Great. We are on our way back from Lake Buchanan. Would 5:30 this evening work for you? We can meet at the Hudson Bend office. Do you know where that is Mr. McCord?"

"Yes, I know where that is. I'll be there at 5:30. See you then, Jack," and with that, Jim McCord ended the call.

~

When Jim McCord hung up the phone he stood and stared out into space. He had thought that the events of 2005 were all behind him, but it wasn't so. A saying popped into his head, "Sometimes the past comes back to haunt us." As a cold fear crept over him, he realized this might be more than a haunting. This could become a nightmare.

Chapter 18 - Stephanie Lake

2014 - The Cold Case Investigation

"WHO WAS THAT ON the phone, honey?" asked Mary McCord as she lay in her bed resting.

"We need to talk, darling. Can you come into the family room?" asked Jim.

A few minutes later, Mary sat down in her normal chair and pulled her robe around her. She stared at her husband with a look of concern on her face.

"You look worried, Jim. What is it?

"They're reopening the case of the woman in the backyard, honey."

Mary gasped, "Oh God, no! We don't need to go through all of that again, do we? I'm not sure that my nerves can stand it. They didn't find out who the girl was when Stan Hardwick had the case back then, and he told us that there was nothing much they could do without an ID. They ran the artist's impression in the *Statesman* and that didn't get them anywhere. What makes them think there might be more information after all this time?"

As Mary rambled and got more excited, Jim McCord felt his mind drift away. He noticed this and snapped back into the present.

"You need to keep yourself together, Mary. We had nothing to do with this and I will try to shield you as best I can.

Don't go talking to your friends about this and if they ask, say that I am dealing with the Travis County police and that because of your condition, there is no reason for you to be involved."

Mary looked to be on the brink of tears. "What new information can they possibly have? I hate when the police get involved in our lives. They make you feel that you have done something wrong even when you're totally innocent. It's just like what happened with that business in Colorado. They kept pressing and pressing and wouldn't stop. I'm really scared, Jim. I think I need to take another Valium and go lie down."

After Mary had left and the bedroom door was closed, Jim stared out the window at the backyard pool.

"The scene of the crime," he mumbled.

As he looked out onto the pool, all of the questions of nine years ago resurfaced. What mad fucker had done that to him back then? What was their possible motive? Jim had his suspicions but kept them to himself. When the cops dig up one pile of shit, there is always the chance that they will find another stack close by. Jim knew that there were multiple piles on this one and it would take all of his skills to keep the police focused on the woman in his backyard. He also needed to keep Mary together so that she didn't lose it and start blabbing about stuff she shouldn't talk about.

He needed to prepare for the meeting with the Travis County detectives. He needed to be mentally strong. No throwaway comments that might give them an opening to dig further. He needed to keep it together.

~

While Jack and Bill were driving back from Lake Buchanan and McCord was having his quiet talk with Mary, Tommy Ross was meeting with the Riverside HOA president, Bill Larkin.

A retired banker, Bill Larkin had bought one of the first houses built in Riverside. They met in Bill's home office. He sat behind a huge oak desk and peered over the top of his gold half-rim reading glasses, his long gray hair flopping over as he did. Tommy felt like he was in a meeting to ask for a loan and that Bill Larkin was already predisposed to refusing the request.

"Thanks for agreeing to meet with me, Bill," said Tommy. "You spoke with my dad, Bill Ross, a week or so ago and he told you he was doing a survey. I have to come clean, it's not a survey. We are actually reopening an unsolved murder case. You might remember the body that was found in the backyard of the McCords' residence back in 2005?" said Tommy apologetically.

"Oh, I see," said Bill Larkin, more than a little offended by the deception. "If you had just been honest with me initially, Detective Ross, I think that that would have been more professional."

Tommy could sense Bill Larkin's tone and could tell the ruse had touched a nerve with him.

With the initial tense exchange over, Bill Larkin attempted to take control of proceedings. "I was not the HOA president back then. Stephanie Lake, our current treasurer, was the HOA president in 2005. Would it help if I asked her join the meeting if she is available? She only lives around the corner on Angel Way."

"I think that would be *very* helpful, Bill," said Tommy.

Bill made the call, and within fifteen minutes Stephanie Lake entered the room like a defense attorney about to rescue her client. She carried a laptop in one hand, a designer handbag in the other, and wore a dark two-piece business suit over a pink blouse. Tommy couldn't take his eyes off of her.

"How can I be of assistance to you boys?" she said in a sultry southern drawl. Tommy shifted uncomfortably in his seat.

"This is Detective Ross," said Bill Larkin. "The Travis County police are reopening the case of the dead woman found in Jim McCord's backyard back in 2005."

Tommy wanted to stand up and shake her hand but thought the better of it.

"Pleased to meet you, Miss Lake," said Tommy. He hoped his face didn't reveal his acute embarrassment.

"It's Mrs., but you can call me Steph," said Stephanie Lake, basking in the knowledge that she had succeeded in making the young officer feel uncomfortable. "Yes, I remember that awful event! How can we help, Detective Ross? What is it you would like to know?"

Her southern drawl was intoxicating. Regaining his composure, Tommy outlined what he needed to know.

"One of your homeowners reported seeing a dark-colored Ford Explorer with Alabama plates in the neighborhood the night before the dead woman's body was discovered. We wondered if Riverside had rules regarding overnight parking of vehicles in driveways without a parking sticker. In particular, a vehicle with out=of=state plates. Do you have such a rule?"

"Yes, we do!" said Bill and Steph simultaneously and almost in harmony.

"And we enforce it diligently," said Steph. "Our management company has people drive around the neighborhood between midnight and 4:00 a.m. a couple of times a month to note any violators."

Tommy fought back the stirring in his groin and said, "I know it's a long shot, but do you keep records on violators going back to 2005 and could there have been an inspection carried out the night in question?"

"The answer to your first question is yes; we have records that go back to when the neighborhood was first formed," said Steph proudly. "The answer to your second question is I don't know, but let's see."

Stephanie Lake opened up her laptop and smiled invitingly at Tommy while she waited for it to boot. "Here we are," she said, opening an Excel spreadsheet. "What date in 2005?"

"The body was discovered Thursday, September 15, so it would have been the previous night, September 14," said Tommy.

"Well, you are in luck, Detective Ross, there was indeed a patrol that night. And let me see, there were 107 violations. We record vehicle make, color, registration, address and name of the property owner. We issue a warning if it's a first offense, but we fine the habitual offenders. That night, there were six fines imposed and posted on the door of the owner, so let's look at those first, shall we?" said Steph, deliberately taking her time to reinforce her administrative efficiency.

"Wow, here it is!" Steph was shocked and surprised that she had actually found this needle in a haystack.

Tommy's jaw almost hit the floor. This was potentially the major breakthrough they had been hoping for. His voice was actually quivering when he asked, "What house?"

For maximum effect, Stephanie Lake read the entire record.

"Grey Ford Explorer, Alabama license plate KAA 20C, driveway of 2014 Braker Lane, home of Mr. & Mrs. Harvey Cohen."

"*Bingo!*" exclaimed Tommy.

"She paid the fine the following morning," said Steph with surprise.

"I'll bet she did!" said Tommy.

Tommy thanked Bill Larkin and Stephanie Lake and asked that they keep the conversation confidential. They agreed. Tommy was walking on air as he entered the cruiser and grabbed the radio to call Marie. He hoped that she had not yet tracked down Dawn Cohen.

"Marie, have you tracked down Dawn Cohen yet?"

"No, not yet, Tommy, why?"

"I just finished up with the HOA and they confirmed that the Explorer was in the Cohen driveway that night."

"Outstanding, Tommy!" exclaimed Marie. "We can go right at her now on her relationship with McCord. That's great news, Tommy."

After the call with Marie, Tommy called Jack Johnson.

"Great news, Tommy. I just hung up with Jim McCord and arranged to meet him tonight. I'll call him back and postpone that meeting until we have more information on his Dawn Cohen relationship. Good work, Tommy," said Jack.

Chapter 19 - Sindhur Wadawadagi

2014 - The Cold Case Investigation

THAT EVENING, THEY ALL sat together in the conference room.

"Major breakthrough and good work, Tommy. McCord came up from San Antonio that night, I'm sure of it. That said, we need to find the evidence to prove that he did," said Jack.

Bill picked up where Jack left off and said, "I also believe that he was the one driving the Explorer, but we need to get more evidence to squeeze him."

Bill thought for a moment and said, "Rental car companies, especially the big national chains, churn cars. When you rent a car from them, it is often a vehicle registered in an adjoining state. Let me get hold of the big name rental guys at the San Antonio airport and see if they still have the rental records from 2005. I can have them look for the Explorer using the Alabama license plate," said Bill.

"Good idea, Bill. Go do it and get back *ASAP* if you find out anything interesting," said Jack.

Marie looked up from her notes and said, "And what about Dawn Cohen? I bet she paid that fine fast so that hubby wouldn't find out who had come calling."

"Are we speculating that Jim McCord and Dawn Cohen had a thing, Marie?" asked Bill.

"Had 'a thing'? Look what she did to the pool boy. She rode him hard and put him away wet! I'll bet she was fucking him senseless and he loved every minute of it. Why else would he drive all the way up from San Antonio?"

After the meeting broke up, Jack walked up to Marie and said, "You need to get off the Dawn Cohen thing, Marie. I know you don't particularly like her. I get that, but we need to focus on the main issues and I don't want you to be off on a Dawn tangent every time we turn around."

Marie's face flushed as she said with embarrassment, "Got it, boss. It won't happen again. Sorry."

~

Bill had found the San Antonio Airport website and written down the names of all the car rental companies both on and off airport, and called each of them. After striking out with the first four, Bill Ross finally nailed it on his fifth try. A pleasant young lady at Hertz recommended he call Sindhur Wadawadigi at the main office. It took Bill several attempts to get the spelling right and twenty minutes of transfers before he was eventually connected to Sindhur.

"Miss Wadigi, this is Officer Bill Ross of the Travis County Police Department," began Bill, completely butchering the poor woman's name. "I'm told that you are the right person to talk to regarding historical rental records."

"I will do my best to help, Officer Ross. Tell me what it is you need," responded Sindhur.

Bill Ross explained the details to Sindhur. She had been with Hertz for four years and was in charge of their Big Data project.

"Let's see if we can help, Officer Ross. We have spent the last two years getting all of our historical data onto SAP powered by HANA," explained Sindhur.

Bill Ross had no idea what Sindhur was talking about but let her continue in the hope that it might produce the information he so urgently needed.

"The Big Data infrastructure allows us to search on multiple elements and link them together using very powerful analytics," explained Sindhur. "So let's start with the vehicle. It's a Ford Explorer, Alabama license KAA 20C."

There was a very brief delay as Sindhur ran the analytics. "Good news, Officer Ross. Hertz owned that vehicle from November 2004 to January 2006. We then sold it at auction."

"Fabulous!" said Bill, now confident that he was at last on the right track. All of this was fascinating to him. The speed with which information could be gleaned from millions of records on file could revolutionize law enforcement.

Sindhur continued, "Now we can link this information to the rental records. You said September 14, 2005?"

A few moments passed before Sindur proudly said, "Yes, we have a rental record. A Mr. Jim McCord, giving an address in Austin, Texas, rented it from our San Antonio Airport location. His original reservation was for a mid-range sedan but as he is a corporate executive gold card member, he was given a two-car upgrade and accepted the Ford Explorer. He had it for twenty-seven hours, returning back to the airport at 15:37 on Thursday, September 15."

"It is quite incredible that you can retrieve this information so fast," said Bill with appropriate admiration.

"That is the power of Big Data, Officer Ross. The Hertz Corporation has invested millions in this technology, which integrates to our mobile applications and CRM system, greatly enhancing the service we can provide to our customers."

"Well, I must say it is impressive," said Bill. "On behalf of the Travis County Police Department, I must thank you for this vital information."

"I just did my job, Officer Ross, and we can thank SAP for developing the incredible technology to help me do my job more effectively."

She sounded like a commercial for SAP, whoever they were. He hoped that they were appreciative of such a glowing reference for their products.

~

"Change of plan!" announced Jack Johnson, coffee in hand, as he sat at the end of the conference room table for the evening briefing with the team.

He had just come from the breakroom, and Bill had already updated him on his success with Hertz. It was almost 8:30 and they had been at it all day. Everyone looked tired and they weren't looking forward to their drive home. Six inches of rain had fallen in a little under four hours and there were abandoned vehicles all over the county as drivers misread road conditions and got caught in the heavy flooding.

"The information on the rental car will allow us to squeeze McCord. He has lied to us and there may be more to this than a fuck fest with Dawn Cohen. So let's back off Dawn for the moment and if we don't get McCord to come clean, we can always track her down and put the squeeze on her later."

The team agreed, but Marie Mason was obviously disappointed and didn't try to hide it.

"We should still interview Harvey Cohen and make sure that he was in Vegas," said Marie.

Jack nodded his head and said, "Agreed. You and Tommy take that and I want it done in the next couple of days, if possible. Bill and I will get McCord in and try to get to the truth. I am beginning to have a really bad feeling about him. He may hold the key to unraveling this mess."

Chapter 20 - Spiders

2014 - The Cold Case Investigation

IT WAS ALMOST LUNCHTIME WHEN Marie and Tommy drove up the driveway to the home of Harvey Cohen. Harvey had agreed to meet them at his house, as he was leaving for Las Vegas later in the day.

"He seems to like Vegas," said Marie in a derogatory tone as they approached the front door. They rang the doorbell, and within a minute Harvey opened the door.

"Hello, officers, please come in," said Harvey Cohen. Tommy stifled a snigger. Harvey Cohen could have been mistaken for the actor Danny DeVito, and framed in 12-foot high, double-hung entry doors he looked even smaller. He guided them through the marble foyer and into the huge living room.

As she thought back to the last time that she had been in the room, Marie noted that the white sectional was gone, the house didn't have the smell of expensive perfume and the annoying little dog was nowhere to be found.

"Can I offer you some refreshment?" said Harvey.

"No, thank you, Mr. Cohen, this shouldn't take too long," said Tommy.

"Oh, please, call me Harvey," said Cohen, the words dripping like honey from his tongue.

Marie felt the hackles rise up on the back of her neck. She was sure that she wasn't going to like Harvey Cohen any better than she did his ex-wife.

"We would just like to confirm some facts relating to your travel back in 2005 when a woman's body was discovered in your neighbor's backyard," said Tommy as Marie glowered at Cohen.

Marie swallowed hard and said, "Your wife said you were attending an orthodontist's convention in Vegas. Is that correct, Mr. Cohen? Were you in Las Vegas?"

"I'm surprised that bitch knew what time of day it was let alone that I was at a convention," snapped Cohen.

A hint of a smile came across Marie's face.

Harvey continued, "Yes, it was our annual convention. That's where I met Dawn back in 2000. A bunch of us went to a club off the strip and she was there looking radiant."

Harvey ran his fingers through his thin black hair and paused before continuing.

"Dawn Sunshine," sneered Harvey. "I mean, who calls themselves Dawn Sunshine, for God's sake? She was born Dawn Sunshine Daniels, the only daughter of a Baptist minister from Fresno, California. I should have known asking her to come out to Austin was a bad idea. Marrying the bitch was the dumbest thing I ever did. The divorce cost me a fortune!"

Marie and Tommy glanced at each other. Their look said, "Not a smart guy, that Harvey Cohen. Not smart at all."

"Can you prove that you were in Vegas at that time, Harvey?" said Tommy.

"Of course I can. I was the keynote speaker on Monday and taught workshops during the Tuesday and Wednesday sessions. I'm sure if you contacted the American Association of Orthodontists, they will be able to provide you with the prospectus for the 2005 annual session. I can also provide you with names of colleagues who attended my workshops and were present for my keynote presentation. I got back to Austin that Thursday night."

Harvey stood and walked to the minibar at the far end of the room. "Sure you don't want anything to drink? I think I'll have a Scotch. I'd be happy to make you both one to take the edge off," said Harvey, trying to lighten the topic of the discussion.

"No, thank you, Harvey, we are both on duty but thanks for the offer," said Tommy, having a brief thought about the Patron Silver shots he planned to have when he got off work later that day.

"Can I use your restroom, Harvey?" said Marie.

"Of course you can," said Cohen with a sultry inflection in his voice.

Marie thought about the first line of the poem *The Spider and the Fly*, by Mary Howitt. *"'Will you walk into my parlor?' said the spider to the fly."* There was something about Harvey Cohen that made her skin crawl.

She walked down the hallway in the direction Cohen had indicated and saw the guest bathroom on the right. A little further down the hallway, she saw a door that she guessed was Harvey's bedroom.

"I wonder," she thought.

Marie passed by the guest bathroom and opened the door to Cohen's bedroom. She walked in, opened the door to his bathroom and sat on the commode. The bathroom was spotless. Marie guessed that Harvey had a regular cleaning person.

She continued to look around for anything suspicious and saw an airing cupboard. Marie flushed the toilet and opened the cupboard door. From the floor to the ceiling, there were towels of every size, neatly organized on four shelves. She looked at the floor, and on the bottom right-hand corner saw what looked like a location for a wall safe with a little door. It was locked with a simple latch.

Marie looked over her shoulder, lifted the latch and stared inside. There were piles of magazines. Grabbing one called *Bondage Babes*, she let it fall open at a random page. The face of an Eastern European woman stared back at her. Her face was contorted in pain and terror as a muscle-bound freak wearing a leather mask was mounted behind her.

Marie felt puke rise from her throat as she quickly stuffed the magazine back into the hole.

"Holy crap!" exclaimed Marie. "This Cohen guy is a sick motherfucker!"

Harvey Cohen saw the strange look on Marie's face as she walked back into the room.

"Everything okay?" said Harvey.

"Not really," responded Marie. "I feel really sick. Tommy, can we go please? I think I might throw up at any time."

"Sure we can," said Tommy, "and thank you for your time, Harvey. You have been most helpful."

"Not at all, Detective Ross," said Harvey with his spider's voice. Marie thought she might have an episode of projectile vomiting right there, and in some ways wanted to do it.

"Let's go, Tommy, *please*," said Marie and with that, they left.

As she was about to get back into the car, Marie grabbed the open door for support. Her nausea was intensifying and her head was spinning. She got herself back in control and flopped down in the passenger seat. Tommy could see that she was sweating heavily.

"What was that all about, Marie? Are you really sick?" asked Tommy.

"Really sick, yes, but not for the reason you think, Tommy. I hate pornography and in particular sadomasochism. Harvey Cohen had a stash of magazines in his bathroom. I picked one up at random and it featured Eastern European women being abused by men in leather masks. According to Sven Stevenson, the medical examiner, the dead woman was Eastern European and had been sexually abused, including anal penetration. This can't be a coincidence," said Marie.

Tommy called Jack Johnson from the car.

"We're just leaving the Cohen place. Marie found a stash of sadomasochistic magazines in his bathroom featuring Eastern European women. The ME's report suggested that Reese might have been Eastern European. May be a link, boss."

Jack sighed and said, "As we all know, there are lots of things done behind closed doors in the most perfect of neighborhoods that would make your hair curl. So, he confirmed he was in Vegas. We can sure as heck prove if he was or not. If he was in Vegas, how did he get back to Austin and plant the body in his neighbor's backyard? As of right now, he's not our killer. We may not like the creep, but I don't think he's the one."

Tommy ended the call and sat back in the driver's seat. It was the end of the day at the tail of a tough week. Marie didn't look that great. Her partner, Shelly, was visiting her sick mother in Corpus Christi over the weekend and Tommy knew that she would be on her own.

"Let me buy you a drink," offered Tommy. They had never been out socially before but Tommy felt bad for Marie. It's not every day you stumble on a stranger's porn collection.

"What about Claire?"

"I had planned to go out with my buddies tonight, so Claire is having a sleepover at Papa and Mimi's house."

"Okay, then," said Marie. "Just a couple of drinks."

"I know the perfect place," said Tommy. "Let's get out of here."

~

The Brooklyn Heights Pizzeria was Tommy's favorite joint. Amongst the giant pizzas and generous pours, his favorite was a Saturday morning breakfast sandwich called the "Bronx Bomber." It was a leviathan of steak, eggs, bacon, and French fries all on a hoagie bun. If you ate enough of them, you would look like Babe Ruth in less than a month, so Tommy limited his indulgence accordingly.

The owner of Brooklyn Heights, Dan Brody, was like Tommy: a rare breed. He was a Raiders fan in the middle of Dallas Cowboys and Houston Texans country. When Tommy walked in that night, it was high fives all around as the patrons gathered for preseason football. The Raiders were playing the Giants.

"This is why Claire is at my mom and dad's house tonight," explained Tommy.

Marie was in no need of an explanation. She was in need of a drink. A pitcher of Dos Equis was ordered and arrived along with a couple of shots of Patron Silver.

"Your health!" said Tommy.

"And yours!" said Marie, as the first shot of the night hit the spot.

"We should get some food. I have a ritual that I need to explain to you. Each time the Raiders score, I order another shot of Patron," explained Tommy.

"You must leave this bar pretty sober most times then," laughed Marie.

And so the evening went. Two work colleagues and friends enjoying a good time together. They both needed it. Neither of them knew that very soon, their friendship would be tested to the fullest extent, but for tonight, it was all about a few laughs at Brooklyn Heights. The Raiders won 31-3 and they watched the whole game together joking with the patrons and teasing Giants fans who now had resigned themselves to drowning their sorrows.

Tommy lifted the pitcher, filled his glass and slurred, "Have you always been a lesbian, Marie?"

"Have you always been an asshole?" responded Marie.

They both laughed.

"Ever been tempted?" asked Tommy.

The Patron Silver had now hit the part of the brain that controlled good judgment.

"Never!" said Marie, "but if I ever did, you would be close to the top of the list for my 'dark side' experiment."

Marie laughed and drained her glass in one, long pull. "Time for us to go home, *separately*."

"I agree!" said Tommy, and asked Dan Brody to call two cabs.

Fifteen minutes passed before the first cab arrived. Marie opened the door but before she got in, she gave Tommy a kiss on the cheek.

"Thanks, buddy. You were a lifesaver tonight." She got in the cab and left.

When Tommy finally arrived home, he laid on the bed fully clothed and sleep came fast. He dreamt he was a quarterback dressed in the silver and black being interviewed after winning the Super Bowl. When Erin Andrews asked him what his plans were after his historic win he replied, "I'm going to Disney-land."

In the dream, Tommy was at Disneyland spinning on the teacup ride with the Oakland Raiders cheerleaders. As they spun, he suddenly felt sick, and the next thing he knew, he was hugging the toilet bowl, praying to the porcelain god, the euphoria of the Raiders Super Bowl win and his celebration with the cheerleaders at Disneyland a fading memory.

Chapter 21 - Let the lying begin

2014 - The Cold Case Investigation

"GOOD MORNING, MR. McCord!" said Jack Johnson as Celia showed Jim McCord into the interview room where he and Bill Ross were waiting.

"As I said, Jack, please call me Jim," said McCord, casually taking a seat and not immediately realizing that this was a formal interview room.

"I think we will keep it to Detective Johnson today, Mr. McCord," said Jack. "This is Special Reserve Officer Bill Ross, who is helping me on the case."

Jim McCord's eyes grew wide as he realized this was not the type of meeting he was expecting.

"What the fuck is this all about?" exclaimed Jim McCord, now scared and on the defensive.

Jack leveled his eyes at Jim and said, "I have reason to believe that back in 2005 you were not quite truthful with Detective Hardwick,"

"What do you mean 'not quite truthful'? I told him everything he wanted to know. Everything he asked me." McCord could feel his chest tighten and his pulse race as he spoke.

"I understand that you were at a conference all that week in San Antonio. Did you leave at any time and drive up to Austin?" asked Jack.

"No, I did not!" said McCord indignantly. His stomach was now convulsing.

"Are you sure, Mr. McCord? A resident in the neighborhood claims to have seen you the night before the body was discovered. The night of Wednesday, September 14th."

"The resident is mistaken," responded McCord as he shifted awkwardly in his seat. Bill and Jack could tell he was trying to put up a good front and continued.

"The resident said they saw a dark-colored Ford Explorer with Alabama plates driven by you just as it was turning dark that night."

"Bullshit!" said McCord. "This is a fabrication and I will be speaking to Chief Dunwoody about this." Jack and Bill knew Jim was caught in trap, but like a fox caught in a snare, he still believed that escape was possible.

"There must be two Jim McCords then. Two Jim McCords who both live in Austin and were in San Antonio that day!" said Jack.

Bill Ross chimed in for the first time. "We've checked and there is only one you, Mr. McCord."

"Who is this limey? Why is he here?" exclaimed McCord, his face getting redder as the noose tightened.

"He's here because I want him to be here and he is a special reserve officer, Mr. McCord. Please afford him the courtesy that his position entitles him to. Less of the limey language."

McCord did not see the look in Bill Ross's eyes. The worst thing you can do is to call a Scotsman a limey. Bill Ross was readying his claymore sword to cut this prick in half if he called him a limey again.

Jack Johnson laid it all out for a now defeated Jim McCord.

"I have a copy of a rental car agreement here that clearly shows you rented a Ford Explorer on Wednesday, September 14, 2005 and returned it to the San Antonio airport the following day. I believe that in the late afternoon, you met and killed the deceased and transported her to your home in Austin. I believe that you did this thinking that law enforcement would not believe that the killer would be dumb enough to dump a body in their own backyard as part of an elaborate plan. You thought planting the body in plain sight would be a smart move? Well, you were wrong, Mr. McCord. In a moment, Chief Dunwoody will enter the room, at which time we will charge you with capital murder. We will be seeking the *death penalty*."

Jim's breath hitched as tears began to stream down his cheeks, now in full panic mode. "No, no, none of this is true. I didn't murder anyone! Okay, I was in the neighborhood that night. I was having an affair with Dawn Cohen. I rented that car and drove to Austin, but I didn't kill anyone. You have to believe me!"

Jack leaned in tight and said, "So why did you lie to us?"

"I didn't want Mary to find out!"

The elaborate plan to make Jim McCord believe that he would be charged with the murder had worked. They had smoked out the truth.

"Okay, Mr. McCord, I believe you," said Jack. "I now want your full cooperation in our investigation. No more lies. Do we have your agreement on this?"

"Yes, of course," said McCord, visibly shaking with fear. "Does Mary need to know about this?" He felt broken and battered.

"Can't promise that she won't find out, Mr. McCord, but Bill and I don't plan to get in our cars, drive down there and tell her tonight. I would strongly suggest that you come clean with your wife as you have done with us today. Honesty is always the best policy, Mr. McCord."

The meeting ended, and Jim McCord left.

When Jim reached his car and got in, he grabbed the steering wheel and squeezed it so hard that his fingers turned white. His heart was pounding, on the verge of a panic attack. He tried to slow his breathing and calm down. It took him several minutes before the episode subsided. He gunned the engine and accelerated out of the parking lot, the rear tires kicking up gravel as the car sped away.

Jack and Bill shook hands. Jack thanked Bill, as it was he who had devised the plan to smoke out McCord, including the "hiding-in-plain-sight" reasoning that had been the final coup de grace.

The plan for Jim McCord was a success, but they were no closer to finding the killer. The woman was dead and someone killed her; those two facts were as absolute today as they were back in 2005. Problem was, they were the only real facts that could be proven. They needed a breakthrough and soon, or this would be thrown back into the cold case files. The team's reputation was now at stake, as was the reputation of Bill Ross.

~

On his way home, Jim McCord stopped at Duffers Bar adjacent the Rolling Oaks golf course. His shirt was soaked with sweat and it wasn't just from the 90-degree summer heat. He had four large Jack Daniels in the space of a few minutes, trying to calm the shaking in his hands and the feeling of panic growing in his chest.

"Are you okay, buddy?" said the bartender.

McCord nodded, still staring straight ahead. Outlined on the wall at the back of the bar, he thought he could see the police artist's impression of her face. He could still feel her fingernails digging into his back as he thrust his rock-hard penis inside her.

"Oh, Jim, I never thought it could be like this," she had whispered in his ear.

Jim McCord knew who the dead woman was, and if anyone found out the truth, his life as he knew it would be over.

This was another one of the piles of shit that Jim McCord did not want the police digging around in. But now they had him by the balls. He would need to start damage control with Mary. The police had agreed to not tell her about his affair with Dawn. If she learned about that, she'd start to unravel and everything might begin to fall apart. The most important thing right now was to cooperate with the police. So he fucked her and she ended up in his backyard. He didn't put her there. Some other crazy motherfucker did and he had to help the police find out who that was. Everything depended on that.

Chapter 22 - Glenmorangie

2014 - The Cold Case Investigation

"I WOULD LIKE TO invite Tommy and Marie Mason over for dinner next Saturday, Elaine," announced Bill Ross after the dishes were cleared away from their Monday evening supper.

"What is the occasion, Willie?"

"I was talking with Jack Johnson on Friday and he's headed down to his ranch in Giddings next weekend. Every couple of weeks or so he goes down there to check that his cattle are doing okay and to ensure that the water holes are holding up in the heat. He also found out from a neighbor that a few of his fences broke and his cattle are wandering out of the property. So, I just thought I could take the opportunity to provide some leadership when Jack is gone," responded Bill.

"Have you told Jack that you plan to do this?"

"Not yet. I wanted to ask you first and make sure that it was okay."

It was agreed that Bill had the green light to invite everyone, provided that Bill did not leave all the preparation and cooking to Elaine. When Bill asked Jack for permission, he thought it was a fine idea. Bill made sure that Jack also knew he was on the guest list for the next time.

When Saturday rolled around, Bill bought a pork shoulder, bone in, at H-E-B. Later that morning, he got the oak lump charcoal up to temperature in the Green Egg and placed pieces of pecan wood in strategic locations on top of the coals. The chunks had been soaked overnight for maximum flavor.

He had prepared the butt with his own special dry rub. When he arrived in Texas from California, he learned that any good Texan had his own special rub for meat and poultry and that there were secret recipes guarded with their lives. Bill's rub contained garlic powder, cayenne powder, paprika, cumin, and several other secret spices. He smoked the pork butt for two hours at 250 degrees and then took it off the Green Egg and wrapped it in a three-layer blanket. Reynolds wrap was the first layer, the second Saran wrap, and then a third and final layer of Reynolds wrap completed the job. This ensured that all the juices and steam were trapped inside. Bill left it on the Green Egg for another four hours at 225/250, removed it and let it rest for another hour. The result was the most tender, flavorful pulled pork they had ever tasted.

They all arrived at Bill's home together. Tommy had Claire in his arms as he walked up the driveway. Marie and Shelly followed close behind. Tommy had never met Shelly and Marie had made the introductions on the driveway. Shelly was a couple of inches taller than Marie and, in contrast to Marie's dark hair, Shelly had long blond hair.

"I like your hair," said Claire.

"And I *love* yours," replied Shelly as she admired Claire's mass of blond curls that made her look like a little Shirley Temple.

Tommy opened the door of his parents' home and the wonderful aroma of pecan smoke and barbecue engulfed them.

"Mom, I would like you to meet Marie and her partner, Shelly," said Tommy as Elaine emerged from the kitchen.

"Very good to meet you, Marie. I've heard so much about you. Good to meet you also, Shelly."

Marie shook Elaine's hand and said, "Good to meet you, Mrs. Ross and thank you for inviting us to your beautiful home. I brought some wine and Shelly brought a salad. Should we put both in the kitchen?"

"That would be great, Marie, and you can call me Elaine!"

They all sat around the huge teak table out on the deck. There was unbridled excitement and anticipation of the delicious BBQ that was about to appear. Shelly helped Elaine set the table and opened the wine as the sun set over the greenbelt and the birds enjoyed their supper from Bill's bird feeders.

The pork was fantastic, with a choice of South Carolina style on a bun with coleslaw or Southwestern style with tortillas, pico de gallo, cilantro and El Queso Cotija de Montana, a delicious cheese often referred to as the Mexican parmesan. There were many buns and a lot coleslaw left as no one could resist the tortillas and the Mexican parmesan.

After dinner, Shelly helped Elaine clean up and then sat with Claire on her lap and watched several episodes of "Peppa Pig." Claire fell asleep on Shelly's lap and Elaine put her to bed. Once Claire was put down, Shelly and Elaine sat in the family room together with a bottle of caramel-flavored Bailey's Irish Cream.

The two women had been laughing and joking for an hour before Elaine asked, "So, do you and Marie plan to get married, Shelly?" Typically she wouldn't have been that forward but the Baileys was having the desired effect.

"Yes we do, Elaine. We met several years ago when Marie transferred down from Smith County. I was a paralegal on a case and she was testifying. Our eyes met and that was it."

"Tommy told me that Marie was brought up in Tyler. Were you born in Austin, Shelly?" asked Elaine

"No, I was born in El Paso and, just like Marie, I had problems with my parents when they realized that I was gay. I also had to leave home and, just like Marie, I found my way to Austin."

Shelly took another sip and said, "Marie had it a lot tougher than I did. Her father was a mean drunk and a gambler. He lost everything playing poker and took it out on his wife and daughter. She has three brothers but they left when their father became bankrupt. They still live in Tyler and are pillars of the Southern Baptist community there."

Elaine grabbed the bottle of Baileys and refilled Shelly's glass. "Wow. That must have been rough on her."

"It was. When her father found out that she was gay, the beatings got worse. After he passed away in 2000, she and her mother thought that their lives would take a turn for the better. That's when her mother found out that she had breast cancer. She died a couple of years later and that's when Marie transferred to Austin."

"What a terrible story, Shelly. It is clear to me, at any rate, that you are both very much in love. I hope you will be able to marry but, as you know, that might take till hell freezes over given where Texas is politically," said Elaine and she gave Shelly a huge hug.

Meanwhile, Bill Ross held court out on the deck. He sipped on Glenmorangie while Marie and Tommy enjoyed the contents of a bottle of Del Maguey Single Village Mezcal from the village of ChiChicapa high in the mountains of the Oaxaca region of Mexico. Bill had bought a bottle after watching an episode of Anthony Bourdain's *Parts Unknown* on CNN.

"Why did you decide to bring your family to the U.S. and leave the London Met job?" asked Marie.

"There were a number of factors," replied Bill, "but it was a really good financial package with the California software company as well as a great opportunity for an adventure with the family. I had to admit to myself that if I progressed further in the Met, it would have meant taking a position with more administrative tasks and more politics. This was not something that appealed to me."

"I'm sure you have tons of stories about your experiences in London," continued Marie. "Is that where you got the scar across the bridge of your nose? It looks like it has been broken a couple of times."

Bill touched the scar and said, "No, I didn't get that from my time in London. It was much earlier. I was a young cop in the Govan area of Glasgow when I was first introduced to the Glasgow Kiss."

"The Glasgow Kiss...what on earth is that?" laughed Marie.

"It's a head-butt. Very effective and often used when there are up-close-and-personal confrontations in the pubs of Scotland. Effectively delivered, the assailant drives his forehead into the bridge of the nose, shattering it. The pain is excruciating! My nose scar is the result of being on the receiving end of that particular combat technique on two occasions.".

"Holy cow, that must have been painful!" said Marie.

"Well, it did make my eyes water a bit!" joked Bill.

Bill got the conversation back on the Riverside case.

"I'm convinced that other pieces of vital information might lay hidden in the file. We have to work together and go through every page, checking and double checking and looking for inconsistencies."

Bill continued to explain this process to Tommy and Marie, who both listened intently. He told them about clues he had found using this technique working cases back in the day in Glasgow and London.

"Before I joined the police force in Scotland, I read in the newspapers about the Mary Bell case. It was 1968 and Mary Bell was the daughter of a Glasgow prostitute. She was still a schoolgirl when she lured two young boys into the woods and slashed their throats. In those days, it was very unusual for children to be discovered to be manipulative, scheming killers. This caused the police to pursue several dead-ends until a team of detectives put the puzzle together by critically examining every piece of evidence and cross-checking for inconsistencies."

Bill went on to explain the vital role that Glenmorangie played in all of this.

"You know, the Gaelic name for Scotch whisky is Usquebaugh, pronounced 'oosh-kee-ba,' which means the water of life. In my opinion, Glenmorangie has secret powers that help unlock the mysteries of any case. This single malt influence helps me see what others cannot. It's very similar to the North American Indians who go into sweat lodges to smoke peyote or the Australian Aborigines with their dreamtime rituals," sniggered Bill.

"Is this true?" asked Marie.

"Of course it's not true, Marie. He's just messing with you," laughed Tommy.

No, it wasn't true, but on a balmy night in Austin, Texas, staring at the stars and listening to the sounds of the night, they were good stories.

Chapter 23 - Nora McConnell

2014 - The Cold Case Investigation

IT WAS SUNDAY MORNING AT the Hudson Bend office and all three were nursing minor hangovers from the night before.

They had sat out on Bill's deck until after 2:00 a.m. when Shelly suggested to Marie that it was time they headed home. Tommy stayed the night and the next morning, while Claire was having breakfast with Mimi, he and Bill drove to the office to meet up with Marie. They all had their own well-tested remedies to clear their heads and focus on the work. Marie had her customary three-shot grande latte from Starbucks, Tommy his thick black coffee in his "Raiders" mug, and Bill brought a coffee from home that contained a small shot of a certain golden elixir.

Bill opened the Riverside file and began separating it into logical sections. For Tommy and Marie, who had both helped work the case as rookies back in 2005, it was "deja vous all over again," as Yogi Berra would say.

Most of the content consisted of the medical examiner's report plus statements that had been obtained by Marie and Tommy. There was also significant content from Stan Hardwick plus a large folder containing all of the phone records and interviews created by the *Statesman* article with the sketch of the likeness of the deceased.

"Why don't you two concentrate on the content from the *Statesman* article and I'll take everything else," said Bill. "The *Statesman* follow-up was done by Stan on his own and you two might be able to see something with a fresh pair of eyes. I will look at all the interviews."

"Sounds like a good plan, Dad," said Tommy and with that, the team got to work.

~

Six hours later, not a single loose end had turned up. Thirty minutes later, they got their first break.

"Take a look at this!" said Bill. "It's from a woman who called in after the *Statesman* article was published. She lives in South Padre Island."

"Listen to what she said on the phone." Bill then read the phone call transcript aloud to the team.

> *It's about the woman found dead in Austin! She was found close to water! She had been cleansed! Her soul will find peace like the others! The instrument of her passing is still restless and looking for more! The pain will never cease, the longing will never end and the broken heart will never be whole until they are together again.*

"What do you make of it?" asked Bill.

"Sounds like another nutcase," said Marie.

"Why did she say, 'like the others'?" said Tommy.

"That was my thought. I think we've found a piece of the jigsaw that doesn't fit," said Bill.

~

On Monday morning, they met with Jack Johnson. He looked a mess with scratches all over his face and hands.

"Had a disagreement with a raccoon?" quipped Tommy.

"No, this is what you get when you own a ranch and you don't pay attention to broken fences," replied Jack. "So what were you guys up to on the weekend?"

"Let's go to the war room," suggested Tommy.

Tommy Ross took the lead to explain what they had found and to update the whiteboard.

"The three of us spent all day yesterday going over the file and we came up with a few things," began Tommy. "Everything we have suggests Jim McCord is the key to this. It could be that he killed the woman and hid her in plain sight as my dad suggested, thinking that we would be dumb enough to write him off as a suspect. If not, why was she left in his backyard? It's not like we weren't going to find her. Why didn't the killer just dump her in a remote part of the Hill Country? Why was she laid out that way?"

Tommy took a sip from his coffee and continued.

"This took a lot of thought, planning and preparation. Nothing could be left to chance and the timing had to be perfect. Not only did the killer have to know the McCords weren't home, they also had to know when they would be back. There's no chance a murderer this careful would risk the McCords walking in on him.

"So why did the killer choose Jim and Mary McCord's place? We need to think at a core level on this and go back to basic instincts. Why do people kill? Three main reasons: hate, love, or money. We need to find the connection. We need to find out everything we can about Jim and Mary McCord, in particular, Jim. As you would say, Dad, we need to construct a jigsaw puzzle of Jim McCord and ensure every single piece fits. If there is one that doesn't, then it may lead us to the killer."

Jack stood up, smiled and said, "Great summation, Tommy. You guys *have* been busy. Anything else turn up from the file?"

"Marie, why don't you take that one," said Tommy.

"Nora McConnell!" said Marie with a smile.

"Nora McConnell? Who the heck is Nora McConnell?" asked Jack.

"Nora McConnell called the help line number given out as part of the *Statesman* editorial piece. She had called at the end of September 2005, left her phone number and simply said that she lived in San Padre Island. Stan Hardwick had spoken with her and no further action was taken.

"I checked White Pages last night for a Nora McConnell in San Padre and found nothing; however, there is a Nora Anne

McConnell listed who lives on East Jefferson Street, Port Isabel, which is on the mainland side of the Queen Isabella Causeway that links Texas to South Padre Island," explained Marie.

When they read the transcript of the McConnell call to Jack, he picked up on the same anomaly. She had said "they," obviously referring to more than one dead woman.

Jack nodded his head and said, "It may be nothing but then again, it may be something, so we need to check it out. Give this Nora McConnell a call and if she's the right Nora, then drive down there, interview her and see what else she knows. Bill and I will continue to trawl through the file again and see if anything else jumps out at us."

~

Marie and Tommy went off to make the call to Nora McConnell, and they returned a few minutes later to update Jack.

"The Nora McConnell in Port Isabel is the Nora McConnell who had made the call. She sounded a bit frail and it was difficult to understand her on the phone, as she kept drifting off into random topics. She claims to have seen the murderer of the dead teenage girl who had been found raped and strangled on the beach in Corpus Christi last year. She might be a real flake but we need to go down there and check her story out," said Tommy.

"Agreed," replied Jack.

~

The following morning, the team was back in the office bright and early.

"Hi, boss, you got a sec?" said Tommy, sticking his head around the door to Jack Johnson's office.

"Sure, Tommy. Please tell me you have some more good news."

"No, not really, boss. I have an idea and a request," said Tommy.

"So, carry on then, Tommy," said Jack, impatient to hear what Tommy had on his mind.

"To get to Port Isabel to visit with Nora McConnell, we have to take the I-35 through San Antonio to pick up the I-37 to Harlingen and then on to South Padre," said Tommy.

"So what? Am I now your travel planner?" said Jack, irritated and impatient for Tommy to get to the point.

"While we're on the road, why don't Marie and I track down who Jim McCord met with for the security audit at Lockheed Martin in San Antonio before he took the detour back up to Austin to get his rocks off with Dawn Cohen? They might be able to give some further background on Jim McCord. We might be able to get a feel for his general personality, what he was like to do business with, did they socialize with him, etc."

"Great idea and good thinking, Tommy. Go do it," said Jack. "Just no fancy meals and no hotel. Up and down on the same day."

Chapter 24 - I see things

2014 - The Cold Case Investigation

LOCKHEED MARTIN AT KELLY AVIATION Center was a joint venture between Lockheed Martin and Rolls Royce, the British aircraft engine manufacturer. Kelly was a repair and overhaul center for both military and commercial engines. The person they needed to talk with was Herman Lutz, the center security compliance officer. When Tommy called him, he picked up the phone after one ring.

"Lutz!" he said with no polite preamble.

Tommy explained the need for meeting him, to which Lutz replied, "Absolutely. C'mon down!"

They arrived at the facility at 0900 hours, the time agreed on with Herman Lutz. They checked in through the extensive security process at the front gate and were then escorted to his office.

"Please take a seat, he's wrapping up a call with Washington. It shouldn't be too long," said his assistant, Margie Grant.

A few minutes later, the door to Herman Lutz's office flew open and he was in their face, hand outstretched, full of apologies for his tardiness. Herman Lutz was a dead ringer for General Norman Schwarzkopf. "Stormin Norman," as he was called, was the commander of the U.S. forces in the first Gulf War and Herman Lutz not only was the spitting image of the general, he had exactly the same demeanor.

"Sorry about that. Have to keep the top brass happy. Coffee, water, shot of Jack?" Herman laughed at his own joke.

"Coffee would be great," said Marie.

"I'll have a coffee," said Tommy.

"Margie!" yelled Herman. "Two Java Joes for my guests!"

Herman turned back to Tommy and Marie and said, "So what do you want to know about the great Jim McCord?"

The way Herman referred to Jim McCord made Marie and Tommy inch forward in their seats. Maybe this would be worth the trip.

After Margie brought the coffees, Herman took a slurp from his Air Force mug and said, "Jim McCord. Don't like the man. Never did, never will. Don't mean to be so direct, but I tell it how it is."

"How so?" said Tommy, using a two-word question so that he could sit back and let the faucet flow.

"He is a blowhard, full of his own importance. Thinks he knows more than anyone else about cyber security risks and countermeasures. What he knows he picked up in textbooks. He has no real-world experience and has never been on the front line. Apart from that, love the man!" chuckled Herman, laughing at his own joke.

Based on the framed photographs on the wall showing Herman Lutz in his younger days in the air force, it was obvious that he did have the real-world experience that was lacking in Jim McCord.

The conversation continued in the same vein for another thirty minutes with Herman questioning Jim McCord's credentials. After a frank conversation about Jim's work in the U.S. Department of Defense, Marie got to the meat of why they were there.

"What about his general personality, Herman? Anything there that you think we should know? Did you spend time with him socially?"

"I tried to spend as little time with him as possible. However, there were social gatherings involving folks from Lockheed, Rolls-Royce, the DoD and the air force that I attended," continued Herman. "He was like a praying mantis, playing best pals with the three stars and hitting on any good-looking broad who would give him the time of day."

"He was a womanizer?" pressed Marie.

"Hell yeah! He tried to get into the pants of every broad he met. Real letch is the great Jim McCord. Sorry for the language, ma'am."

The three spoke for a few more minutes before they thanked Herman Lutz for the information, left Kelly Aviation Center and continued on to Port Isabel.

"Wow," said Marie as they drove south.

"Wow is right," replied Tommy. "We need to recommend to Jack that we turn over every rock in Jim McCord's sorry life. He could be the bastard who did this, Marie; the guy's a real prick!"

"I was disappointed that I didn't get another go at Dawn Cohen, but sweating Jim McCord might be even more satisfying." said Marie.

They both agreed as Tommy put the pedal to the metal on the way to Port Isabel.

~

It was 4:30 when they pulled into the driveway of Nora McConnell's home on East Jefferson Street in Port Isabel. It was a quaint little house on a quaint little street. Nora was in her early seventies, and had iced tea and lemon ready for her guests' arrival.

"Please do come in, why don't you?" said Nora with hints of an English upbringing in her accent.

"Thank you, Mrs. McConnell," said Tommy.

"Oh, it's Miss, young man," said Nora. "Never found Mr. Right, but you never know. He might still turn up one day. Are *you* married, Detective Ross?" she said with a cheeky grin.

They settled into the comfortable surroundings in the main room of her tiny home. Photographs took up every available space on the tabletops in the room. Nora McConnell was obviously an avid reader, as part of the room looked like a mini-library with books stacked from floor to ceiling. As she sat there in her favorite chair, Tommy could not help but think about the image of Miss Marple, Agatha Christie's famous English sleuth.

"Have you always lived in Port Isabel, Miss McConnell?" asked Marie.

Nora McConnell offered them no informality about calling her by her first name, further evidence of her strict English private school upbringing.

"I lived most of my life on the island," said Nora, referring to South Padre. "I moved to this little gem in 2006 to live out the rest of my days."

Getting down to the subject of their visit, Tommy asked, "So you saw the article in the *Austin Statesman*, Miss McConnell. May I ask how you came by a copy of the paper?"

"Oh, my sister lives in Onion Creek in Austin and she sends me the weekend edition every week. I return the favor and send her the *Port Isabel-South Padre Press*," replied Nora. "I understand that both newspapers are now available online but we both much prefer the print version."

"Ah, I see," said Tommy. "I read the transcript of your call to the police hotline and your subsequent interview with Detective Stan Hardwick. Do you recall what you said, Miss McConnell?" asked Tommy.

What happened next took their breath away. Nora McConnell's eyes took on a peculiar trance-like state and she repeated word for word what the transcript in the file had said. It was if she had a photocopy of it in her brain.

It's about the woman found dead in Austin! She was found close to water! She had been cleansed! Her soul will find peace like the others! The instrument of her passing is still restless and looking for more! The pain will never cease, the longing will never end, and the broken heart will never be whole until they are together again.

"That's amazing, Miss McConnell," said Marie. "How do you know this information?"

"Oh, that's also an easy question, Detective Mason. *I see it!*" said Nora without a moment's hesitation, as if she were explaining how she found the winning lottery numbers in the newspaper on a Sunday morning.

Marie was astounded. "Have you always had this gift, Miss McConnell?"

"Oh yes," responded Nora. "I have seen things, mostly tragic events, since I was a little girl living in Hampshire. It continued on when Mummy and Daddy brought us to the USA when we were in our early teens." *Mummy and Daddy* is also very English, and when she used the term her voiced changed to the one of a little girl in Hampshire, England.

"Is there anything else you remember about what you saw, Miss McConnell?" pressed Marie.

"No, my dear. I just get flashes. Sometimes I see them use the same technique on television shows I watch to suggest something that might have happened in the past."

"What shows do you watch, Miss McConnell?" asked Tommy.

"I love *Law & Order* and I also like that other show *Bones*. She is a very pretty woman, that one in *Bones*," said Nora.

They were both beginning to feel that this had been a wasted journey and they prepared to leave. Perhaps Nora was concocting a story based on what she had seen on TV. They thanked Nora for her time and for the iced tea. Nora stood at the door and watched them as they got into their car.

"Oh wait!" she shouted. "I do remember one other thing about the flashes of those girls. They all wore *white dresses and had bright red lipstick!*"

Marie and Tommy literally ran back into the house to talk some more to Miss Nora McConnell. The details on the white dress and the red lipstick were never released to the public. Nora McConnell had *"seen"* the body of the dead woman in the yard of Jim and Mary McCord.

Chapter 25 - The jigsaw

2014 - The Cold Case Investigation

THEY WERE BACK IN AUSTIN by midnight. It had been a long and tiring day, about six hours each way to Port Isabel. However, neither Tommy nor Marie got much sleep that night. Their minds were on fire. Elation would not have been too much of an exaggeration on how they felt.

They decided not to call Jack or Bill from their car but rather wait until morning so that they could give a comprehensive report and answer any questions they might have face to face rather than over the phone. They would also have to update the catalog of facts now overflowing on the white board.

The next morning in the conference room, they provided their briefing on their trip to meet with Nora McConnell.

"There is no doubt in our minds that Nora McConnell saw the dead woman," said Tommy. "We have no idea how this little old lady can possibly have such a gift but there is no doubt that she has it."

"Were you able to get any more detail from her?" asked Jack. "For example, did she say the body was next to a pool or on a recliner?"

"No, she didn't. She said that all she saw was a face and shoulders, so she could tell that it was a white dress of some sort. She did say again that she was close to water and that she had been cleansed."

"Did she say anything about the hat and the sunglasses?" pressed Bill.

Tommy's heart dropped as he said, "No, she said that the woman she saw had blond hair. No hat, no sunglasses."

"How the heck can that be? She had those on when we found her," said Jack with some degree of incredulity.

Marie's eyes widened as she said, "Perhaps the 'snapshot' she saw was before the killer put the hat and sunglasses on her. There are definitely questions, Jack, but I believe she saw the dead woman."

Jack looked at both Marie and Tommy and said, "Okay, her transcript said that she saw 'others.' How many others did she say she saw?"

"Good question," said Marie. "We forgot to tell you that she reckoned it was five or six but she wasn't sure."

"Five or six! Are we saying we could have a serial killer here?"

"If what she says is true, it sure sounds like it," chimed in Bill.

"If it turns out we have a serial killer on our hands, we would have to bring in other agencies, including the FBI. If we went to them with what we've got right now, they would laugh us out of Dodge. No, we need to gather more evidence before we go down the serial killer route," concluded Jack. "Let's switch gears here and get to husband of the year."

"According to Herman Lutz, he's a real piece of work," said Marie.

Jack turned to Bill and asked, "What do you think? How do we take it from here on McCord?"

"We need to validate. We need more opinions," responded Bill. "We need to talk to everyone who knows him reasonably well and start to build a mosaic of Jim McCord. It would be wrong for us to run off half cocked with only Herman Lutz's ranting."

They decided to split the McCord contacts for interview into five categories:

1. Family
2. Friends in Austin
3. Friends in Pagosa Springs
4. College friends
5. Work friends and acquaintances

"This is going to be a slog, people, but there's no other way to do it," said Jack.

"Tommy and Marie, you guys take the Pagosa Springs connection. Get up there and interview neighbors and friends. Bill, you take college friends and the research on other murder cases involving women, white dresses, water, etc. I'll take Austin and talk with everyone here who knows him," continued Jack.

"The clock is running on this and Chief Dunwoody is getting antsy. We will have regular update meetings as needed, and for those of us who cannot be here in person, you must find a way to call in for the briefings. Bill, can you set up Google Hangout so we can use it for real-time video collaboration? That's it for now, team, so let's get back at it." Jack left to brief the Chief.

The pieces of the jigsaw were beginning to fit, but as of yet no clear picture was emerging. It was clear that there was a guy with a beard and glasses in the picture, but was Jim McCord the killer? More pieces of the puzzle would have to be found and assembled before they could reach that conclusion.

Chapter 26 - A single dad

2014 - The Cold Case Investigation

TO ENABLE HIM TO MAKE the trip down to Port Isabel, Tommy again had to rely on help from Elaine. She made sure that Claire was picked up from daycare and brought to Mimi's house for dinner and a sleepover. She then took Claire to daycare the following morning and Tommy picked her up later that night.

Life was tough as a single parent and a police officer. It had taken him a couple of years to get over the death of his wife. He tried to talk with Claire about it as best he could, but the older she got the more questions she had about why others in daycare had mommies *and* daddies to pick them up.

He tried to explain that Mommy was in heaven, but the concept was tough for a four-year-old.

Once he had come to terms with the death of his wife, Tommy had tried online dating sites. He was lonely and came home every night to an empty house. After a long day in the office, having to get Claire fed, bathed and off to bed was exhausting. He then had to get on with the other normal household chores. The laundry needed to be washed, folded and put away. Claire's toys had to be picked up and dishes had to be washed. All this sapped what remaining energy he had and he would routinely collapse into bed at midnight, totally exhausted.

He needed to find another mate. He needed to find love again. The dating sites were a disaster. All of the thirty- and forty-year-olds had baggage, some more than others. Tommy was a single dad, so he thought the best approach would be to find a single mom. He was shocked at how many were out there. He met a couple of dates for early morning coffee on the weekend. He was careful not to involve Claire and he again got help from Elaine to enable him to do that. The first few he met were disappointing. It was obvious that they were just looking for a man to help them raise their kids and protect them. They were desperate and it showed.

He then met Sylvia and really liked her. She had one young son, a year older than Claire, and they decided to go out for a drink together one Saturday night while Claire slept over at Mimi's house. It turned out to be a great night. There was no sex involved on this first date. Tommy simply dropped Sylvia off at her mother's house and went home.

Later that night, he heard a knock on the front door. He grabbed his handgun, placed it within easy reach and asked who was at the door. It was 4 a.m.. It was Sylvia's ex. He had been following them all night and now was at Tommy's front door throwing out obscenities and threats. Tommy didn't open the door, and when he calmly explained he was a cop, the ex-husband left in a flash.

Afterward, Tommy couldn't get back to sleep and was even more exhausted the next day. It couldn't go on like this, he thought. He had to find someone, and while it might take time, the dating sites were not the answer. The bars were not the answer either. He would have to meet someone in a social gathering and, although he was not particularly religious, he decided that church might be an answer. He could take Claire with him to church so she could get benefit from the support of the Christian community.

He made up his mind. He would look for a church close by and give it a try.

Chapter 27 - Fran Taylor

2005 - A Great Adventure

PAVEL KEPT THE TRIUMPH CLOSE behind the Cadillac SUV as they drove north on I-25. Galina sat on the back with her arms wrapped tightly around Pavel. He was the love of her life but she still had reservations about the change of plan. They had spent months planning their escape from Pikesville and all it took was a chance meeting to toss those carefully prepared plans out the window.

But when they made the exit off I-25 on to the 84 North to Pagosa Springs, her mood instantly brightened. The scenery took her breath away.

Growing up in Pikesville, Galina had never traveled out of the state. Her parents worked every hour they could to make the restaurant a success and never took vacations. Even her high school trips were all within the state. For the first time in her life Galina witnessed firsthand the spectacular diverse landscape of the U.S. She had only read about this in textbooks and she now realized that photographs did not do justice to this amazing scenery. Galina drank it all in. This must have been what it was like for Lewis and Clark, minus the roads, homes, and overhead power cables.

The 84 North wound its way through northern New Mexico and into southern Colorado. Her fears about the side trip to Vail began to subside as the Triumph ate up the miles passing through the Santa Fe State National Forest, Carson National Forest, past Lake Heron National Park and crossing the border into Colorado.

The scenery in Colorado was even more dramatic. They entered the Rio Grande National Forest, passed within a few miles of Pagosa Springs and arrived at the River Bend Campground nestled in the pines on the south fork of the Rio Grande.

That night, they fell asleep to the gurgling of the river, the scent of pine and the gentle hooting of a tawny owl calling his mate.

~

After a good night's sleep, they awoke, ate breakfast and continued on the second leg of their journey to their new home. Within a few miles of Vail, the road wound its way through the majestic mountains and the towering firs of the national forest. After passing by the Breckenridge and Copper Mountain ski resorts, Galina saw, for the first time, the stands of towering Aspen trees with their shimmering silver bark. They were standing in formation to welcome her to her new adventure in Colorado.

Vail was like an alpine village with taverns and every Swiss-German restaurant imaginable. It is the playground of the rich with expensive upscale boutiques and craft stores, offering every luxury item designed to relieve the seasonal, well-healed visitors of their wealth. Skiing is the sport of choice in the winter and golfing and fishing in the summer.

The LSU crew had rented an apartment in West Vail, a sister township, where those who worked in the businesses in Vail Village lived. Luckily, it had four bedrooms, so the living accommodations worked for the three couples and Fran. Last year, they promised their bosses they would return again in 2005, so they all had jobs waiting for them in town.

Gail had a waitressing job in the Lions Head Tavern. Back in Albuquerque, she called the owners to ask if they could use more help for the summer. To her delight, they said that they needed another waitress, and after hearing about Galina's experience, she was hired. Pavel, on the other hand, had to look for work and the morning after their arrival, he went off to find a job.

It took Pavel two weeks to get a job as a waiter and busboy at the Sonnenschein Resort and Spa. He worked the late shift in the main restaurant from 3:00 p.m. to 11:00 p.m.. Galina worked at the Tavern from 11:00 a.m. to 7:00 p.m. and often got some overtime, finishing at 9:00. It was hard work for both of them. When Pavel arrived back in the apartment after midnight each workday, he was so tired that he climbed in to bed and was instantly asleep.

They had fun on their days off. They both had managed to work their schedules so they could spend their free time together. They met a guy who was a regular in the Lions Head Tavern who worked in a bike rental place. He helped them score free bikes whenever they wanted. Every once in a while, they went off on their own and made sandwiches to picnic by the river. They were making great money and saving every penny that they could. They both agreed that it had been the right decision to take this three-month side trip. This opinion would soon change.

~

Galina and Pavel planned their wedding for the 3rd of July, as they all had the 4th as a holiday. Pavel chose Rocky as his best man while Gail, Adelaide, and Fran were the bridesmaids. They had filed the necessary documents to get their marriage license almost immediately after they had arrived in Colorado, so all of the necessary paperwork was in order.

The ceremony was set to take place at the Eagle County Office of Clerk and Recorder in Eagle Vail. Afterward, they would take the gondola to the top of the mountain to the wedding platform where the "rich" wedding ceremonies took place. It was agreed that Lani, who had taken photography as one of his elective subjects at LSU, would take the official wedding photographs.

It was July 2nd and Galina got out of bed as the rising sun broke through the curtains. She grabbed a breakfast bar, kissed the sleeping Pavel on the cheek and left for work. She caught the bus every day at the end of the street and today was no different. When she arrived, Sabine Ruess, the owner of the Lions Head Tavern, told her to lay the tables for the lunch crowd and then to take the rest of the day off.

"You need to go home and take time to prepare for the big day, dear!" said Sabine.

Galina thanked Sabine, set the tables, and left the Tavern at about 12:30 to catch the bus back to West Vail.

When she opened the door to the apartment, she knew instantly that something was not right. She could hear what she thought were voices coming from inside. She expected to find Pavel preparing to leave for his shift but "voices"?

She opened their bedroom door. Fran Taylor was naked and bent over their bed, her legs spread, with Pavel thrusting from behind. Fran looked up, saw Galina and smiled. Galina ran into the bathroom and threw up.

She ran out of the apartment with no idea of where she was going or what she was going to do. In the last fifteen minutes, her life had fallen apart.

"Why did you do this to me!" she yelled at the top of her voice as she ran. "You bastard, Pavel, and you fucking whore, Fran!"

A few minutes later she was bent over a railing, looking down at the river. She thought about jumping. The torrent below could take her and in an instant wash away all of her pain. She was hysterical.

Galina was shaking almost uncontrollably. She pulled out her phone and called Gail Anderson at the Tavern. When she told Gail what had happened, she was not as shocked as Galina had expected her to be.

"Where are you?" asked Gail.

When Galina responded, Gail said, "Well, stay there. I will borrow Sabine's car and I'll be there as soon as I can."

About twenty minutes later, Gail arrived in Sabine's Toyota SUV and Galina jumped in.

"So tell me again, what happened?" asked Gail.

As they drove back to the Tavern, Galina explained the situation to Gail. How she found the love of her life deep inside a whore named Fran. How her whole life felt shattered and broken.

Twenty minutes later, they were back at the Tavern and sitting with Sabine Ruess.

"This must be devastating for you, Galina. I am so sorry!" said Sabine. "You have your job here at the Tavern for as long as you need it!"

"I'm not going back to that apartment," sobbed Galina.

"You can stay in one of the bedrooms here in the Inn. We have one empty room tonight and tomorrow. Then we're full for the next six days. I can give you some toiletries and Gail can go back to the apartment and get your clothes and stuff."

Gail nodded and said, "I can do that. You just need to tell me where everything is in your room."

Over the next day, the others in the LSU crew rallied around her and offered their support. They told her that they had sensed that Fran had been trying to seduce Pavel and, like everything else Fran did, saw it as just a challenge, another conquest to be made. They suspected that she never had any desire for a lasting relationship with Pavel. They all agreed that Fran was a piece of work.

Pavel and Fran were nowhere to be found. He called Galina constantly on her cell. She ignored the calls. Adelaide and Gail tried to spend as much time as they could with Galina to make sure that she was okay and didn't do anything stupid.

For the next two nights in the bedroom at the inn, Galina lay awake for the longest time, trying to make sense of it all. Whether he was seduced or not, he had betrayed her trust and, in an instant of lust, destroyed her life and her dreams. Her sixth sense had kicked in when she first met Fran. There was something about her that didn't feel right. She vowed that she would never make that mistake ever again.

~

The following morning, Galina met with Sabine. Galina had decided to return home to Pikesville. Sabine suggested that she might want to take some time and not just run home, that perhaps she should stay the summer in Colorado and then make a decision when she was less emotional.

"I can't stay any longer in the inn and I can't stay here in Vail," cried Galina, "I have to get out of here!"

Sabine offered an alternative she had been working on.

"I have a good friend who owns a sports bar in Pagosa Springs. If you would like, I could call her and see if she needs help for the remainder of the summer?"

Galina agreed that it would be an option she would consider, and Sabine made the call.

Heidi Braun owned the San Juan Sports Bar and Grill on San Juan Street in Pagosa. She offered Galina an ideal scenario. If Galina was willing to help out around the restaurant, Heidi would allow her to stay in an Airstream trailer that was parked out back of the bar, rent free.

It was the first good thing Galina had heard in days. This was a way for her to get out of Vail quickly and, as Sabine had suggested, a way to buy time to get her head straight. She took the job.

That weekend, Adelaide, Gail, Rocky, and Lani drove with Galina to Pagosa Springs. Heidi Braun was a good woman; she welcomed Galina with open arms and, just like Sabine, offered to support her through this difficult time.

The LSU crew each hugged Galina, agreed to stay in touch, and left to make the drive back to Vail. It was Saturday July 9th. In just over two months, Galina Alkaev would be dead.

Chapter 28 - Vanderbilt University

2014 - The Cold Case Investigation

"EVERYONE IN THE WAR room now!" announced Jack Johnson, "Bill has found something of interest in his research of Jim McCord and his college days!"

Bill Ross laid out for the team what he had found.

"Jim McCord graduated from Vanderbilt University in Nashville with a Masters in Computer Science. During his time there, he and two other male students had been accused of raping a female student. The student had dropped the charges, which often happens in rape cases, but her attack had been quite violent and she had been sodomized. I found the medical records of the student, Pauline Lawson, in the Nashville Police Department archive."

"McCord could still be our guy, people!" announced Jack, "Tommy and Marie, you guys need to get to Pagosa Springs ASAP and talk with the folks there who know McCord. Let's be diligent. No stone left unturned!"

Tommy contacted the sheriff's office of Archuleta County and briefed them on the investigation. Sheriff John H. Gordon was happy to help in any way and assigned Detective Raul Ortiz to help them.

They flew from Austin on U.S. Airways, connecting in Phoenix and arriving 11:15 a.m. into Durango. Raul Ortiz was there to meet them. Raul was a muscular 40-year-old and looked a little bit like the boxer Roberto Duran. When Tommy shook his hand he was convinced that Raul could probably give Duran a run for his money in the ring. During the ninety-minute drive from Durango to Pagosa Springs, Raul updated them on the research that he had done on Jim McCord.

"The guy appears to be squeaky clean," said Raul. "No traffic violations, no problems with neighbors and no unpaid bills with any local business."

Tommy sighed and said, "We can tell you from experience that he's anything but squeaky. What about the neighborhood?"

"The community where he has a home is very upscale. Most properties have ten-plus acres and a minimum of four bedrooms and four baths. He has three neighbors that back on to his property directly. There's Scott and Rachel Shultz, who are only around in the summer. Then there is Josef and Cornelia Jacobsen and Luther Fisher, who live there year round."

"Does Mr. Fisher have a wife?" asked Marie.

"Nope. Luther's wife passed away a few years back. Really tragic story."

Raul checked his mirror, turned into the right-hand lane and said, "I took the liberty of calling all three residences and we have an interview scheduled with Scott and Rachel Shultz later today. The Jacobsens and Luther Fisher cannot meet with us until tomorrow. You guys must be hungry, so let's grab some lunch. I normally eat at Wayne's Diner. The food is good and I went to school with Wayne, so the conversation is always good too. We were both on the high school baseball team. He was a pitcher and I played catcher. Our meeting with Scott and Rachel Shultz is at three o'clock, so that gives us enough time to grab a quick burger. That okay with you guys?"

"Sounds great, Raul," said Tommy.

~

They arrived at the Shultz residence right on time.

"Come in, please!" said Rachel Shultz as she guided them into a huge public room with spectacular mountain views.

As they walked into the room, Scott Shultz, dressed in shorts, flip-flops and a San Diego State tee shirt, entered from his adjoining office. With his blond hair and California tan, he looked like he had just come from surfing Trestles, the world-renowned surf beach north of San Diego.

"Hi there! I was just wrapping up a call when you arrived. How can we help the investigation?" asked Scott, wasting no time getting down to the reason for the visit.

Tommy shook Scott's hand and said, "What business are you in, Mr. Shultz?"

"I import fine furnishings from Europe. My main show-room is in San Diego but I have another one in New York. Mainly furniture, but I also import carpets from Iran and paint-ings from Holland and France. By the way, please do call me Scott!"

"Do you work, Rachel?" asked Marie, making the assump-tion that she would also be okay with the informality.

"No, I do not," said Rachel. "We entertain a lot and I deal with that. Our suppliers visit the U.S. frequently, so we enter-tain in our San Diego home and also here in Colorado."

"Do you socialize with Jim and Mary McCord when you are here in the summer?" asked Marie.

"We have in the past," replied Rachel, "but I would not say that we are best friends or anything like that. We have dined at their place and they have at ours."

"Would you care to offer your opinion about them?" asked Tommy.

"Not sure what you mean," said Scott, jumping into the conversation, looking a little concerned. "He is not a suspect in the murder, is he? Detective Ortiz, you had said that this was an interview for general background information. Is that still the case?"

"Yes," replied Raul Ortiz. "We are just trying to build the best background picture we can of Jim and Mary McCord. It must have been a shock for them when they found the dead woman in their backyard."

Marie flipped to a fresh page in her notebook and said; "We understand that Mary McCord has undergone extensive therapy since the murder. Do you know anything about that, Rachel?"

"Yes, she has been in therapy for years, even before the murder," said Rachel, instantly realizing that she should not have said that as it opened up a door. Marie walked right in.

"Can you elaborate?" asked Marie.

"It is not our place to pry but I do believe that they were having marital problems and Mary was trying to work through them with the help of a counselor," said Rachel.

Tommy turned to Scott and asked, "What's your impression of Jim McCord?"

"Seems like an okay guy. Perhaps a little full of himself, but decent enough," replied Scott.

"Would you have them over for dinner again?" asked Marie.

"Can't see why not," said Scott, but Rachel didn't look like she totally agreed with her husband. Marie picked up on her negative body language.

"And what about you, Rachel? Do you agree with Scott that Jim McCord and Mary would be on your guest list for your next social gathering?"

Rachel squirmed in her seat and said, "Sometimes I do feel a little uncomfortable around him."

"Why is that?" pressed Marie, as Scott looked on somewhat perplexed.

"I just feel sometimes that he is undressing me with his eyes." responded Rachel.

Scott shifted uncomfortably in his seat again, obviously feeling that Rachel perhaps had gone too far with her critique of Jim McCord.

Afterward, Tommy and Marie thanked the Shultzses and asked if it would be okay to call them again if they thought of any other questions. Rachel said yes but Scott looked less than thrilled with the idea.

"I'll bet there will be some words between those two after we leave," said Marie as they walked back to their SUV.

"A real sleaze ball, our Jim McCord," said Tommy as they drove off.

~

The following morning, Raul, Tommy and Marie drove up to Luther Fisher's place. Compared to the almost pristine condition of the Shultz home, Fisher's home looked rundown. It was obvious that he didn't care about first impressions. The garden was overgrown and there was an old tractor with a snowplow attachment in the middle of the yard. It probably hadn't moved since the previous winter.

They rang the bell several times before Luther Fisher, dressed in what looked like military fatigues, opened the door. Whereas the outside of the home looked rundown, the inside looked spotlessly clean. The surroundings were not luxurious, almost the opposite; everything looked like it had a place and was functional rather than opulent.

After the introductions were made, they sat at the kitchen table. Luther had prepared a pot of coffee and he gave them each a mug. Tommy couldn't help but notice that a rifle was propped up at the end of the kitchen island and a handgun lay by the side of the phone.

"You need to be careful with weapons laying around your home, Mr. Fisher," said Tommy.

"I am careful!" said Luther abruptly. "So how can I help? You want to know about Jim McCord?"

Raul poured himself some coffee and said, "Yes, Luther, as I explained on the phone, these detectives are here for background on Jim and Mary McCord. They are reopening the case of the body found at the McCords' residence in Austin in 2005."

"Does Jim know you are here?" said Luther aggressively.

"He doesn't know we are in Pagosa Springs today but we have told him we are reopening the case and he has agreed to provide full cooperation."

"Is he a suspect?" asked Luther.

"There are no suspects at this time, Mr. Fisher. We are just trying to construct as much of a picture of Jim and Mary McCord's life as we can. We think that in doing so, we might find some connection that will allow us to find out who did this."

"Makes sense, I guess," grunted Luther.

"You live here year-round, Mr. Fisher?" asked Marie.

"Yes, I do!" said Luther.

"What line of business are you in?"

"I'm retired."

"Do you have hobbies?"

Luther grimaced and said, "I thought you were here to talk about the McCords. What do my hobbies have to do with that?"

Sensing the interview wasn't going well, Tommy jumped in. "As we said, we are trying to construct a whole picture, Mr. Fisher. We need to see where the McCords fit into that, so if you would just try to answer the questions we have, we'll try to keep this short and sweet and get out of your hair as quickly as possible."

Luther relaxed and said, "Okay, sorry about that. There is too much government interference into people's business these days and what I do with my time is my business, no one else's." He was clearly laying down the boundaries for the conversation.

"So let's switch gears, Mr. Fisher. How long have you known the McCords?" said Tommy.

"Quite a while. I built my place a couple of years after they did."

"Do you socialize with them?"

"I don't socialize with anyone. I'll occasionally have a beer with Jim if he is going into town and I have some businesses to take care of down there."

"What kind of guy is Jim? Do you like him?" asked Marie.

"Can't say I dislike him. Never did anything to me. Pretty straight shooter, I would say."

The conversation continued along the same lines for about an hour. It was tense and uncomfortable, but they got the information they felt they needed. As the interview wound down, Tommy was struck by an idea: Luther Fisher was almost certainly a "Doomsday Prepper." Preppers are convinced that there will be a catastrophe that will cause the social and economic collapse of civilization as we know it. Their lives are dominated by the need to prepare for every eventuality and they do so by stockpiling firearms, ammo, and food. They see conspiracy in everything and hate anything that smells of government interference in their lives. Not only that, they feel law enforcement agencies are an instrument of the government and treated with suspicion. Yes, Luther Fisher was a Prepper.

As they were preparing to leave, Marie did her "Is there a restroom I could use?" routine.

"Let me show you," said Luther and walked her along an adjacent corridor. As she attended to business, Luther hung around, pretending to adjust some pictures on the wall. There was no way he was going to let her out of his sight so she could stick her nose where it wasn't wanted.

While they waited in the kitchen for Marie's safe return, Tommy and Raul spotted an elaborate and expensive floor-mounted telescope in the living room pointed in the direction of the mountains. Tommy walked across to the scope and peered through the lens. He had expected to see mountains but instead, it was pointed across the valley at a small cabin with an RV and a boat parked alongside it.

"Don't touch that!" roared Luther. "That is a very delicate and expensive piece of equipment!"

Tommy jumped back and said, "Oh, sorry, Mr. Fisher, I didn't touch it. Just admiring the view."

As they were preparing to leave, Marie asked, "I understand that you are a widower, Mr. Fisher?"

"Yes, I am. My wife passed some time ago," replied Luther.

"There is a photograph in your hallway with you and a tall blond lady taken by a lake. Is that your late wife in the photograph? She was very beautiful," said Marie.

Luther's eyes looked off to a faraway place as he said, "Yes. That is my Summer."

"Her name was Summer, Mr. Fisher?"

Luther barked, "Yes, her name *is* Summer! What's that got to do with anything?"

"Background, Mr. Fisher. Just further background."

On their way back to the car, Marie shook her head and said, "Her name *is* Summer, as if she were still alive. What a fruitcake!"

Chapter 29 - The drowning at the lake

2014 - The Cold Case Investigation

AFTER THE FISHER INTERVIEW, Raul, Tommy and Marie drove a couple of miles to the Jacobsen home.

Josef and Cornelia Jacobsen had relocated from their native Minnesota to Colorado fifteen years ago, having spent three years getting their home built and then furnishing it to their satisfaction prior to making the move. Josef Jacobsen met them at the door and took them into their family room. The inside of the home smelled like a bakery and Marie suddenly had a yearning for fresh baked apple pie.

"Please have a seat," said Josef, as his wife, Cornelia, arrived from the kitchen, cleaning the last remnants of flour from her apron. "May I offer you some coffee and perhaps a blueberry muffin to go with it? They're freshly made."

Once the coffee and muffins arrived, they began their interview.

Marie took a bite of her still warm muffin, washed it down with some coffee and then said, "We are trying to construct a complete picture of Jim and Mary McCord's life so that we might get a break in finding who killed the woman found on their property in Austin back in 2005."

"What a life Mary has had over the past few years," said Cornelia. "First there was the death of Summer Fisher and then they find a dead body in their yard. Not surprising that she has been receiving therapy, poor woman."

"Yes, we were told that she was getting help. How was Jim McCord during this time? Was he supportive of his wife?" asked Marie.

"I'll answer that," interrupted Josef. "I want to make it clear that I really dislike Jim McCord. I have told him that to his face, so I guess there is no reason not to discuss that openly. He is a braggart, a liar, and a womanizer," said Josef.

"Josef, please don't speak like that," interrupted Cornelia, uncomfortable with her husband's directness.

Marie pressed, "A womanizer, Mr. Jacobsen? Why do you say that?"

"I have seen him about town with different women in his car, some of them no older than our granddaughter and she's eighteen. He lied to me about the financial stability of a computer software company he was involved with some time back and I lost a packet on that. Jim McCord is not to be trusted. Not that I am trying to suggest any connection to the dead woman, but he's just not good people!"

Marie turned to Cornelia, "You mentioned that Mary was emotionally affected by the death of Summer Fisher. Can you tell us about that?" Marie had taken the lead in this interview and was doing a fine job in the opinion of Tommy and Raul.

"Yes, it was back in 2003, I think. The Fishers and the McCords took a trip to the lake at Navajo State Park. It's less than an hour south of here. They drove down in Luther Fisher's RV and took the boat with them. They had been there a couple of days, and the second night before dinner, Mary and Summer laid out on recliners at the end of the jetty to watch the sun go down. By all accounts, they had been drinking wine most of the day while Jim and Luther were fishing on the lake. Summer got up from her recliner, tripped and fell into the lake. Mary, a good swimmer, dove in after her. It was later discovered that Summer couldn't swim and that Mary had tried in vain to rescue the poor woman."

Tommy looked up and said, "We just met with Luther earlier and he told us that he didn't socialize with Jim and Mary."

"While they may not do so today, Luther spent a lot of time with both of them back then," said Cornelia.

Cornelia then continued with her memory of the drowning death of Summer Fisher.

"The state police investigated the drowning and initially concluded that it was a tragic accident. However, that changed when then heard a rumor that Jim McCord might have been having an affair with Summer. They thought that Mary might have intentionally pushed Summer into the lake and then dove in to create the illusion of trying to save her. This scenario was eventually ruled out and the final verdict was accidental drowning, but the emotional damage the episode caused to Mary had a lasting effect. The discovery of the dead woman in her yard accelerated her emotional decline. She has been seeing a psychiatrist and taking medication for acute depression ever since."

After a few minutes, they said their goodbyes to the Jacobsens and Raul drove them back to Durango for their flight back to Austin.

"Thanks for your help in setting this all up for us, Raul," said Tommy.

"Not a problem, Tommy. Come back and see us anytime. I love to fish, and have a cabin a few miles from Pagosa, so if you get the inclination to catch some of the best trout in the world, grab your rod and get on up here," replied Raul.

As the plane taxied for take off, Tommy looked out of the window to get a final glimpse of the Colorado landscape. The trip to Pagosa had yielded a treasure trove of information on the McCords. The opinions offered by Herman Lutz on the character of Jim McCord were confirmed beyond the shadow of a doubt. But could he be the killer? That was still the million-dollar question.

Chapter 30- The sexual predator

2005 - A Great Adventure

GALINA QUICKLY SETTLED IN TO her new waitressing job at the San Juan Sports Bar and Grill. She worked double shifts every day starting at 9 a.m., and after midnightshe would climb into the Airstream and cry herself to sleep.

Pavel called her on her cell constantly but Galina ignored them. The LSU crew did not share with Pavel or Fran where Galina had gone, so it was impossible for them to find her and for Pavel to try to explain his betrayal. The crew shunned them both but still allowed them to stay in the apartment till the end of the summer. They all made it clear to Fran that her relationship with them would never be the same and that when they returned to Baton Rouge, they wanted her out of their lives.

Galina hoped that time would heal her pain and threw herself into working all the hours she could to keep her mind clear of the memory of that terrible day. That's when Jim McCord entered her life.

Each time he came into the bar, he sat in the same corner table. He kept to himself mostly but had an eye for the ladies. Galina watched him as he floated around the bar from table to table spinning his bullshit lines. She sensed that Jim was a bit of a rogue but despite his being much older and even a little dangerous, she still found him interesting. There was something about him she liked.

The predator was sucking her into his web with well-practiced, artificial compassion. "Why do you look so sad? A beautiful girl like you shouldn't be sad!" The words dripped off his tongue like a wolf salivating over an imminent kill.

Then one day his sleaze-ball tactics worked. She told him her story and the tears rolled down her cheeks. She felt that she needed to tell someone. It felt like her memories were boiling up inside her and she needed to tell someone to relieve the pressure. The predator saw this as the opportunity he was looking for; he offered her a Kleenex to dry her tears and touched her hand. The feeling of her skin on his electrified him and he felt a tingle of excitement in his groin.

"Each day will be better, Galina. You will get stronger and you *will* get over this!" It was the coup de grace. He had her and his heart raced at the prospect of the pleasure to come.

~

Over the years, Jim McCord had a routine that he had established for his Pagosa Springs summers. He would have dinner with his wife, Mary, and then bed her down for the night. The medications she took ensured that she slept soundly, leaving McCord free to go on the prowl. He didn't do it every night and not on weekends. He typically went out Tuesdays and Wednesdays so that tongues wouldn't wag and no gossip would find its way back to Mary's ears.

Jim's habits were methodical. He made sure he wasn't seen in the same bar on two consecutive nights, and stayed sober enough so he wouldn't run into trouble with police. The last thing he needed was a DUI. Jim McCord was not out looking to get drunk. He was out looking for some action to satisfy his sexual appetite.

Over the next few weeks, Jim worked his charm on Galina. By the time mid-August rolled around, he made his move.

One night, Jim met her on her night off and took her to another bar on the outskirts of town. She got drunk quickly and was drowning in his charm. He said that he would look after her. Galina agreed that was what she needed. She needed to feel the warmth again of someone who cared. She needed a shoulder to cry on to let out all the pain.

After drinks, they drove back to the rear of the San Juan Bar and crept into the Airstream together. They sat on the bed; Jim brushed away her tears and stroked her hair. He kissed her softly on the cheek and neck and placed a hand on her breast. As he touched her, Galina pushed up into him, surrendering to his caresses. He undressed her slowly and took off his clothes. Their bodies combined, hands touching and exploring. He kissed her deeply and then slowly entered her. Their lovemaking was slow and sensual and she gave herself to him completely.

"Oh, Jim, I never thought it could be like this," she whispered in his ear.

He waited until she fell asleep. Her breathing was soft and low and he felt good that she had obviously enjoyed the lovemaking of a master of the art. With the conquest complete, he dressed and left the Airstream.

Another notch on the belt! he thought to himself as he drove home.

After Jim McCord left the Airstream, Galina awoke, saw he was gone and cried uncontrollably. Her head cleared and the full realization of what had happened hit her like a runaway train.

"How could I be so stupid? Jim just used me and I let it happen. I let it happen with that whore, Fran, and now this. How could I be so stupid?"

Galina cried herself back to sleep. She felt like a lost soul adrift on the ocean and the sharks were circling.

Chapter 31 - The doomsday prepper

2014 - The Cold Case Investigation

A WEEK LATER, THEY were all back in the conference room. Tommy and Marie had written up their report on their trip to Pagosa Springs. Bill Ross had done considerable research on the Internet but nothing had popped up indicating that this might be a serial killer. Jack Johnson had interviewed everyone in Austin in the Riverside neighborhood.

Jack sat at the head of the conference table and kicked things off. "I suggest that we take the next couple of hours to white board a timeline and then populate that timeline with what we know. We can then highlight any missing pieces in the sequence and develop a plan to target those for further investigation."

Bill stood up, walked to the whiteboard and said, "So let's write down what we know for sure."

1. The body was discovered on Thursday, September 15, 2005.

2. Jim McCord was tripping the light fantastic with Dawn Cohen the previous evening, September 14.

3. Bobby McCord and friends were at the McCord house over Labor Day weekend and left Friday morning, September 9.

4. The cleaning crew was in the home on the Sunday and Monday and completed their work on Monday night, September 12.

5. We know nothing of the events at the house from Monday night until the body was discovered on Thursday.

6. We know Jim McCord returned his rented Ford to Hertz at San Antonio Airport late afternoon on Thursday.

Bill looked over his handiwork and said, "Now let's create a list of supposition and speculation."

1. We suspect that Jim McCord didn't do it because we currently have no evidence to suggest he did.

2. We are pretty sure that aliens didn't do it, but we don't know that for sure.

3. We think that Mary McConnell may have "seen" the face of the dead woman and is suggesting there may be others. We think we might have a serial killer but we have no evidence to suggest that.

"Now, let's catalog the work from the investigations we've done over the last couple of weeks. Jack, why don't you go first with Jim McCord's friends in Austin and your interview with Bobby?"

Jack pulled out his notes. "Unfortunately, I got nothing of substance from the Riverside neighbors. The women felt sorry for Mary and her emotional problems, and while many of them tried to involve her in social activities, Mary constantly found excuses not to participate.

"Jim's golf buddies responded like golf buddies normally do. He's a good guy, doesn't cheat (most of the time). I also talked with McCord's son in Oklahoma, Bobby. Lately, Bobby hasn't been able to come home to spend time with his parents. He loves his mother very much but he didn't stray from the 'party line' about his father. His dad was a cyber-security expert, a subcontractor with the U.S. government and traveled a lot. That's about it from me," concluded Jack.

"I'll go next," said Bill. "I found the Vanderbilt connection. Jim grew up in Nashville but other than the rape allegation, there's nothing to report. His father was a doctor and he worked in Vanderbilt Medical Center, as did his mother, who was a research chemist. They were killed in a plane crash when Jim was in his second year at college. He inherited close to $8 million from the estate. I got nowhere on finding other murders with similar modus operandi but I'll keep at it."

Bill looked over to Tommy and Marie and asked, "Last but not least. What did you two dig up?"

Tommy handed out their printed reports and walked the team through the content. He cataloged the meeting with Scott and Rachel Shultz and wrapped it up by saying they confirmed what Herman Lutz at Lockheed Martin had said about Jim's character. They had even gone further to paint him as a womanizer. Clearly, Jim was not to be trusted.

"Our next interview was with Luther Fisher," said Tommy. "Based on the way that interview went, we're surprised that he even agreed to meet with us. He is without doubt a Doomsday Prepper. He had various guns on display and has survivalist magazines lying around all over his house. He was deeply suspicious of our motives for being there and behaved every second of our interview with him like he wanted us gone. He has a fancy telescope that I thought was pointed at the mountains but when I looked through the lens, it was pointed at another property on the other side of the valley. It was a cabin of some sort with an RV and boat parked alongside. When he saw me looking through the telescope he went ballistic.

"In addition, there were inconsistencies in what he told us. During the interview, Luther said that he thought Jim McCord was an okay guy but that was because he 'didn't do anything bad to him.' He made it sound like McCord let Luther Fisher be Luther Fisher. But then we met with Josef and Cornelia Jacobsen."

Before Tommy could continue, Bill Ross stood up with a look on his face like he had just won *America's Got Talent*.

"I knew that I recognized the name! *Luther Fisher!* Luther Fisher and Jim McCord were two of the three guys accused of raping the female student at Vanderbilt!"

"Wow! Another piece of the puzzle," said Jack. "But let's continue with Tommy's findings for now."

Tommy thanked Jack and continued, "When we met with the Jacobsens, it became obvious in the early part of the interview that Josef Jacobsen hated Jim McCord. He called him a liar and a cheat."

"His wife had even more interesting revelations!" continued Marie. "She told us that the McCords and the Fishers were best friends before Summer Fisher drowned in the lake at Navajo State Park in 2003. In the initial part of the investigation, Mary McCord was considered a suspect in her death because it was rumored that Jim was having an affair with Summer. The theory was that Mary deliberately drowned Summer in a fit of rage. Mary had been close to a nervous breakdown and is still receiving treatment today."

While Tommy and Marie were presenting their report, Bill had continued to Google *Luther Fisher*. When they finished, Bill spoke up.

"According to Google, Luther Fisher graduated Vanderbilt with a degree in pharmacology and worked in the medical center for a couple of years. According to *Who's Who* in Nashville, he inherited over $70 million when his mother died in 1999. His father had been a music executive in Nashville and died from a drug overdose a few years earlier. Luther quit his job and built a home in Pagosa Springs with some of his inheritance."

Jack nodded his head and said, "I say it's time we circle the wagons on this and figure out where we are. Bill, why don't you go first?"

"From my perspective, it gets down to motive and opportunity," began Bill. "I don't see motive with Jim McCord. We might not like him but I don't think he did it. Regarding opportunity, he could have tried to pick up a girl on his way up to Austin from San Antonio just to have her reject him. He freaks out, kills her and then dumps her body in plain sight. But the body wasn't dumped. It was staged, and when would he have had time to do that? Also, why would he pick up someone a few hours before he was due to meet Dawn Cohen for sex?"

Bill continued on, "Luther Fisher had possible motive. He may have found out that his wife was having an affair with Jim McCord and wanted to hurt him. He finds some random girl, kills her and then somehow makes his way to Austin to put the body in McCord's backyard. We need more evidence for this to be a credible option. There are still pieces that don't fit. Why was the body staged?"

Bill sighed and sat down at the table. "And the biggest question is who was she? We are still no closer on that and we need to be. That's about it from me."

"I'm with Bill," replied Marie. "Two weeks ago, we thought that Jim McCord held the key. I now feel that Luther Fisher is the missing piece. We need to sweat him some more and he's not going to like it. He's a Prepper and I would wager has enough firepower in that house to start World War Three. I also think that there is a connection to the drowning of Summer Fisher. I don't know what it is, but we need to press Luther Fisher on that."

"I agree with both Bill and Marie," said Jack.

"I do too," said Tommy.

"I guess we will be making another trip back to Pagosa Springs," continued Marie.

Jack nodded and said, "Yes, and this time I will be coming with you. But before we head out there, there is more work we need to do. We need to go talk with Jim and Mary McCord. I will brief Chief Dunwoody and also Sheriff Gordon of Archuleta County, as we will need his help again. Bill, you continue with your research on the serial killer angle and check out the available information online regarding the drowning of Summer Fisher."

"Will do, boss," replied Bill.

Chapter 32 - Mary's story

2014 - The Cold Case Investigation

AFTER EVERYONE HAD LEFT THE conference room, Jack called Jim McCord and set up a time to meet.

Jim sounded stressed over the phone. "Do we need to involve Mary? She has been through enough. There's no need to tell her about my indiscretion with Dawn Cohen, is there?"

"I don't make promises, Jim, but at this time, we don't believe that your affair had any connection to the dead woman," said Jack, deliberately trying to ensure that McCord's guard would not be up. He needed McCord to feel less at risk in answering their questions.

Jack hung up with McCord and stared at the phone. "You're trying so hard to keep Mary out of this, McCord, could it be for other reasons than your infidelity? Let's see what Mary has to say." Jack then left his office and went off to the breakroom for another caffeine fix.

~

The following morning Jack and Marie arrived right on time at the McCords' home in Riverside for the meeting with Mary. Jim McCord opened the door after the first ring of the doorbell. *He must have seen us arrive and has everything planned out. He's ready for us. Thinks he's so smart*, thought Jack.

McCord led them into the living room where Mary McCord was waiting. She was seated on their leather sofa with a pot of tea, cup and saucer on the coffee table in front of her. When she saw them enter the room she picked up the cup and took a sip of tea. She was shaking so hard that the cup rattled on the saucer when she laid it back down again.

"Good morning, Mrs. McCord. My name is Jack Johnson and this is Detective Marie Mason. I'm sure Jim has told you the reason for our visit here today."

"Yes, it's about the dead woman found out by our pool in 2005," replied Mary McCord, looking tired, pale, and drawn. The stress and the medications over the years had taken their toll. Marie stepped in to pick up from Jack, as they had planned. She would lead the questioning of Mary.

"We are collecting background information, Mrs. McCord, so that we can try to piece it all together, so please relax and don't feel that our questions are in any way accusatory. We are simply here to gather what information we can," began Marie.

"Let's begin with your friendship with Summer and Luther Fisher, your neighbors in Pagosa Springs."

Without warning, Jim McCord interjected and shouted, *"What's that got to do with anything?"* He was visibly angry at this line of questioning.

Jack Johnson jumped in immediately and cut McCord off.

"As we said, Jim, we are trying to gather information. We have spoken with your neighbors both here and in Pagosa Springs to see if anyone knows anything. Someone killed this woman and we plan to find out who did it. So please *cooperate* with us on this. " Jack stressed the word *cooperate* for deliberate effect.

Mary put her head in her hands and sobbed, "Summer Fisher died some years ago! We don't have a friendship!"

"Yes, but you did, didn't you," continued Marie. "It all ended when she drowned in the lake at Navajo State Park. Can you tell us what you remember about that terrible day?"

Mary McCord looked decidedly uncomfortable, and her husband tried to come to her rescue again.

"Is all this necessary? Do we need to dredge up the past?

Jack drew him a look, and he backed down.

Marie glared at Jim, looked back at Mary and pleaded, "Please, Mary, what do you remember?"

Mary fought back tears and said, "We had parked the RV overnight by the lake. Jim and Luther launched the boat in the morning after breakfast. They went out on the lake for a day's fishing while Summer and I had a lazy day." The memories of 2003 were slowly beginning to resurface.

Marie looked over her notes and said, "According to the police report, you and Summer had consumed quite a bit of alcohol. This was confirmed by the autopsy. Were you both drinking that day?" asked Marie.

"Yes, but not all day."

Mary reached for the tea again and took a sip. Her shaking was getting worse and she needed both hands to put the cup back on the saucer.

She continued on. "We had a glass or two of wine with lunch and then later in the day, as the sun went down, we decided to take the recliners out to the end of the dock where the boats tie up. Summer took a bottle of Chardonnay and two glasses in her tote and we set up to drink some wine and watch the sunset until the men came back from their day on the lake."

"Please go on, Mary, this is very helpful," said Marie, trying to keep the conversation on a positive tone.

"All I remember is that Summer got up from the recliner to use the restroom and as she turned, the hem of her dress caught on a dock hook and in she went."

"So she was wearing a long dress. What type of dress was it, Mary?" asked Marie.

"It was a white cotton dress. She wore it a lot. She loved the coolness of it."

"What else was she wearing, Mary?" asked Marie with growing excitement.

"She had on her favorite floppy hat to keep the sun off, a pair of sunglasses, and flip flops."

Marie was elated; this was the way that the dead woman's body had been staged. She pressed on with her questioning of Mary.

"You then jumped in to try to save her?"

"Yes, I knew she couldn't swim. The dress had wrapped around her head and shoulders and she was panicking. I tried to get to her but she went under fast. I yelled to a couple of men tying up their boat some ways down the dock but they couldn't hear me. I dove under to get her to the surface but she was flailing around. Her weight and the wet dress made it impossible for me to grab hold. She was trying to pull the dress over her head but before she could, the flailing subsided," sobbed Mary. She paused, took a Kleenex from the pocket of her cardigan and wiped her tears.

"I got out of the water and ran for help. The two men I saw earlier heard my screams and came running along the dock. They dove in and after several attempts, eventually found her and pulled her to the dock. They tried mouth-to-mouth but she was dead!" Mary paused again to use the Kleenex but she seemed to be gaining some strength from cleansing her soul, letting it all out.

Another sip of tea and she continued on.

"When Jim and Luther came back on the boat and were within a few yards of the dock, they yelled at me to tell them what was going on. All I could say was, '*It's Summer!*' Luther jumped off the boat and swam to the dock. After one of the men pulled him up, Luther ran to her. I was rambling, trying to tell him what had happened. He pushed me out of the way so hard that I almost went in.

"Summer was laid out on the dock. Her white dress and blond hair had a strange aura as the sun set. Luther sat there on the dock with Summer cradled in his arms and he stroked her hair. The police arrived some time later. They interviewed all of us about what had happened and that was it. Summer was gone!"

Marie, trying to sound convincing, said, "Mary, you have been incredibly helpful. Not sure that Summer's drowning has any connection to the murdered woman in your yard but we need to tie up all loose ends."

Jim McCord got up from his chair in the corner of the room and sat by his wife. He held her in his arms as her shoulders went limp and she sobbed uncontrollably. As he did so, he shot a glance at Jack Johnson.

You're doing this for effect, you son of a bitch, thought Jack as he watched McCord stroke his wife's hair.

Marie closed her notebook and said, "I think we are done for the day. No need to take more of your time, Mary. This was obviously incredibly stressful for you going back over all the details. Thank you so much for doing that."

Jim McCord looked relieved until Jack asked him to walk out with them to the car, and at that moment his mood changed. McCord kissed his wife and said, "I'll be right back, honey."

McCord walked down the steps from his front door and over to the car where Marie and Jack stood waiting. Marie opened the back door of the Ford and asked McCord to get in, which he did somewhat unwillingly. Marie closed the door and got into the driver's seat. Jack was already in the front passenger seat and he turned around to face a very nervous Jim McCord.

"When did you first meet Luther Fisher, Jim?"

Jim's eyes grew wide. "When they built their home in Pagosa Springs."

"Don't screw with us, McCord, or I will get out of this car, go back in and have a quiet word with Mary. The *truth*, please!"

"Okay, I went to college with him at Vanderbilt University in Nashville."

"Jim, you only have one shot at giving a truthful answer to this question. Did you have an affair with Summer?"

With what looked like tears in his eyes, Jim McCord finally gave a truthful response. "Yes, I did. But can I explain?"

"Go right ahead," said Jack.

Jim McCord told his story.

"Summer was locked in a nightmare of a marriage and on the verge of a nervous breakdown. She came to me looking for a shoulder to cry on. I tried to help her, listen to her and be supportive. and it developed in to a physical relationship," said Jim McCord. his eyes pleading for Jack to believe him.

"You are a real knight in shining armor," sneered Jack. "What about the rape of the female student at Vanderbilt?"

From McCord's reaction, you would have thought that Jack had stabbed him through the heart with a Bowie knife. He was clearly terrified.

"It wasn't me!" yelled McCord.

"Why should I believe you? You've lied to me about everything else up until this point, so tell me why I should believe you now?" pressed Jack.

"I didn't do it. I swear!" said McCord with tears running down his face. He drew his right arm across his face to wipe the snot dripping from his nose.

"But you *do* know who did, don't you?" Jack had him by the balls and was not going to let go.

"Luther Fisher did it," said Jim McCord, trying to wriggle his way out of Jack's iron grip.

"So tell me about it then," said Jack.

"Luther was majoring in pharmacology and was experimenting with various drugs. He told us that he wanted to get a girl drugged up and screw her, so he asked Billy Pell and me if we wanted in. We agreed. We went to a bar, he found a target and we took her with us back on campus. After we had a few more drinks, Luther slipped a drug into the girl's glass. When she was passed out, Luther stripped her and told us to watch. He told us that he had to be first and that after he was done we could have a turn. It was like he was possessed. When he got violent with her, Billy and I got scared and ran off. I don't know what happened after that."

Jack was about to ask another question but Jim McCord wasn't finished.

"It was the same with Summer. Luther knew that I was building a place in Pagosa Springs and asked if he could come visit with us with his new fiancée. I agreed and they came and stayed for a week. They loved the area and he decided to buy the land adjoining our property and build a place. They stayed with us while their house was being built and Summer became good friends with Mary. It was after their home was completed and they had moved in that Summer started to confide in Mary about Luther's perversions."

"What kind of perversions?" asked Jack.

"He wanted her to dress up in weird leather outfits that he had bought. He would tie her up and the sex would be very rough. A few times, she had to have medical treatment."

Jim's mouth was a rushing faucet that wouldn't stop flowing. "Summer would come visit with us when Luther was out of town, and sit and drink wine. When Mary went off to bed, Summer and I would continue to talk and drink. And that's when the relationship between us became physical."

With his "confession" over, McCord stared at Jack Johnson with the look of a little boy, his eyes pleading that Jack believe him.

Jack stared at Jim and said, "If what you say is true, we need to take a long, hard look at Luther Fisher. I want your complete cooperation. You discuss this with no one. We'll have to contact the authorities in Tennessee about what you have told us. If what you say is true and they can prove that Fisher did this, your cooperation may be taken into consideration. You are in deep shit, Jim, and we are your only hope. We need your *total* cooperation and your *total* silence—*clear*?"

Jim McCord stumbled out of the car and plodded back up the driveway to his home, hunched over like every ounce of life force had been drained from him. He knew that this was just the beginning and that they would keep digging. His world was collapsing around him.

Chapter 33 - Chubby Checker

2014 - The Cold Case Investigation

THE FOLLOWING DAY, JACK updated the team on the Jim and Mary McCord interviews.

"Sounds like it is beginning to point to Luther Fisher," said Tommy.

"Yes, but there are still a lot of loose ends and I don't want us going back up to Pagosa Springs without more information. Bill, have you uncovered anything else?" asked Jack.

Bill cleared his throat, looked down at his notes and began.

"The first thing I want to say is that none of what I am about to share could have been uncovered without the help of the folks at the sheriff's office in Archuleta County and, in particular, Detective Raul Ortiz. Firstly, I have the full report from the drowning of Summer Fisher that Raul found in the archives and everything jives with what Mary McCord told you in the interview."

"Initially, there was strong suspicion that Mary may have deliberately drowned Summer but that could not be proven. The official ruling of the medical examiner was accidental death from drowning."

Bill paused, took a sip of water and then continued on.

"After Tommy and Marie mentioned Luther's explosion at the use of his telescope, I asked Raul to pull the county property records. Survivalists often have multiple 'fall back' zones and

I wondered if there was any connection. Why else would he have eyes on another property? Raul said that Cemetery Road accessed that part of the valley and that there were only three large properties over there. When we searched the property records, we hit pay dirt."

Bill had the team's full attention at this point. Celia opened the conference room door and stuck her head in. "Not now!" yelled Jack and her head disappeared as she closed the door.

Bill continued with his report. "One of the properties is owned by Crystal Light Promotions of Nashville, Tennessee. Crystal Light Promotions is headquartered in the Cayman Islands and the president and CEO is listed as Britney Fisher, Luther Fisher's dead mother. All communication with Crystal Light in the USA is via a P.O. box in Nashville, and the property taxes for this property are paid using a Crystal Light corporate credit card drawn on a bank in Grand Cayman. Raul also accessed the county vehicle registration database and Crystal Light owns an RV, a boat, a boat trailer, a Jeep and a Toyota Land Cruiser."

"I would say from my viewpoint that many pieces of the puzzle are beginning to fit," concluded Bill as he leaned back in his chair, allowing himself a little smile of satisfaction.

"Well, you've been busy," said Jack. "Anything else?"

"Raul and I are working on something but it is premature to comment on the results. We are turning up nothing on women killed and left staged wearing white dresses. I called Nora McConnell and asked her if she could tell me how many women she had 'seen.' She wasn't certain but she thought that it might have been more than six. Again, that gave me pause to think that we might be off on a tangent. Since rape seems to be up Jim McCord and Luther Fisher's alley, Raul and I are now looking at all sexual offenses in Archuleta County. I will update everyone when I have more information.

"Oh and one final request, boss," said Bill. "Don't you think we have enough evidence that points to a Pagosa Springs connection that might justify requesting the Archuleta sheriff to circulate the artist's impression of the dead woman in their county and see if we get any hits?"

Jack couldn't hide his smile. "Great idea, Bill. I will call Sheriff Gordon and get back to you rather than go through Detective Ortiz. *Great work*, Bill!"

Jack stood up and addressed the team. His eyes were alight with a fire they hadn't seen up until this point. They all felt they were closer to the truth than ever before.

"Keep at this, team. We are getting closer, but no jumping to conclusions. This case has taken more twists than Chubby Checker! Let's meet again here on Friday."

Chapter 34 - In the clutches of a killer

2005 - The Killing

IT WAS SEPTEMBER 9, 2005 and the crowds that descended on Pagosa Springs for Labor Day weekend had returned home to get their kids ready for the new school term. Galina finished her shift at the bar and made her way to the Airstream. As she opened the door of the trailer, she sensed that something was wrong. An arm shot out from nowhere and wrapped around her neck. As she struggled for air, a hand with a pad soaked in chloroform was pressed hard against her mouth.

He had her in his grasp, unconscious. He expertly balanced her weight and lifted her off her feet. Looking around to make sure that no one had seen the struggle, he quickly moved from the trailer to his Jeep, which he had parked at the rear of the bar, and bundled her into the back.

He drove from the San Juan Sports Bar to his cabin off Cemetery Road. As he drove, his eyes constantly flashed to the rear-view mirror to make sure that no opportunistic police officer looking for drunks was on his tail. He drove cautiously, always at the speed limit, never too slow or too fast, so as not to attract attention. He was skilled at this and he wasn't going to allow a momentary lapse in concentration result in his demise. This was always the most risky part when he abducted girls: driving them in the Jeep to the cabin. If he were to be pulled over, that would be it. No risks to be taken at this stage.

He arrived at the cabin gates and keyed in the passcode for the security system. As the gates opened, he threw doggy treats out the window of the Jeep to Tweedle Dum and Tweedle Dee, the two Dobermans that patroled the yard. He parked the Jeep beside the RV and opened the rear door to the cabin. He wheeled out a gurney that was parked behind the door and transferred the still unconscious Galina onto it.

He wheeled the gurney down the central hallway of the cabin, past the small kitchen on the left and the viewing room on the right. There were two bedrooms at the end of the hallway, one named Summer and the other named Winter, an evil and twisted play on words. He wheeled the gurney into the Summer room and placed Galina on the bed.

He fastened one ankle to a manacle connected to a long chain that was connected to a tether on the central wall of the room. He had other manacles on either side of the headboard that would be used later so that when he abused her, she couldn't fight him off.

There were photographs of a young woman everywhere on the walls and on the side tables of the bed. In the majority of these pictures, the woman wore a white cotton dress, floppy sun hat and shades. In the closet, more than a dozen white dresses were hung, just like the ones in the photos. On the shelf, he had exact copies of the hat and sunglasses shown in the pictures. The dressing table had every conceivable high-quality cosmetic product and, in a prominent position, bright red lipstick tubes placed on end like tin soldiers on a mock battlefield.

In the corner of the room was a sink and, alongside it, a refrigerator containing bottles of water. The refrigerator also contained transparent plastic containers with green salad and others with fresh strawberries. There were no utensils or any other sharp objects anywhere in the room. When he had Galina restrained and he felt everything was in order, he left the Summer room, closed the door and opened the door to the Winter room.

This was where the bad girls went. He always liked to stand at the door and look inside, reminding himself that everything was there and in order if needed. The metal operating table complete with leg stirrups. There were syringes and adequate supplies of morphine and others drugs plus every device imaginable to be used on the girls to inflict pain and fuel his sexual depravity. There were also huge speakers in all four corners of the room for him to be able to play his music as he performed his art. The room was totally soundproof.

He closed the door of the Winter room, smiled and walked across the hallway to the "viewing room." This is where he stored all of the records of his life's work. He chose one of the videos from his collection and a beer from the fridge, settled himself into his recliner and hit the play button.

Chapter 35 - The seeds of evil

2005 - The Killing

LUTHER FISHER WAS THE ONLY son of Britney and Alvin Fisher. He was born and raised in Nashville, Tennessee where his father was a music producer. In the '60s and '70s, drug and alcohol abuse was commonplace in the Nashville music scene. Britney and Alvin were substance abusers and Luther, an only child, had very little love or nurturing from either parent.

In addition to the drug and alcohol abuse, Britney and Alvin had an "open" marriage. They each enjoyed sex games that frequently involved bondage. Britney was always the submissive where Alvin would play the dominant male. The open marriage allowed them the flexibility of sex with multiple partners.

In his early childhood, Luther witnessed his mother and father perform these sexual acts. He was frequently left alone in the house and ignored. However, he was a clever little boy and he would try to play with his toys or watch TV while the sex sessions were going on in another part of the house. Over the years, he found himself drawn to the sounds from the bedroom and he would deliberately hide in the bedroom closet so he could watch through the louvers in the door. He witnessed his mother in submissive sexual positions restrained by cuffs and ropes, with her husband or another male partner of her choosing performing the dominant male role.

This environment created a child with a desperate need for love and attention that never was received from either parent. As he entered puberty, his sexual development was distorted by what he had experienced firsthandgrowing up. Bondage and the subjugation of women for sex were primary elements of his sexual personality. His abandonment as a child distorted this even further, resulting in the creation of a true hatred of women: misogyny.

An event in school was a harbinger of things to come. When Luther was thirteen, he was in morning classes and left the classroom to use the toilet. He saw that a young girl from another class had done the same and as she left the toilet, Luther grabbed her from behind and forced her back into the restroom.

Luther always carried a knife with him and he forced the terrified girl back into one of the cubicles. He told her to keep her eyes shut and that if she didn't he would slit her throat.

He used the knife to cut off all of her clothes. He stuffed toilet tissue in her mouth, wrapped her blouse around her head and tied it loosely so she could still breathe. With one of the sleeves cut from her blouse, he tied her hands behind her back and he then used her school tie to tie one ankle, wrap the tie around the commode and tie the other ankle. She was completely naked, blindfolded, gagged and secured on the commode with legs splayed. He molested her. He then wrote, "whore" on her naked stomach, locked the cubicle door and climbed over the metal partition. He returned to class like nothing had happened.

Later at morning break, the restroom rapidly filled with girls and when they couldn't get into the locked cubicle, one of them was given a boost to look over the top. Full panic ensued and school staff escorted the humiliated and terrified girl from the restroom and called her parents. When interviewed, the little girl was incoherent.

The teachers and the police suspected that it was Luther but they could never prove it. The victim never returned to the school and she and her parents left the area.

Chapter 36 - Psychosis

2005 - The Killing

LUTHER HAD BOUGHT THE CABIN soon after he and Summer had completed their main Pagosa home. The original plan was that this would be his bunker that he would fortify with heavy defenses and stock with food, water, and ammo. If there was to be a breakdown in society and a final war to be fought, he could defend his primary residence and then fall back to this secure bunker if the house was compromised. The death of Summer changed this plan.

Summer drowned in August of 2003. In 2004, almost a year to the day from the drowning, Luther had seen a young woman walking along the street in Pagosa. In an instant, he was convinced she was Summer. It made perfect sense to him that Summer had returned and was searching Pagosa looking for him. He abducted the woman, took her to the cabin and spent several days raping and abusing her before killing her.

When the woman was dead, he cleaned her thoroughly using a diluted bleach mixture. He shampooed her hair, combed it and blow-dried it until it shined. He worked on her fingernails and toenails, giving her a French manicure. He then dressed her in a white cotton dress. The final touch was the facial makeup along with a dab of Chloe perfume. She was now ready to be returned to the lake so that she might come to him again.

Luther put the body in his RV and drove to the lake at Navajo State Park with his boat in tow. When he arrived, he parked the RV and launched his boat with the dead girl's body on board. He then sailed to the middle of the lake, secured weights to her and dumped the body overboard. As she sunk to bottom, his twisted mind imagined how she would return to him; when she did, he would be better prepared for those visits. That's when the cabin was remodeled for a different purpose than being his bunker of last resort.

~

Luther heard Galina stir in the Summer bedroom. He entered the room and could see that she was disoriented. She was sitting up on the bed, trying to focus and figure out where she was. When she realized she was shackled, she panicked and began screaming uncontrollably. Luther took a vial of drug cocktail he had grabbed from the Winter room when he heard her stir and injected her with it. The mixture of morphine and Rohypnol calmed her down almost immediately and she entered a semiconscious state.

After she settled down, he fastened the headboard manacles to each wrist and lay down beside her and began whispering in her ear. Her eyes stared blankly outward as his lips brushed against her earlobes.

"I am so happy you're home again, Summer. I thought that I had lost you at the lake but I've have worked hard and found a way to bring you back to me."

His psychosis had reached such a state that he believed he could bring the long dead Summer back to life on demand by kidnapping young women whose physical attributes were close enough to those of his dead wife. His deluded mind allowed him to fill in the gaps.

He began kissing her passionately, and when the semiconscious Galina did not fully respond in the way he thought she should, pent-up anger filled his body. This had also happened when Summer was alive. She refused to submit to his fetishes and extremely deviant sexual demands. Whenever she refused, Luther would lose control and lash out.

Galina's response brought the same result. He lost control and started to deliberately do things to her to cause pain and to "teach her a lesson." Luther grabbed her by the throat and penetrated her roughly to exercise his control and power. He followed that up by assaulting her with dildos, metal tubes and other instruments of torture that he had assembled ready for use. His perversion knew no bounds. In some cases, in the Winter room, he had gone too far and killed the poor girls.

With his anger spent and his sexual desires met, he again lay down next to her and kissed her tenderly.

"I love our games, my love, and I know you do too. I'm so happy that we give each other so much pleasure. Sleep well, my love, as tomorrow we go off on a grand adventure."

Luther left the cabin, "It's good to have Summer home," he whispered to himself as he drove off.

Chapter 37 - It's Galina Alkaev

2014 - The Cold Case Investigation

SHERIFF GORDON FROM THE ARCHULETA Sheriff's Department agreed to circulate the artist impression. Every deputy was provided with a copy. The sheriff also had the editors of the *Pagosa Springs Sun* and the *Pagosa Daily Post* run the picture simply saying that the Pagosa Sheriff's Department was looking for anyone who might recognize the woman and to contact them ASAP to help them with their inquiries into an ongoing case. They got fourteen hits.

Two days later Raul called Bill. "Hi, Bill, this is Raul. We have a number of positive IDs on your artist's impression."

"Let me get Tommy and Marie in here and put them on speaker. Jack is out today or I would have him join us," said Bill.

A few minutes later, Tommy and Marie joined Bill in the conference room to listen to the update from Raul.

"Go ahead, Raul, we're all here."

Raul's voice sounded crackly through the conference room speakerphone.

"Thanks, Bill. We got fourteen hits on the artist's impression we circulated. I've already spoken with all of them. Two of them sound a little flaky, but the other twelve seem like they are genuine for one specific reason. *They all drank at the San Juan*

Sports Bar and Grill here in town back in 2005. Many of them *still* drink there regularly."

"One of them was the owner of the place until 2010. Her name is Heidi Braun. Heidi is sure that the dead woman's name is Galina Alkaev and that she worked in the bar for about three months until she disappeared just after Labor Day, 2005. She also lived in an Airstream trailer that Heidi parked at the rear of the bar."

Marie had her hand over her mouth and was stifling a scream as she stared at Tommy. *Galina Alkaev!* After ten years could they have finally put a name to her?

Raul continued, "She said that when Galina Alkaev disappeared, she left everything she owned in the Airstream. She simply vanished into thin air without a note or any communication. Heidi said that she was concerned at the time as it wasn't like Galina to just up and go. Heidi also said that she had hired her as a favor to a friend in Vail after Galina had some boyfriend troubles. She called her friend to see if Galina had gone back there but she hadn't."

Tommy interrupted Raul. "And she left it at that? She didn't do anything else to try to find her?"

"Good question. Heidi had tried to locate Galina to return her things to her but never managed to track her down. One of the things that she left was an address book that contained names and phone numbers for people back in Pikesville, Maryland, her hometown. Initially, Heidi had thought to call her parents but then thought it better not to interfere. Over the years, Heidi forgot about it. She still has a box with all of Galina's stuff in her garage."

Raul paused for a second before saying, "Oh, there is one other thing that Heidi Braun told us that you guys are going to really love."

Raul paused to increase the tension of the moment and to playfully piss off the audience.

"Well, go on and stop keeping us in suspense!" yelled Tommy.

"Galina had an up-close-and-personal relationship with Jim McCord!"

There were gasps around the room. Then Bill broke the tension.

"Chubby Checker is at it again. Another twist!" said Bill.

The team thanked Raul for his hard work on the case and hung up. Tommy called Jack Johnson on his cell and debriefed him on the Ortiz call. To say Jack Johnson was angry and frustrated was an understatement.

"Have this Heidi Braun woman package up the stuff and send it down here to us. Give our FedEx account number to her to bill the cost and tell her to overnight it. When it arrives, let's go through it together and then we get that bastard McCord back in. As God is my witness, I am going to string him up by the balls before I hand him over to the Tennessee people."

The box arrived the following morning. Apart from clothes, shoes, and other miscellaneous items, there were photographs and the address book. One photograph was of a young man and woman standing by a motorcycle, taken at the side of the highway with a *Welcome to Vail* sign in the background. The woman was a tall blonde who looked like Reese Witherspoon. They now knew for sure: "*Reese*" was Galina Alkaev.

Chapter 38 - You're under arrest

2014 - The Cold Case Investigation

JIM McCORD WAS SEATED IN the conference room when the team walked in. Celia had gotten him a cup of coffee and he was leaning back in his chair as if he didn't have a care in the world. His demeanor changed when he saw Jack Johnson's face.

Jack stared at Jim and said, "I despise murderers, pedophiles, and rapists. They are all in the first division of my hate leagues. Just below them and in the top spot in division two are liars. Jim McCord, you are a liar of the highest order. You're such a liar that you've told yourself you're not a liar. So, now that we're all clear on who you are and what you are, tell me about Galina Alkaev!"

The blood drained from Jim McCord's face and drops of sweat sprung from his forehead. He covered his face with his hands and said, "I didn't kill her, I swear!"

"Is that another one of your lies, Jim, you piece of shit? Back in 2005, when you saw the artist's impression, you knew exactly who the dead woman was. You said nothing and wasted police time. You probably hastened the end of a good detective's career. Today, we are spending taxpayer dollars to pursue a cold case that could have been solved years ago, and the killer is likely to have killed many other women because of your inability to tell the truth and own up to your actions. Give me one reason why I shouldn't throw you to the wolves?"

McCord started to say something, but before he could, Jack interrupted him. Jack and Bill had decided on their next move before Jim had entered the room.

"Jim McCord, I am arresting you on the suspicion of your involvement in the rape of a female student at Vanderbilt University on or about April 7, 1988. You will be held here, pending your extradition to the State of Tennessee.

- You have the right to remain silent when questioned.

- Anything you say or do may be used against you in a court of law.

- You have the right to consult an attorney before speaking to the police and to have an attorney present during questioning now or in the future.

- If you cannot afford an attorney, one will be appointed for you before any questioning, if you wish.

- If you decide to answer any questions now, without an attorney present, you will still have the right to stop answering at any time until you talk to an attorney.

- Knowing and understanding your rights as I have explained them to you, are you willing to answer my questions without an attorney present?

Jim McCord had his hands over his face as his head shook slowly from side to side. He was going to jail and they might throw away the key. "Can I call my son? I need to call my son. Please!"

McCord made the call and he was then led away to the holding cell.

Chapter 39 -Search warrant

2014 - The Cold Case Investigation

THE FOLLOWING MORNING, JACK kicked off the status review meeting. "Are we all in agreement that we suspect that Luther Fisher abducted Galina, transported her to Austin in his RV, killed her and staged her body in the backyard of the McCord residence?"

There was a unanimous show of hands.

"Bill, would you like to summarize where we are with the evidence we have gathered and any developments in your research with Raul Ortiz on sexual assaults in Archuleta County?" asked Jack.

Bill Ross cleared his throat and said, "Luther and Summer Fisher moved into their new home in Pagosa Springs on May 2, 2001. Starting in 2002, there was a marked increase in walk-in rape victims to hospitals and trauma centers across Archuleta, La Plata, and San Juan Counties. Many of the victims had significant injuries and had no recollection of what had happened to them.

"Most of these women had been out partying and the next thing they remembered was waking up the following morning lying in the backseat of their cars. They couldn't remember what had happened and therefore no charges were brought in any of the cases, as there was a lack of evidence to work with, not even semen. They each had chlorine residue on them and the medical examiner suggested that they might have all been assaulted in a health club with a swimming pool or a hot tub. He later revised this earlier supposition, as the levels of chlorine were too high. He concluded that they might have been deliberately washed to remove the possibility of gathering forensic evidence.

"Over the same time period, there were four women found dead in different locations with significant injuries suggesting that they may have been raped and tortured. They also had the same chlorine residue on them. So let me summarize where we are.

1. "We have no evidence connecting Fisher to Galina Alkaev. We may be able to get a search warrant and go through his house and the cabin with forensics to try to find that link.

2. "We do not know why or how he transported Galina to Austin. Again, we may be able to get a forensic team to pull the RV apart and find, as we suspect, that the RV was his mode of transportation.

3. "If he did do this, we don't know how he got the body into the backyard of McCord's home. If he had driven there and came in through the Riverside neighborhood, he risked being spotted. Tough not to spot an RV with Colorado plates in a neighborhood like Riverside."

Jack nodded and said, "Thanks, Bill, any other issues or concerns from the team?"

When no one responded, Jack said, "Okay, here's what I suggest as next steps. I'll call Sheriff Gordon and ask him to get a search warrant via the La Plata County District Attorney's Office based on the evidence we currently have. If the DA thinks that we have enough and we get a warrant, then I suggest that we form a joint team consisting of the Archuleta Sheriff's Department and the three of us to conduct the search. We can get specialist support from Archuleta or from state resources in Denver or both. Ultimate jurisdiction will depend on where the actual murder took place and, while that might be difficult to prove, we need to get the warrant first.

"Also, so everyone is on the same page, part of my reasoning in charging McCord was for us to be able to tell Fisher that we have arrested him. If our theory holds up that the reason he did this was revenge for McCord screwing his wife and perhaps a longer-term resentment of McCord for running away from the rape in Nashville, then he will think his plan has worked and his guard will be down. There is still a risk, however. He's a Prepper and almost certainly mentally disturbed. He may not take kindly to us invading his privacy again. I will brief Chief Dunwoody and then call Sheriff Gordon. Stay tuned, team!"

As the meeting broke up, Marie walked up to Tommy and asked, "What are you and Claire doing this weekend?"

"We have no plans," replied Tommy. "I thought I might take her to Zilker Park for the day and go swimming in the Barton Springs pool. We've been there a few times and she loves it."

"Why don't you come to Lake Travis with Shelly and me on Saturday? We want to take our boat out one last time before winter and this weekend is supposed to be real nice. We can come pick you up around 8:30, we'll get to the lake before 10:00 and get the boat launched before the big crowds get there."

"That could be fun. Let's do it," said Tommy.

Chapter 40 - Let's push the boat out

2014 - The Cold Case Investigation

ON SATURDAY MORNING, SHELLY and Marie arrived right on time at 8:30. Claire had been up since 6:00, jumping around excitedly about going to swim. For the past year, Elaine had taken Claire to swimming lessons at Little Tots Swim Center in Cedar Park and ever since, she became hyper-excited when anyone mentioned swimming.

"Is this a new truck?" said Tommy as he carried out the towels and his and Claire's backpacks.

"Yes, it is, Tommy. Shelly bought it a couple of weeks back. She traded in her old Toyota and the folks over at Henna Chevrolet gave her a great deal on this beast. It's a Silverado four-wheel-drive crew cab. It's great for towing the boat and we can get all our friends in the cab comfortably, along with our stuff in the back."

Tommy drooled, as this was the truck of his dreams, but at a $60,000 price tag, it was a little outside his range.

Shelly had bought Claire a pink life preserver and matching pink baseball cap. After they put it on her, they all agreed she looked adorable. They then climbed into the truck and headed to the lake. On the way they stopped at the storage center on 2222 and got the Sea Ray hooked up. It was a Sea Ray 280 sundeck, great for spending a day on Lake Travis.

To be able to live the American Dream these days, two incomes are needed. It was obvious to Tommy that Shelly and Marie were living the dream. He knew that their dream was not quite complete, as they wanted to marry, but that wasn't going to happen any time soon given the Texas legislature's stand on same-sex marriage.

They reached the village of Volente on Lake Travis before ten after stopping off at the 7-Eleven on 620 to load up the cooler with ice, bottled water and beer. Marie and Shelly had brought sandwiches, chips and juice for Claire, so they were all set for the day. They got the Sea Ray launched, parked the truck and trailer and they were off.

Once on the water, Shelly and Claire became fast friends. She let the four-year-old take the wheel of the boat as they sped across the lake. Claire was laughing and screaming at the top of her voice, "Look at me, Daddy!"

Marie and Tommy sat back relaxing with a beer. "So, you grew up in Tyler. What was that like?" asked Tommy.

Marie looked over the water, hesitated for a moment and then told Tommy about her early life in Tyler.

"My dad was a cattleman. His parents owned a ranch that he inherited when they died. I have three brothers and I am the youngest. My earliest memories were of my dad teaching my brothers how to operate the ranch. They often involved frequent *trips to the woodshed*, as he would say, to teach them a lesson if they messed up, which, in the eyes of my father, they did frequently.

"My father was a bully, a drunk and a gambler who lost the ranch in a poker game. When that happened, he went to work for another rancher who allowed my parents to rent a house on the property. Not long after, my three brothers left and got jobs in manufacturing companies in and around Tyler."

"With my brothers gone, my dad took his anger out on Mom and me. Being 'different' from the other girls didn't help. In the early days, he didn't understand why I was different and then, when he eventually came to terms with the fact that I was gay, the beatings got worse. I knew that I needed to get out of there as soon as I was able," said Marie as she grabbed another beer from the cooler.

"I'm sorry, Marie, I didn't mean to pry," said Tommy, feeling a little uncomfortable.

"I wanted to tell you. You weren't prying. I needed to get it off my chest, I guess. As partners we need to trust each other, and I trust you, Tommy."

Tommy took a swig from his beer and asked, "Did you always want to be in law enforcement?"

"No, just like you, I thought about the military. Not the Marine Corps, but the navy. I almost signed up one day when the recruiters came to the high school. I chose the police instead and got a job with the Smith County Sheriff's Office in Tyler."

Marie wasn't done and as the beer flowed, she continued to tell Tommy about her life as a deputy in Tyler and the challenges of being a lesbian in a male-dominated profession.

"In the beginning I thought I had made a terrible mistake, but, as they say, what doesn't kill you makes you stronger. And I got stronger. When my father died in 2000, my mother and I rented an apartment in town. Soon after, she was diagnosed with breast cancer and I cared for her until she died a year or so later."

Tommy put his hand on Marie's shoulder and said, "I'm sorry to hear that, Marie. That must have been tough for you. What brought you to Austin?"

"Many people in Tyler talked about Austin. It's the capitol of the state but the talk was about what a great city it was and how it was possibly the most liberal city in Texas, with a great music scene. I talked to my boss about my interest in moving to Austin and he reached out to the folks here in Travis County. A year later, I made the move and here I am," concluded Marie.

While Tommy and Marie were talking, Shelly and her first mate, Claire, found one of the many coves on Lake Travis and tied up alongside other boats while they ate lunch. Music echoed around the cove from the many boats as everyone was whooping and hollering and enjoying the last days of summer.

Claire was having great fun jumping off the deck at the back of the boat into the shallow water of the cove.

"She'll be tired tonight," said Tommy as Claire yelled, "Watch me, Daddy!" for what seemed like the hundredth time as she cannonballed over Shelly, who was trying to cool off with a quick dip behind the boat.

While his daughter played, Tommy told Marie about his life in the Marine Corps. Not all of it, just the good parts about forming a trust in your brothers-in-arms and friendships that would last a lifetime. There was no way he was ever going to share some of the atrocities that he witnessed during his tours of duty in the Balkans. He still had nightmares about that. He remembered his father talking about the poetry of Robert Burns, the Scottish bard, and a line from one of his poems about man's inhumanity to man. There was no more devastating example of inhumanity than the events of that war.

As the day drew to a close and the sun began to sink toward the horizon, they headed to shore. They got the boat back on the trailer and drove back to town as Claire slept in her car seat in the back of the truck.

Not much was said on the drive home, as nothing much needed to be said. It had been a great day and everyone was tired in a good way. Stories had been shared and, in the sharing, a depth of friendship had been established.

Yes, it had been a good day. When they got home, Tommy tucked Claire into bed, looked down at her rosy cheeks and kissed her on the forehead. "Sweat dreams, my love." With that, Tommy took himself off to bed, as tomorrow there would be more baddies to fight.

Chapter 41 - We're going on a trip

2005 - The Killing

GALINA WOKE IN THE MIDDLE of the night. She felt sick and had terrible pain in her groin. Her eyes tried to focus and make some sense of what had happened and where she was. Before leaving the cabin, Luther had undone the shackles on her hands, so she was now just tethered by the single manacle on her right ankle. She rose from the bed, stumbled around and found a light switch. She went to the toilet and as she urinated, she felt a terrible pain. When she was done, she looked down and saw blood in the toilet bowl. The pain in her stomach was almost unbearable but she was starving and saw the fridge in the corner of the room.

Galina ran to the fridge, opened it up and saw stacks of full salad containers. She grabbed one of the containers, tore off the lid and stuffed the salad into her mouth with her fingers. A nearby bottle of water followed to wash it down, which made the pain in her gut even more intense. Her eyes scanned the room.

"Where am I? What is this place! Who is this sick motherfucker?"

Galina tried to hold the tears back as she thought of her family. She was terrified and began to shake and convulse uncontrollably.

~

Luther returned to the cabin midmorning. When he entered the Summer bedroom and switched on the light, he saw the bed empty, the fridge open and half-eaten salad strewn on the floor.

As he entered the room and closed the door behind him, she attacked. Galina had been hiding behind the door and she jumped on, causing him to lose his balance and fall forward onto the floor. Using the power cord that she had managed to rip from the refrigerator, she wound it around his neck. As Luther gagged, Galina pulled on the cord with every sinew in her body, straining with the effort. After a few seconds, the pain in her abdomen was too much for her to bear and she lost the power in her arms. Luther swiveled around and threw her to the floor. She tried to struggle to her feet but Luther slapped her with the back of his hand and she lay at his feet sobbing. He lifted her up back onto the bed.

Galina had no energy left to resist. Panting, Luther reattached the wrist restraints and injected her with another cocktail of drugs.

"Now you feel better, Summer. You've had a good night's sleep and now we can plan the day," whispered Luther as he caressed her and smoothed her hair.

He lay down beside her and told her what he had planned.

"When I saw you, I was so excited that you had once more returned to me, my love. But you were with Jim McCord again and you know that I must be the first to enjoy our games. Once we're done, Jim can have his turn."

~

Luther met Summer when he attended Vanderbilt. He had never met anyone like her. As the relationship developed, Luther found, for the first time in his life, someone who truly loved him. It took time but he finally fell in love with her. He had never experienced love before. He loved Summer with every fiber of his being.

After graduating they wed, and it was after their marriage that Luther's base sexual needs began to seep into their lovemaking. In the beginning, he asked her to role-play the bondage, like a playful game. Over time, the games became more intense.

As he became more sexually demanding, Summer reached out to Jim and Mary McCord and confided in them. Jim saw this as an opportunity to feed *his* sexual appetite and an affair with Summer developed. Thanks to his parents' open relationship, Luther didn't care about Jim and Summer's affair, provided that he got what he needed first.

When Summer drowned in the lake, Luther was devastated. He had lost the only woman who had ever loved him. For months after her death, Luther was a lost soul until he saw "her" walking around Pagosa Springs. In his mind, the young girl with the long blond hair *was* Summer. She had returned and was searching for him. He abducted her, drugged her, abused her, killed her and then "returned her to the lake" so that she might come to him again.

To him, Galina was the return of Summer. Problem was, when she went with Jim McCord first, she broke the rules. Luther had watched her make love to Jim in the Airstream trailer. To Luther, this was not the way the game was played. He *had* to be first. He constructed a plan.

"For the rest of the day, we will have our fun and then tonight, we will go on a trip. Jim McCord can have you *this time* but this will be the last. When you return to me again, there will be no more Jim. Just you and me, my love. Just you and me."

He played with her for the rest of the day, his sick mind imagining that she was enjoying every moment.

As Galina slept, Luther thought back to Jim McCord. He realized Galina wanted McCord more than him. Luther's solution was simple: McCord could have her after he was done and then McCord would have to return her to the water. He knew that the McCords would be at their home in Austin after Labor Day and that the house bordered Lake Austin.

The plan became very clear: after he was done with his enjoyment in the cabin, he would take Summer to Austin and leave her for McCord to enjoy. McCord would then know to return Summer to the water in the lake at the rear of his home.

Somehow, in his demented mind, this all made perfect sense to Luther Fisher.

When it got dark, he transferred Galina to the RV and secured her by shackles he had fitted in the vehicle. He took with him a couple of dresses, in case one got soiled, plus a hat, sunglasses and makeup. He also had a gallon container of bleach solution, as he didn't want to leave any traces of him being with her, given that he was leaving her for McCord.

As he was making his preparations for the journey, Luther mumbled to himself. "If you hadn't wanted to be with McCord, I would have returned you straight to the lake at Navajo State Park. All of this extra work was for you. You chose to be with McCord. It's your fault. You changed the rules of the game. I will give you what you want this time, but never again. This will be the last time you will be with Jim McCord."

That night, the RV hauling the boat set out on the journey to Austin. It would take two full days, so, all being well, he planned to arrive late afternoon on Tuesday, September 13.

~

Everything did go according to plan and the RV entered the outskirts of Austin just after noon on the 13th. He was on the 183 entering Austin from the northwest. He then took the 620 toward Lake Travis and then left on 2222 before turning on City Park Road to his final destination, the Emma Long Metropolitan Park that sat on the shores of Lake Austin, downstream from the McCord home.

Lake Austin was formed by the runoff from Lake Travis via the Mansfield Dam. The dam was built across the Colorado River to store the water that fed Austin. Lake Austin was actually the Colorado River but the locals called it a lake. Many expensive homes had lakefront property and boat docks. One of these homes was part of the Riverside neighborhood and belonged to Jim McCord. Luther planned to stay two nights at the park. The second night, September 14th, he would leave Summer in Jim McCord's yard for his enjoyment.

Luther got to the park in the late afternoon, paid his fee for two nights and found a convenient place to set up. The park was deserted. One week earlier, it had been overflowing with campers and RVs enjoying Labor Day weekend. Now it was like a ghost town. It was perfect. No nosy neighbors to interfere with his plan.

Luther spent the following day continuing to satisfy his sexual perversions with Galina. Later in the day, with Galina completely sedated, he began the process of washing her down. He shampooed her hair and gave her fingernails and toenails a manicure. The final facial makeup could wait until she was relaxing beside the pool. He also had the bottle of wine and the wine glass chilling in the RV refrigerator.

Later in the day, as the sun began to sink toward the horizon, Luther launched the boat. Galina was still sedated but not to such an extent that she couldn't stagger along with Luther supporting her as she went. She was dressed in the white cotton dress and Luther had the sun hat, sunglasses, the wine and wine glass already in the boat. As the sun went down, the boat cast off and headed for McCord's dock.

A few minutes into their trip across the lake, Luther saw and heard a boat coming toward him as he headed north. His heart started to race and his mouth suddenly went dry.

"Everything okay there?" said the officer on the police launch.

"Yes, officer. It's a beautiful night and my wife and I thought we might enjoy it on the lake," replied Luther as both boats slowly passed each other.

"Make sure those running lights don't get obstructed and you folks enjoy your evening," said the river patrol cop as he continued down river.

"That was a close call, wasn't it, Summer!"

Twenty minutes later, they slowly drifted up to the McCord boat dock. Luther secured the boat on the opposite side of the dock from a suspended Malibu Wakesetter. Checking around to make sure that the coast was clear, he jumped up onto the dock. With Galina still sedated in the boat, Luther went around the side of McCord's house and located the TV cable box. McCord had boasted to him about the integrated security system he had installed in both of his homes and how the security system was part of the cable TV service. Luther located the exterior control box and cut the wires.

Luther returned to the boat and lifted Galina onto the deck. He supported her as she staggered up the steps from the dock and up to the pool in the backyard. Once by the pool, he laid her down on one of the recliners and gave her one final injection of the drug cocktail.

"Goodbye, my love, and enjoy your time with Jim. I will be waiting anxiously for your return."

He kissed her passionately and then placed a plastic bag over her head. He held it there and watched as she convulsed and died. He leaned down and whispered, "I will see you again soon, my love. I will be awaiting your return as my life is never complete unless you are by my side."

Luther then returned to the boat for the makeup, sun hat, sunglasses, wine, and wine glass.

With the aid of his flashlight, he combed her hair and tucked it up under the sun hat. He did her facial makeup, applied the bright red lipstick that had been Summer's favorite and made sure that her white cotton dress was perfect. He then uncorked the bottle of wine, pressed the glass to her lips to make a mouth mark and returned the glass to the table beside her. After half filling the glass with wine, he placed her right arm over the side of the recliner, just touching the top of the wine glass.

Luther Fisher stood back to admire his work. It was perfect.

"Goodbye, my darling," he whispered in her ear. "We will be united again soon."

Luther Fisher then turned and walked back to the boat with the aid of his flashlight.

In the distance, a man's voice said, "I'm telling you, Ethel, there is someone in Jim's backyard!"

Chapter 42 - G Men

2014 - The Cold Case Investigation

THE WEATHER WAS BEGINNING TO turn in Austin. There were dark skies and heavy rain and the Monday morning commute was a nightmare. Bill Ross headed to the conference room with nervous anticipation. He expected the green light from the Archuleta County DA for a search warrant of the Luther Fisher place in Pagosa Springs. When he walked into the conference room and saw Jack Johnson's face, he knew that it was not going to be a good start to the week.

"Bad news, team. We were turned down for the search warrant. The DA doesn't think there is enough evidence connecting Fisher to Galina and he doesn't want us to go on a fishing expedition to try to get that evidence," announced Jack. "We need to connect Fisher to Galina or we're dead in the water."

The mood was somber as they all stared at one another, searching for a flash of inspiration. It came from Tommy Ross.

"I suggest we look at this in a different way," began Tommy, looking up from his laptop.

"I am online right now looking at the Rape Abuse and Incest National Network (RAIN) and according to them, the Vanderbilt rape falls under Tennessee code 39-13-502 which is aggravated rape. Also, there was more than one perpetrator, the female student was injured and it's likely that the sodomy was committed using some sort of foreign object, i.e., a weapon. According to Tennessee Code 39-13-502, that's a Class A felony. We can get the FBI involved!"

Bill Ross looked across the room at Tommy. He had a huge smile on his face and the brief nod of his head and wink conveyed it all. "Well done, son," he whispered to himself. "Diligent research and attention to detail will always be the cornerstone of good police work.

"We can turn Jim McCord over to the Feds. We can tell them that he confessed to us about seeing Luther Fisher commit the rape. Whether he actively participated or just watched, he was involved and is therefore guilty," added Bill.

Jack Johnson jumped in, "Once they get the tip, the Feds will issue an arrest warrant and pick Jim up. We would have to get approval to help them search the properties looking for any clues regarding that rape and our case, but that shouldn't be a problem. We can brief them on the evidence gathered to date. Federal jurisdiction would trump ours, Jim would be tried on the Nashville rape and, if found guilty, it could be a death sentence."

Jack briefed Chief Dunwoody. The chief got Sheriff John Gordon on the phone.

"Good morning, John. My team met this morning after I gave them the news that your DA had rejected our request for a search warrant of Fisher's place. A suggestion has been made that we bring in the FBI," said Bill Dunwoody.

There was a brief pause and then John Gordon responded.

"Why would we do that, Bill? You're going to have to walk me through your rationale. I've had limited experience working with the Feds but they have the reputation of a bull in a china shop on cases like this. Help me understand why your team wants to go down this route."

Dunwoody cleared his throat and said, "As you know, John, our problem with the warrant is that we have no evidence linking Luther Fisher to the dead woman. We have circumstantial evidence and we wanted the search warrant to help us get what we needed. The DA was right to reject our request."

"Where we do have strong evidence, based on Jim McCord's confession, is the rape of the woman at Vanderbilt by Fisher, McCord and Billy Pell. Based on the reading of the Tennessee statute, the rape is a Class A Felony with the possibility of a death sentence. We have an obligation to turn it over to the Feds."

Gordon replied, "I see. Now it makes sense. Not that I like it but we might spend weeks and months trying to get the evidence linking Fisher to Galina Alkaev. This is the most expedient approach and, as you say, based on the evidence we have on the rape, we have an obligation to pass it to the Feds."

"I agree, Bill. How do you want to handle it? My suggestion is that you make the call, as your team has the evidence on the rape. We'll have to remain involved, as the arrest will be made on our turf, but the Feds will coordinate that with us."

Dunwoody replied, "Agreed. I'll make the call and send you an email confirming everything we've discussed. I'll give you a heads-up when I've talked with the Feds. Stay tuned."

Chief Dunwoody ended the call and asked Jack to stay while he made the call to the FBI.

~

The main FBI field office for Tennessee is located in Memphis. Bill Dunwoody made the call and was connected with Special Agent Harold DeWalt. DeWalt was acting regional director for the FBI for the State of Tennessee. Harry listened to what Bill had to say and then said that he would discuss it with his colleagues and get back to him ASAP. It only took a day before Bill got a call back.

"Hi, Bill, this is Harry DeWalt. I spoke with my team here in Memphis and with our satellite office in Nashville. When we go to a state to arrest a suspected felon, we work with the local law enforcement agencies. In this case, that would be the Archuleta Sheriff's Office. If you've been cooperating with them, as it sounds like you have, and they have no issue with you tagging along, then it's fine with us. Just stay out of our way and let us run the show."

With the FBI now involved, this was a whole new ball game and Bill knew it.

"Fucking Feds," said Bill under his breath, and then regained his composure,

"Okay, sounds good, Harry. We'll talk with the Archuleta boys and then coordinate back. Does that sound like a plan?"

"Sure does, Bill. Now remember when we do get rolling on this one…"

Bill Dunwoody interrupted the FBI agent before he could say it. "Stay out of your way, right, Harry?"

"Right, Bill!"

Bill imagined that Harry DeWalt had a big smile across his face as they ended the call.

~

The team set up a conference call with the Archuleta Sheriff's team. Sheriff John Gordon and Detective Raul Ortiz were on the line from Pagosa Springs, and in the Travis County Police Department conference room were Chief Bill Dunwoody, Jack, Tommy, Marie, and Bill.

John Gordon spoke first. "Biggest risk in bringing in the Feds with a guy like Luther Fisher is that this could end up like *The Gunfight at the OK Corral.* Feds and survivalists are a volatile mix. Throw in the fact that if found guilty, Luther Fisher could face a death sentence. He would likely opt to shoot it out rather than face execution."

Bill Dunwoody stepped in and said, "With your permission, John, I would like to send three of my officers up there to be part of your team when the Feds make the arrest.

"I see no issue with that, Bill. We will all be working in a supporting role with the Feds anyway. Our teams have worked hard on this, so it's only fair that they be there to see the cuffs put on this son of a bitch! I'll call DeWalt and let him know that this is our plan. We can then coordinate with them on timing. That okay with you, Bill?"

"Agreed, John. We will stand down and wait to hear back from you then," said Bill as they ended the call.

Dunwoody turned to the team and said, "Jack, Tommy, and Marie should be the ones to go. Sorry, Bill. I don't want to put a civilian in the line of fire. You have done great work on this and I'm sure you would have wanted to go, but we should leave it to these guys. Hope you're okay with that."

"Fully understand, Bill. I'm in complete agreement," said Bill Ross. Tommy noticed a touch of disappointment on his dad's face. Once again, he was playing the good soldier.

~

Three days later, Jack got a call from Harry DeWalt.

"I'm sending a couple of agents down to arrest Jim McCord and bring him to Memphis. They will interview him there and get his agreement to cooperate for the chance that the judge might consider some reduced sentence. We need to get all our ducks in a row before we go charging into Colorado!"

There was no hint of a request. The FBI was in charge and this was their show now. A couple of days later, the federal agents landed at Bergstrom Airport and were met off the flight by agents from the Austin FBI field office and Jack Johnson. Later that day, they sat in a Travis County interview room across from Jim McCord and his attorney, Marilyn Williamson.

A young man in his early thirties walked into the room and sat down across from Jim and his lawyer. With a thick Tennessee accent, he introduced himself as Special Agent Vernon Bailey and began his questioning.

"This is your chance to tell your side of the story, Mr. McCord. You're going to a federal penitentiary, and for how long will depend on what you tell us now and what you are prepared to testify to in court."

Jim instantly became panicked. "I didn't rape anyone, Agent Bailey! I was so sick at what I saw and the ferocity of the attack that I took to my heels and ran!"

"So you say, Mr. McCord, but we only have your word for that, don't we. You told Detective Johnson that there were three of you, the third being Billy Pell. Have you any idea where we might locate Mr. Pell?"

"The last I heard he was somewhere in Florida. Perhaps the Vanderbilt Alumni Association could help locate him."

"If he is alive and breathing, we will find him, Mr. McCord. Are you confident that he will confirm your version of events?"

Jim's eyes were wide with fear. "Yes, Billy will confirm. He was just as disgusted as I was and ran off with me."

Vernon shuffled his papers and glanced at Jack Johnson. Jack had a satisfied smile on his face. Everything was going exactly as they planned.

"We can't make any promises on what sentence you might end up with, Mr. McCord," continued Vernon. "That will be up to the federal prosecutor and the judge. However, if you and Billy Pell can testify on your version of events, then there may be some consideration given. That is all I can say right now."

McCord's attorney, Marilyn Williamson, made the normal statement on behalf of her client.

"Mr. McCord is fully cooperating with you, Agent Bailey, and he has made it clear that he did not participate in the rape. He is a person of good standing in the community and I would ask that he remain here in Austin until such time as a trial is set and his testimony is required at that trial."

"This is a Class A felony case, Ms. Williamson. However, I will call my boss right now and get his reply to your request."

Vernon Bailey left the room and returned a few minutes later.

"The best we can offer is that he will remain here in Austin in federal custody. We need to track down Billy Pell and get his side of the story. Until that time, he will remain in custody and then we can perhaps revisit the issue. That is the best we can do."

Marilyn Williamson conferred with Jim and then nodded in agreement. Jim McCord looked like death warmed up. His ashen gray face and his pleading eyes were evidence to the fact that he now knew all was lost. His life was over and he hoped that Billy Pell would tell the same lie as he had done to save his skin. He and Pell *had participated in the rape* but he clung on to this last lie like a drowning man clinging to a leaky lifeboat.

Chapter 43 - They're coming

2014 - The Cold Case Investigation

LUTHER FISHER WAS SEATED AT his kitchen table cleaning his rifle. He sensed that they would be coming back. "Why did that bitch ask about Summer? Why had they been looking at the telescope?" He was running through in his mind all the careful steps he had taken to protect himself from an eventual dooms-day scenario.

Luther had purchased the property across the valley and built the cabin for a reason. It was a key component of his overall defensive infrastructure. This was his bunker if he need-ed to fall back from the main house. His mind went through a systematic review of all of his assets: ordinance, food and water, fuel, transportation, and real-time intelligence. He had installed a network of wireless sensors and cameras that would give him a real-time assessment of any threat. There wasn't an inch of his property that was not "seen" and relayed back to his control center.

The perimeter of his property was not only visible from any angle, it also had motion detectors that automatically alert-ed him to any breach of the perimeter. If a penetration occurred, it triggered the arming mechanism on several antiper-sonnel weapons. The final pieces in this impressive array of assets were a series of smoke and percussion grenades linked into the infrastructure that could be detonated to provide perfect cover for his exit from an engagement, if necessary.

His armory was equally impressive. Handguns, shotguns and rifles had been selected with great care to provide long-, medium- and short-range advantage. His rifle was an AR15 with a free-floating barrel and Winchester 223 Remington jacketed ammo, accurate up to 1,000 yards. His midrange weapon was a Remington 870 Express tactical shotgun, 12 gauge, pump action with an 18.5 inch barrel loaded with Federal Premium LE reduced-recoil buckshot. For his handgun, the Sig Sauer P250 9mm 2SUM had been chosen to allow him to configure two guns with different but complimentary capabilities.

"If they want to fuck with me, they better come prepared!" he mused.

He had spent a considerable part of his inheritance in the design and construction of his main home. From the outside, it looked like any normal, albeit up-market home in the Colorado Hills. What lay behind this benign exterior was a complex network of hidden passages that allowed him to move about the house unseen. One minute he could be in the kitchen or the main living room and then, in an instant, he could disappear via a silent automatic door disguised as a full-length mirror or a decorative alcove.

These hidden passages led to a central elevator that linked the main level of the house to a basement that contained separate living quarters complete with kitchen.

The escape route from this was via an automatic garage door that was unseen from the front of the property and exited onto a gravel road that linked the main house to the cabin property across the valley. His Jeep with a 3.6 Pentastar V6 intercooled engine and JK supercharger sat ready for an instant high-speed exit.

He knew that there was an Achilles' heel in this elaborate, complex and costly compound—gas. If they used gas, he would have to get out of there quickly. He had planned to install a high-capacity exhaust system but had not been able to get it done. This had been a mistake. He knew that and cursed silently at his stupidity.

Luther sat in his control room, looked out across his monitors and weighed his options. His psychosis drove his flawed and twisted reasoning. They had arrested McCord because he had not returned Summer to the water after he had finished with her. Luther couldn't believe what a stupid and weak man he was. If they did come, which he expected they would, it would be to get additional evidence against McCord, wouldn't it? He had been so thorough and meticulous in his planning and execution that they would never suspect him of being involved. Luther thought to himself that maybe he should call the police and tell them that he had seen McCord with Summer in her new job in the bar. That would convince them that McCord had abducted her, taken her to Austin, and killed her.

Luther's mind quickly negated that plan. That Texas detective bitch saw a photograph of Summer in his house. They would know who she was. Fire grew in Luther's eyes. His plan was almost perfect.

"If I get the chance, I'll kill that bitch!" yelled Luther Fisher.

Chapter 44 - A joint operation

2014 - The Cold Case Investigation

BILL ROSS WAS AS GOOD as his word. The weekend following the decision to bring in the FBI, he organized an end-of-summer BBQ and, as he had promised Elaine, invited Jack Johnson since he had missed the last one when he was down mending fences on his ranch. They were all seated together on the deck waiting on the latest succulent output from the Green Egg.

Tommy and Marie sucked on their Dos Equis as Claire ran around the backyard, trying to catch a butterfly as it searched for the last remnants of sweetness from the flowers Elaine had planted in the early spring.

"Have you had much experience working with the FBI, Jack?" asked Bill, who had only read about FBI exploits while growing up in Scotland. He had seen the movie *G Men* with James Cagney and that was the image that stuck in his mind: tough, uncompromising, gun-toting, hard men.

"No, not really, Bill. The only other time was when I was a young officer and was involved in a case regarding a bank robber from Chicago trying to make it to Mexico. He was holed up in a house in San Antonio. They got their man, but he was carried out in a body bag."

Before long, the steaks were cooked to perfection and Elaine had prepared a delicious salad of spinach, walnuts, blue cheese, and cranberries.

As they ate, Tommy was the first to get the conversation going. "They're called Preppers for a reason. For them, it's about survival and survival is about preparation. Many of them follow the methods developed by military strategist Air Force Colonel John Boyd. Boyd developed the OODA Loop—Observe, Orient, Decide, Act. To adopt this rapid decision-making methodology while in the heat of an engagement, there must be complete trust in the assets that have been put in place in advance."

"You sound like you're a fan of Boyd, Tommy," noted Jack.

"The Marine Corps taught me a culture and belief system that will be with me for the rest of my life, Jack. As the Chinese military general Sun Tzu wrote, *If you know the enemy and you know yourself, you have no need to fear the results of a hundred battles.* Winning is about preparation. Good planning and preparation prevent piss-poor performance. He will be prepared. I just hope that the FBI is."

~

The following morning, Harry DeWalt called Bill Dunwoody.

"Hi Bill, Harry DeWalt here. I have John Gordon and his team on the line and wanted to conference you in on our plan."

"Good morning, Harry. Can you give me a couple of minutes? I'd like to get my team in here on the call, if that's okay with you."

"It's okay with me, Bill."

Bill Dunwoody quickly got them all together in his office. The stage was now set for Harry DeWalt.

"We're all here, Harry, over to you," said Bill Dunwoody.

"Okay, thanks, Bill."

Harry DeWalt laid out the plan.

"My second in command, Vern Bailey, and I will fly into Denver on Tuesday morning and have a final pre-arrest coordinating meeting with the local Denver FBI boys at 1100 hours. We will then get a chopper up to Stevens Field in Pagosa Springs with two of our Denver agents and meet up with Sheriff Gordon and his team. Bill, if you want to be part of this thing, you better get your team up there by Tuesday, 1500 hours to meet us at the field. I'll let you coordinate that with John. Any questions from anyone?"

There were no questions and Bill Dunwoody called Sheriff Gordon directly after hanging up with the FBI. Everyone was in sync and Sheriff Gordon was happy that the Travis County team would be involved in the takedown of Luther Fisher.

Tommy Ross had listened in on the call and his first reaction was that he hoped the FBI team was as efficient at execution as they were at theatrics. He hoped the chopper would be large enough to accommodate four FBI agents and their enormous egos.

~

It was the day before the FBI operation to take down Luther Fisher. Jack, Tommy and Marie landed in Durango at 1100 hours as planned and were met by Detective Raul Ortiz. It was mostly silent in the SUV during the drive up to Pagosa Springs, each person lost in his or her thoughts about the drama that might unfold the following morning.

"I hope he doesn't go postal when he sees a dozen folks arriving for breakfast," laughed Marie, trying to ease the tension.

"And four of them G Men," added Tommy. "He sure as heck won't think it's a social visit and we're there looking for a donation to the Sheriff's Department Widows and Orphans Fund."

"I think it's a genuine concern," said Jack. "If what you say about this shithead is true, he may just put up the shutters and start firing."

Both law enforcement teams were at Stevens Field to meet the chopper. After the rotors stopped spinning, the chopper doors flew open and four FBI agents looking like "the men in black" marched in lock step toward the welcoming party.

On arrival at the terminal building, Harry DeWalt shook hands with Sheriff Gordon and introduced his team while the other members of the joint operation stood in the background.

As they moved through the hall of the private section of Stevens Field, to Tommy's complete surprise, Harry DeWalt maneuvered himself to walk alongside Tommy.

"Semper Fi, Marine," said Harry.

Caught by complete surprise, Tommy still managed to reply, "Semper Fi, sir!"

Harry DeWalt strode on. Tommy's impression of the FBI lead agent changed in an instant. DeWalt was a former Marine, probably an officer. *This might get interesting. Very interesting indeed*, thought Tommy.

~

After the short drive from Stevens Field, the FBI team, the Archuleta team and the Travis County team met at the sheriff's office in Pagosa Springs. Harry DeWalt stood in front of the white board and, off to the side, an aerial view of Luther Fisher's home was projected on the wall from Agent Vern Bailey's laptop.

Harry began the briefing of the joint team task force.

"As you can see, this is a two-story residence with a two-car garage. The hillside drops off dramatically from the front to the rear and there is dense tree growth all around. Access to and egress from the building are only from the front and there are no other options available to the occupant to make an escape unless he tries to run into the woods. Given the excessive slope of the terrain, this would not be a smart choice on his behalf."

Harry continued on without interruption.

"We need to split into three teams. I will lead the main team to the front door. Vern will lead the second team covering the garage to prevent an escape from there. Detective Raul Ortiz will lead the third team and take a secure position at the rear of the property, protecting against any, albeit unlikely, attempt to exit from the rear. Questions?"

Tommy initially hesitated and then stood up. "A couple of questions if I may, Agent DeWalt?"

"Yes, Detective Ross, go ahead."

"Are you aware that Fisher owns another property?"

It was like a fart in church. "What fucking property?" said Harry, staring at Vernon Bailey, as he had been the one responsible for gathering the intelligence to plan the assault.

"He owns another property on the other side of the valley. It was purchased through his dead mother's company and he obviously bought it for a reason. It could simply be for storage, as he parks an RV and a boat over there, or it could be that it's his fallback position if his primary home becomes compromised, ir."

"His home becomes compromised? We're not dealing with Jason Bourne, Tommy. This is not some CIA rogue super agent that we're here to take down. We're here to arrest a jackass who is a fucking rapist!" snorted Harry, trying to save the FBI embarrassment for not having proper intelligence on the other property.

"With all due respect, Agent DeWalt, this jackass is a Prepper and my guess is that he has the ability to dig in and shoot it out if he chooses to. I also think that, just to be on the safe side, we should have a fourth team located over the valley at the other property. He may try to fall back there."

Harry relaxed and said, "Good idea, Detective Ross. Good not to underestimate his capabilities. Why don't you take a couple of deputies and position yourselves at the other property."

"May I add an additional comment, sir?" added Tommy.

"Yes, what is it?" said Harry, now getting seriously pissed off.

"I would like to take Detective Ortiz with me to the other property as he and I have a good working relationship," said Tommy, stretching the truth.

"Might I also request that Detective Marie Mason make the approach to the front door with you and your main team? She has previously interviewed Luther Fisher and is therefore known to him. A direct approach announcing you're the FBI might be enough to set him off and the situation might spiral out of control."

Harry nodded and said, "These are all good ideas, Detective Ross. Anyone with any further contribution, please speak up now."

"For the record, I agree with Tommy's assessment of the situation," injected Jack Johnson.

Tommy had succeeded in getting the Archuleta and Travis County teams more actively involved in the operation but also had identified some flaws in the initial plan that had now been addressed.

Harry DeWalt again took control,

"Okay, team, here is the revised plan integrating Detective Ross's valuable input. The main team, led by me, will stay the same with Detective Mason making the 'introductions.' Vern and his team will cover the garage in case he tries to flee with a vehicle from there. Deputy Jack Johnson will lead the team covering the rear of the house while Detective Ross and Detective Ortiz cover the second property on the other side of the valley, just in case Batman flies over there."

Everyone laughed at Harry's attempt at humor.

"We will assemble here at 0500 hours tomorrow and hit him before he's had his Wheaties," said Harry.

The meeting ended and the teams went off to have dinner and an early night. As the senior member of the Texas team, Jack Johnson was invited by Sheriff Gordon to have dinner with him and Harry Dewalt. On the way out to the parking lot, Jack pulled Tommy aside.

"Good job in there, Tommy. You were right to speak up. I think we now have a better plan to get this done without bloodshed."

Jack's comments would haunt Tommy for the rest of his life.

Chapter 45 - Let's get this done

2014 - The Cold Case Investigation

THE JOINT TASK FORCE MET in the sheriff's office parking lot the following morning. Every agent was issued body armor as a standard precaution for this type of operation. It was to be a silent approach to the property. No sirens. Headlights were to be turned off when they made the turn into the driveway. Tommy Ross and Raul Ortiz drove off first. When they approached the cabin entrance, they saw the Dobermans.

Tommy whispered to Raul, "We'll need to set up back from the gate so the dogs don't go into a frenzy. The sound might carry across the valley and that could alert Fisher something was up."

They stopped about a hundred yards from the gate and reversed into a dirt track just off the access road and called DeWalt.

"In position at the cabin property," reported Tommy.

The main team entered the driveway to Luther Fisher's home, lights out and sirens off. They parked their cruisers around the perimeter gate and began taking up their positions. Jack and two of the Archuleta sheriff deputies carefully inched their way around the side of the house and down the steep slope to the rear of the property, crossing a gravel track that seemed out of place with the rest of the undergrowth around the building.

As the deputies approached, a flashing red light and whine of the alarm in the control center woke Luther from a sound sleep. He was out of bed and seated at the control in less than two seconds. Sector two was showing a perimeter penetration, so Luther activated the infrared cameras. He switched the anti-personnel weaponry to neutral as he didn't want to have pieces of red deer to clean up if Bambi had decided to come looking for food. Once the guns were stabilized, he looked to the monitors and saw the outline of a slowly approaching figure holding what looked like a handgun. They were here.

He dressed quickly. Everything felt more than a little suspicious to him. If this was a simple follow-up call to ask more questions about Jim McCord, why were they here so early and why were they creeping around the rear of his house? He activated the sector one infrared cameras that covered the front of the house. He could see the hazy outline of four police cruisers parked out front.

"What the fuck is going on?" he yelled.

Then he saw Marie Mason. She was with guys in suits and body armor with FBI in big white letters.

"The fucking FBI! Why are those fuckers here?"

His mind was now racing. Why would the FBI be involved? He hated the federal government and here they were at his front doorstep.

The doorbell rang and a familiar female voice sounded from the other side.

"Mr. Fisher, this is Detective Marie Mason. We met when I visited with you here a couple of weeks ago. We have a few more questions that we need to have clarified."

"It's a bit early, Detective Mason. Why don't you come back later this morning?"

Luther was speaking to them from the communications center transmitting to the speaker at the side of the front door. There was a brief pause and then the front door was blown off its hinges. Harry DeWalt and his team stormed the house. The agents swarmed the lower level of Luther's home.

"Kitchen clear!"

"Living room clear!"

"Bedrooms clear!"

From the back of the house, a Denver FBI agent shouted, "Agent DeWalt, you need to see this!"

Harry rushed toward the sound and saw the agent standing at a converted closet in the master bedroom. A large monitor with split screen showed infrared images from around the building along with a microphone and other digital controls. As they watched, the screen went black. Luther had deactivated his bedroom control center and was now controlling everything from his secure center in the basement.

Luther had used one of the hidden doors from his bedroom and had taken the concealed elevator down to the basement. He thrust open a set of lockers, changed into a set of military camouflage fatigues and opened the weapons closet. Within five seconds, Luther grabbed his ammo belt and the Sig Sauer, pulled on the armor vest, and finally grabbed the shotgun. This was what he had prepared for. He had the upper hand. He had eyes everywhere and he could take them down one by one.

~

While Luther was gearing up in the basement, Harry DeWalt was baffled. "Where the fuck is he? There must be a basement. Find the access point, dammit! We need to get this guy in cuffs!"

They split up and began searching for the access to the basement. As they looked, Marie crept into the master bedroom, looking for the telltale signs of a door opening. She was staring at a wall unit off to the side of the converted closet with the now-dead surveillance controls, thinking that the door might be there. She didn't hear the full-length mirror behind her slide to the side.

Within an instant, Luther's arm locked around her throat and a pad soaked in chloroform was pressed over her mouth. Luther dragged her through the door and it immediately closed behind them. Marie was till struggling and trying to fight him off when the door closed. With his left arm still around her neck, he stuck a syringe into her with his right hand and she passed out.

~

When Marie came around, her wrists and ankles were shackled to a metal chair and Luther Fisher was standing over her.

"You are going to wish you'd never been born, bitch! Why are the fucking Feds here?" demanded Luther as he slapped Marie hard across her face. "And don't you dare lie to me, bitch!"

Marie saw no reason to lie. When she signed on to be a police officer, she knew that she was putting her life on the line. She just hoped that she wouldn't suffer. She would rather aggravate Luther to the point where he killed her than give him the satisfaction of seeing her in pain. It had been the same with her father as he repeatedly beat her. She retreated to a place in her mind that dismissed the pain. There was never a time when she gave her father the satisfaction of seeing her cry. This son of a bitch wouldn't see her fear either.

"You raped the girl in Nashville and that is a Class A felony. That's why they're here. They're here to arrest you."

Luther's eyes grew wide as he began shifting blame. "I didn't do that. Jim McCord and Billy Pell did it!"

"Jim McCord said you did it when we arrested him and is willing to testify to that effect."

Luther started to speak by Marie cut him off.

"You're not going to argue your way out of this, Luther," said Marie triumphantly. "If you believe you're innocent, then your best chance will be to surrender and tell your side of the story."

Luther punched Marie in the stomach and said, "I have a video of the rape and it shows McCord and Pell doing her!"

Marie coughed and said, "Oh yeah? And who was doing the filming, Luther, Stephen fucking Spielberg? You were there, and you were involved, so you're as guilty as the rest of them!"

Luther hit her again and kicked her in the groin. He was now in a panic. They had him caged. He could hold out for a while but the end was a forgone conclusion. His head was spinning when Marie, rolling the dice with her life, made her move.

She lifted her head very deliberately and, while making sure that Luther was watching her, rolled her eyes back in her head, just as Nora McConnell had done, and said, *"Summer wants you to come to her!"*

Luther's mouth fell open like a bolt of lightning hit him between the eyes. He stared at Marie like she was some grotesque apparition and yelled, "What the fuck did you just say?"

Marie rolled her eyes back again and said exactly the same thing in exactly the same way. *"Summer wants you to come to her!"*

Luther grabbed the Sig Sauer and pressed it to Marie's temple. "I should just shoot you now, bitch! You're making this up!"

"Summer wants you to come to her at the lake!" said Marie in the same melodic tone.

"How do *you* know this?" demanded Luther.

"I talk to the dead," said Marie. "That's why I asked you what your wife's name was the last time I was here."

"Liar, you're a fucking liar!" screamed Luther. "If you're talking to Summer, ask her where she was when she fell in the water?"

Again, Marie rolled her eyes back, *"She's telling me that she was on a recliner at the end of the boat dock drinking wine with Mary McCord!"*

Again, a look of astonishment came over Luther. "You could have read that in the police report, you liar!" hissed Luther. "So bitch, one more question for you to answer. You get it wrong and I shoot you in the head!"

Marie heard the Sig Sauer cock. "Ask Summer what her favorite perfume is," said Luther defiantly.

Marie rolled her eyes. *"Chloe, her favorite perfume is Chloe!"*

Luther almost collapsed in a heap at her feet as his legs turned to rubber. This police bitch was actually talking with Summer.

~

Luther Fisher took a moment to regain his composure. He needed time to think. After a few minutes, he picked up the microphone, pressed a couple of buttons, and began to speak.

"I want you off my property or the bitch dies!"

The sound was deafening as it reverberated around the house from the twenty-speaker system.

"I didn't rape the girl in Nashville, Jim McCord and Billy Pell did that, so back off and get the hell out of here. Do it and I'll make sure that she is unharmed."

Luther watched their reaction from the infrared camera system. He could see them leaving the house but they congregated outside and looked to be trying to decide what to do.

Harry DeWalt grabbed a bullhorn and stood apart from the rest of the team.

"This is Special Agent Harry DeWalt of the FBI. I am the agent in charge here. We will get back in our vehicles and pull back. You will let Detective Mason exit from the front door of your property and when she is back and safe with us, then we can talk and hear your side of the story."

From the cabin property, Tommy and Raul could hear everything echoing over the valley. He jumped up and said, "He's got Marie! I need to get back over there!"

"No! That makes no sense, Tommy. We can't leave our position here," responded Raul.

Tommy was now in full panic. Luther had Marie, his colleague and friend. He had to do something. He called Harry DeWalt.

"Agent DeWalt, do you need Raul and me to leave our positions and come over there to provide support?" yelled Tommy over the radio.

"Hold your position, Detective Ross. We don't know what he's up to and he might make a run for it."

Tommy's heart was aching with fear for Marie but he stayed put as ordered. He wasn't going to let her die. That was not going to happen!

~

Back in the basement, Luther's mind was whirling. If he gave up the bitch, then they would just storm the place and probably gas him out if they couldn't find the secret door access to the basement. They were not to be trusted. He needed time to think.

He needed to get to the lake and see Summer again before he made his escape. He needed to tell her why he was leaving and where he was going; otherwise, how could she possibly find him again?

Luther had constructed a plan for an organized withdrawal to the cabin bunker if the main house was compromised. The cabin was protected by Claymore antipersonnel mines and other ordinance. If he had to flee the cabin, there was a final escape route to the lake at Navajo State Park. He had renovated an old boathouse located on the north side of the lake that had been long since deserted. Inside the boathouse, he had hidden a speedboat that he planned to use to travel south on the lake and cross the border into New Mexico. He had hidden a car near Route 511 that he could then take to make his escape to Albuquerque and then south to Mexico.

Luther clicked on the radio and said, "Okay, I agree! Pull back and when I see you're gone, I will release her!"

Through the infrared monitors, he could see that they were getting into their cars and pulling back.

While this was all going down, Jack Johnson had been updating Tommy and Raul on the radio with every development and asked that they be ready for anything. Tommy and Raul had pulled out from the gravel road where they had parked the SUV and drove toward the cabin. As they got within twenty feet or so, the Dobermans went ballistic. Their barking was irrelevant now. Raul turned the SUV cruiser around so it faced down the road, so any approaching vehicle would come at them head on.

Meanwhile, Harry DeWalt called the chopper crew at the airport and told them to have the engines running and the blades turning so they were ready if they needed to use it in a hurry. It would take them thirty-five minutes to get to the air-

port from the Fisher house as there was no place for the chopper to land at the property.

After the FBI was backed up enough, Luther undid the
shackles on Marie's ankles and led her to a Jeep ready and waiting in the underground garage. He used cable ties to fasten her
wrists to the frame of the Jeep, went back inside and returned
with bags of ammo and the AR15. After loading them in the
back, he fastened the shotgun to a custom-frame structure over
the passenger seat so it would stabilize, allowing him to fire out
of the passenger side window. He had the Sig Sauer pistols on
his lap so he could use them to fire out the driver's side. Marie
was secure in the back. He was ready to roll.

Chapter 46 -Navajo State Park

2014 - The Cold Case Investigation

"WHAT'S TAKING HIM SO long?" said Harry. "He should have released her by now. Something's not right here."

As Harry turned back to the house, explosions erupted all over the property, billowing smoke and debris. The sound was deafening. In the basement, Luther pressed a remote on the Jeep and the concealed garage door flew open. He gunned the Jeep. The V6 blower did its work, engaging the four-wheel traction, and the Jeep roared forward like a bat out of hell.

As the Jeep flew out of the back, one of the Archuleta Sheriff's deputies at the rear of the house was mowed down by the onrushing vehicle and died instantly as his head ricocheted off the grill.

Jack Johnson, driven by instinct, rushed forward, pistol drawn.

~

The Jeep was powering through the forest. Luther had done at least twenty practice runs over the past couple of years, so he knew every bend, turn, dip, and climb. The Jeep had three rows of powerful halogen headlights that lit up the road like a Texas football field on a Friday night. Luther was going fifty when the Jeep shot out from the gravel road where

Tommy and Raul had been parked and took a sharp right-hand turn toward Pagosa Springs.

Raul had seen everything and was ready. The Archuleta Sheriff's SUV lurched forward, churning up gravel as the tires spun. It hit the Dobermans like 12-gauge buckshot and they whined in pain. As they chased Luther down, Tommy updated Harry DeWalt on the radio.

"In pursuit of target down Cemetery Road toward Highway 160!"

Harry and his team scrambled up the hill at the side of the house and ran to the vehicles. "Get that chopper ready!" he yelled down the radio as the vehicles sped off in the direction of the airport.

Luther turned onto Highway 160 East and ran the traffic lights in the center of Pagosa Springs, reaching almost 80 mph as he exited the town. Raul was in close pursuit while Tommy tracked their route with his iPhone.

"Where's he going?" thought Tommy. Fifteen minutes went by, and as the Jeep turned left on to Highway 151, he knew.

"He's headed to the lake at Navajo State Park!" he yelled down the radio. "That's where his wife drowned in 2003!"

The FBI team got to the chopper in record time but thirty-five minutes had passed since Tommy had reported that they were headed south on Highway 151. As the chopper got into the air, Luther was already at the vicinity of Navajo State Park and was turning right onto Route 159 that skirted the northern part of the lake. Ten minutes later, he pulled into the road leading to the boathouse and, as he did, he shut off the lights on the Jeep.

Less than a minute later, Luther saw Raul's SUV flying along 159 going straight past the boathouse turn in his rearview mirror. Luther smiled, activated the remote, and pulled the Jeep into the garage at the rear of the boathouse.

"Shit, we've lost him!" exclaimed Raul.

"Stop and go back. He must have turned off and it can't be more than a mile back!" said Tommy.

A few minutes later, they saw the road to the boathouse and turned in.

The road dead-ended at an old gray beach house and their SUV screeched to a stop. "No sign of the Jeep but this is the only place they can be. Raul, you take the left and I'll take the right."

~

As Tommy and Raul crept around the house toward the lake, Luther yelled, "Get in the fucking boat, bitch. You think I was stupid or something believing that you were talking with Summer? That was all bullshit. I'm free and clear to Mexico and you are going to a watery grave in the middle of the lake!"

Marie, still feeling the effects of the drug cocktail, could smell the stench of marine grade diesel and could see the hate in Luther's eyes as he bundled her into the boat. He secured her hands with more cable ties to the railing of the boat so that she was right next him. He started the engine and raised the door from the boathouse to the lake. With one hand on the controls and the other holding the Sig Sauer against Marie's temple, the boat slowly exited the boathouse.

The exit channel from the boathouse to the lake had a docking pier on either side. As the boat pulled out, Tommy yelled at him from the docking pier on the right side pier.

"Stop right there, Luther, or I shoot!"

Caught off guard, Luther released the boat controls and grabbed Marie around the throat. As he did so, he saw Raul on the other pier with his gun pointed at his chest.

"Back off, or she's dead," sneered Luther.

At that moment, Marie rolled the dice again and looked past Luther out to the center of the lake.

"*Summer? Is that you, Summer?*"

It only took a fraction of a second but Luther turned his head to look.

As he snapped his head back around, realizing the deception, Marie, unpracticed in the art of hand-to-hand Scottish pub fighting, landed the most perfect Glasgow Kiss the world has ever seen on the bridge of Luther's nose.

His nose exploded, blood, bone and snot going in all directions. He released his grip on Marie and fell back, shooting wildly in every direction. Four slugs hit him simultaneously, two in the chest, one in his neck and the final one, fired by Tommy, below the right eye, taking off the back of his head and knocking him out of the boat, into the water.

Tommy jumped into the boat and hugged Marie.

"That was quite a Glasgow Kiss, Marie. My dad will laugh his head off when I tell him what you did." As he was saying this, tears were running down his cheeks. Raul was at his side and he cut the cable ties that Luther had used to secure Marie in the boat.

"I wasn't going to let you die, Marie. That wasn't going to happen," said Tommy as he hugged her again.

The adrenaline rush of the encounter had drained them completely and they flopped down at the rear of the boat. They stared out over the stillness of the lake as the moon beams made it shimmer. It was eerily silent. The silence was briefly broken by the call of a great blue heron gliding slowly across the surface of the lake.

Chapter 47 - Jack Johnson

2014 - The Cold Case Investigation

TEN MINUTES LATER, THE chopper landed. Marie, Tommy and Raul were still recovering when Harry DeWalt and his team ran along the side of the boathouse to the dock with guns drawn.

Harry DeWalt jumped into the boat and, with the assistance of Tommy and Raul, helped Marie out on to the dock. Her heroism and clarity of thought while facing certain death had been astounding. Harry looked Marie in the eye, shook her hand, and said, "Outstanding work, Detective, fucking outstanding!"

"Where's the rest of the team," said Tommy. "Where's Jack?"

"Tommy, why don't you step over here for a moment," said Harry, and the two former Marines went off out of sight behind the boathouse.

"Don't you fuck with me, Harry. Where's Jack, where's my boss?" said Tommy now realizing that something really bad had happened.

Harry's eyes held back tears. Every fiber of his military background told him to be firm. "Jack's dead, Tommy."

Tommy screamed and Harry grabbed him by the arms. "Let go of me!" yelled Tommy. "What happened, what the fuck happened!"

"Get yourself together, Marine!" demanded Harry. "Jack died in the line of fire, he did what he was trained to do. He tried to bring a scumbag to justice!"

"Tell me what happened, Harry, please tell me what happened?" sobbed Tommy, now over the initial shock.

"He rushed that Jeep when he saw it mow down one of the Archuleta deputies. It was instinct, Tommy. He shot at the side window of the Jeep, jumped and tried to grab Fisher as the Jeep roared on its way. We found his body laying fifty yards up the gravel path. Fisher had shot him in the face at point blank range. He probably died instantly."

Tommy's legs gave way and he fell to his knees. Harry put a hand on the back of his fellow Marine and left him to recover from the shocking news. He then made his way back to the boathouse to coordinate the work still to be done.

They loaded the chopper and took Luther's body, the body of the Archuleta deputy, Sam Brown, and Jack's body back to the medical examiner in Denver. The chopper then returned with a full forensics team. Tommy and Marie, although overcome by grief at the death of Jack Johnson, asked to assist in the gathering of the evidence.

Chief Dunwoody arranged for Jack's body to be flown back to Austin and gave the team the go-ahead to stay after talking with the FBI and Archuleta Sheriff's Office.

Tommy called Bill and told him the whole story. Both he and Tommy broke down in tears at the loss of their colleague and their friend.

~

Two crime scene teams were deployed, one focused on the main house and the other on the cabin. It didn't take long for the team in the main house to find the secret doors to the labyrinth of passages. They took the elevator down to the basement and found an environment that could have sustained a long-term siege. There was a huge water tank incorporating a filtration system that injected a small amount of chlorine into the water to ensure that there was no parasitic infestation. Luther had hoarded a store of canned and dried foods that would have sustained him for months. To ensure he maintained sanitary conditions, he had installed a chemical waste-processing unit with venting up through the ceiling and into the roof space of the house. A small generator used the same venting system and provided heat and light. Finally, there was an arsenal of weaponry and ammo that could have equipped a small army.

Further analysis of the cabin yielded the evidence of the twisted mind of a sexual sadist and serial killer. The Summer bedroom was a shrine to his late wife. The Winter bedroom was a torture chamber. Luther was almost certainly misogynistic, as this room was constructed to inflict maximum pain and, in doing so, feed a sexual depravity rooted in the hatred of women. It was difficult to comprehend that any woman who entered that room left alive.

The viewing room held all the confirmation they needed. Like the Nazis and Adolf Eichmann in particular, Luther had created a systemic catalog of everything he did. There were detailed written notes accompanied by videos and a photographic portfolio that was a historical record of all that he had done. This allowed the beast to relive his work on demand and wallow in its savagery as he salivated at the pain and suffering that each activity had bestowed on the victim.

The earliest Super 8 videos were a record of savagery on small animals until he graduated to young girls. There was a detailed record of the rape of the girl at Vanderbilt University. The early part of that video showed his victim, restrained face down on a bed, legs held wide apart with a gag in her mouth. The videographer was either Jim McCord or Billy Pell, but the brutality of the assault by Luther was self-evident. The latter part of the video showed Jim and Billy taking their turn. They were both very timid in their efforts and that upset the videographer immensely. The voice of Luther Fisher could be heard barking instructions. When they failed to implement those instructions, they were ridiculed for their ineptness.

The walls of the viewing room were adorned with headshots of the women. One wall was dedicated to Summer, with her portrait at the top. It was a portrait showing a radiant young woman, full of life, seated at a small Parisian-type round table with a bottle of wine and a glass in her hand. Her look of desire was palpable, her eyes begging for the caresses of an eager lover. This was not a pornographic portrait: this was the work of a world-class photographer who had captured not only the depth of her beauty but also the simmering cauldron of desire that lay beneath.

Below this exquisite portrait hung headshots of a different nature. There were a total of ten, one for each year following the death of Summer. Each woman had excessive facial makeup and bright red lipstick. These headshots had been taken postmortem and, compared to the beauty of the image at the top of the wall, were opposite in the extreme. No life, no beauty, no desire. Like shots taken of a corpse on the coroner's operating table.

The videos and the written records detailed what had happened to them. He had videotaped them upon their arrival in the summer bedroom, when he restrained them and told them about the ordeal that was to follow. It recorded the terror and the look of complete despair. What followed was days of repeated rape and depravity.

The final act was to clean the victim and dress her in a white cotton dress. It recorded the transportation in the RV and the final part of the journey when he took them out into the center of the lake, killed them by suffocation, weighted their bodies down and slipped them slowly into the water. The video continued as in each case the white dress first rose to the surface and then was drawn down into the depths, never to be seen again.

They also found the videos and notes that told the whole story of Galina's abduction and death. Luther had seen Galina soon after she arrived in Pagosa and began stalking her in preparation for her abduction. Then he saw her with Jim McCord. In his twisted mind, Summer had come back and cheated on him again. He wrote in his notes that this was not the way the game was played.

He knew that McCord normally returned to his home in Austin on the Friday of the week after the Labor Day week. In 2005, that was Friday, September 16, so he planned to leave

Summer in his Austin backyard next to Lake Austin on Thursday the 15th.

Was there some part of his mind that constructed this sick scenario to get back at Mary McCord and Jim McCord because they had been there when Summer drowned? Or did he want to punish Jim McCord for his affair with Summer? We will never know.

~

The FBI returned with Tommy and Marie to Austin. Chief Dunwoody requested that he, Tommy, and Marie be present when Jim McCord was finally charged with the Nashville rape. McCord was led into the room in the Austin FBI field office and Vern Bailey did the honors,

"Jim McCord, I am arresting you for the aggravated rape of Pauline Lawson on the campus of Vanderbilt University." Vern continued on to read McCord his Miranda rights.

Jim McCord was then led away and immediately transported to Nashville.

Before leaving the Austin FBI field office, Tommy and Marie cornered Vern Bailey.

"Were there any discussions about Mary McCord and the possibility that she might have been complicit in the drowning death of Summer Fisher?" asked Tommy.

"Yes, we discussed that but the conclusion we reached was the same as the one the Archuleta DA had reached back in 2003. There was not sufficient evidence to pursue a case against her," said Vern.

Vern, Tommy, and Marie said their goodbyes, and the Travis County police team returned to their 34th Street HQ.

Chapter 48 - A final resting place

2014 - The Cold Case Investigation

MARIE AND TOMMY MET WITH Chief Dunwoody in his office on 34th Street. "We need to inform Galina Alkaev's parents about her death," said Tommy.

"Agreed," said the Chief. "Where are her remains?"

"She's buried in the Travis County International Cemetery. We should ask if they would like her remains returned to their hometown or left where they are."

"I agree, Tommy. Go track them down and make the call."

~

"Alkaev Family Restaurant. Nikolay Alkaev speaking. How may I help you?"

"I am Detective Marie Mason of the Travis County Police Department in Austin, Texas. I would like to speak with Mr. Alexi Alkaev please, is he available?"

"My father is dead. How may I help you, Detective? Is it about Galina?"

"Yes, it is, Mr. Alkaev. I am sorry to have to inform you she is dead."

A moment passed before Nikolay asked, "How did she die, Detective?

"She was murdered."

A longer moment passed before Nikolay said, "My mother and I both felt that it was likely that Galina was dead. We never said the words out loud to one another, but we knew in our hearts that she was gone.

"My father passed away in 2010 and the restaurant was too much for my mother, so I stepped in and took over the day-to-day running of the business. My mother still helps on a part-time basis to keep herself busy."

Marie could hear the sadness in Nikolay's voice, so she let him continue. "The disappearance of Galina had hastened the death of my father. The community here in Pikesville rallied around to provide support but it was obvious that the disappearance of my sister and his beloved daughter had ripped his heart out and what was left was a shell that took seven years to die. My mother too suffered but she endured. She is the matriarch of our family and it is her strength that inspires us.

"Let me get my mother. She'll want to hear this," said Nikolay.

There was a long stillness as he fetched his mother to the phone. The two sat in silence as Marie told them what had happened. As she went on, Marie could hear Lyudmila sobbing in the background.

When Marie finished, Nikolay took a breath and said, "Of course, her body must be returned. We will pay whatever it costs. She must have a Panikhida and we must sing the Trsiagion for the release of her soul."

~

And so it was done. The body of Galina Alkaev was exhumed and transported back to Pikesville. Nikolay flew out to be present at the exhumation and then to escort her body home.

Father Vasily Arshavin of the Holy Trinity Church led the Divine Liturgy and then Galina was laid to rest in the Russian Orthodox Cemetery in the family plot alongside her father.

Some one hundred yards to the left of the burial site, standing behind a tree, a solitary figure stood pulling his heavy coat more tightly around him as the bitter wind whistled across the cemetery. Pavel Orlov stood weeping uncontrollably. It was his moment of weakness with Fran Taylor that had led to the chain of events resulting in Galina's death. He would have to live with this for the rest of his life. He turned and left the cemetery, a lonely and broken man.

"They are united again in the arms of our Lord," said Nikolay as he said his goodbyes to Tommy and Marie at the Baltimore Airport. He had asked that they come, and had paid for their flight. He was eternally grateful to them for helping bring closure. They were equally grateful for the gesture and for the opportunity to be there when Galina was finally laid to rest.

Chapter 49 - Giddings, Texas

2014 - The Cold Case Investigation

THE WEATHER WAS TURNING AS the intense heat of the central Texas summer gave way to cooling September showers. Giddings, Texas, lies fifty-six miles east of Austin and, like most small rural Texas townships today, felt run down and tired. Despite its appearance, the town was reasonably vibrant, helped by a prime location on Route 290 linking Austin to Houston. Town center businesses eked out a meager living from the occasional traveler who stopped en route and from the farmers and ranch owners who came into town to get supplies and meet at Stan's Diner to discuss the latest beef prices.

The First Baptist Church was the oldest in Giddings. The first church building was raised in 1872, and during the oil boom of the late 1970s funds were made available to build the current church with its magnificent stained glass windows that captured the rays of the sun and bathed the pews in all the colors of the rainbow.

So it was for the funeral of Jack Johnson, who was born and raised in Giddings. The church was full and overflowing, bathed in glorious sunlight as Jack's coffin, draped in the Texas flag, lay below the cross.

Pastor Tim Richards opened the service with the Lord's Prayer and then stepped aside as several senior dignitaries spoke of the life of Jack Johnson, the early passing of his wife and the years of dedicated service he had given to the citizens of Travis County.

At the end of the service, six pallbearers carried the coffin out to the waiting hearse. Jack Johnson's two brothers and his best friend, Harold Gunderson, had asked Tommy, Marie, and Bill Ross to be the other pallbearers and to help carry the coffin to its final resting place. This honor was overwhelming for them, particularly for Marie, as men typically performed this duty.

As they emerged from the church, rays of warm sunshine caressed the casket, as if the Lord himself was reaching down from Heaven to welcome Jack home.

The attendees numbered in the thousands. Citizens of Giddings, citizens of Travis County and officers from every law enforcement agency lined the route to salute their fallen comrade. As the cortege passed by, hats were removed and held over their hearts. An observer of this mark of respect never failed to be touched by the slow synchronization of this common custom like a silent musical movement, an adagio flowing through the crowd.

At the corner of Austin and Main Street, a solitary Marine Corps officer stood in their midst. His dress blues were immaculate and he displayed the ribbons of his past sacrifices on behalf of his country. Harry DeWalt saluted as the cortege passed, a tear rolling down his cheek.

Jack's body was laid to rest in the family plot in the Giddings Cemetery as a lone piper played "Amazing Grace."

~

After the service, the three of them rode together in Tommy's car back to the Travis County HQ. When they arrived, Chief Dunwoody asked that they join him in his office.

"I know the last few months have been rough on all of you, but the reality is this: we need to move on," said Bill Dunwoody. "We need to continue to serve the citizens of Travis County in the best way we know how. We owe it to Jack Johnson and the others before him who have fallen in the line of duty in the service of this community."

As everyone sighed and nodded, Bill Dunwoody continued. "I have given this a lot of thought and I have reached a decision. I would like Tommy to become the new leader of the cold case unit, with Marie as his second in command. I also approved your continued engagement as a Special Reserve Officer, Bill, if you want to do that. Without your insight and experience, we may have never gotten the breakthrough needed to bring this case to closure and to return Galina Alkaev to her home."

"It would be my honor to continue, Chief," responded Bill.

Tommy and Marie hugged each other and Marie drew him a look that said, "Don't get any ideas, buddy!"

"Congratulations, son," said Bill as he gave Tommy a hug. "And congratulations to you, Marie. I have never in my life served with a better police officer and certainly not a braver one."

Bill gave her a hug and Marie kissed him on the cheek. "Thank you, Bill. I know that I'll continue to learn a lot from you and I look forward to doing just that as we bring down the baddies!"

The three of them left and headed home

Chapter 50 - Reflection

2014 - The Cold Case Investigation

WHEN MARIE WALKED INTO HER townhome in the Westlake Hills suburb of northwest Austin, the smell of sautéed pancetta, onions and mushrooms greeted her. She loved the aromas of Shelly's cooking, particularly when she was making spaghetti carabonara. It was Marie's favorite dish in the world, and washing it down with a couple of glasses of Chianti instantly took Marie to her happy place.

"Hi, honey, how was the funeral? Dinner will be ready in about twenty minutes. I've opened a bottle of Barolo since we appear to be out of Chianti. Can I pour you a glass?" said Shelly as she grabbed the bottle of wine and sat down on the sofa in their family room.

"That would be great, Shell. I've got some news to share. Let me get my sweats on and I'll be right there."

A few minutes later, Marie, wearing her favorite sweats and a "Keep Austin Weird" tee shirt, flopped down on the sofa, kissed her partner and grabbed the waiting glass of Barolo. She closed her eyes briefly as she stretched back on the couch and allowed the wine to have the desired effect.

"God, Shell, it was so emotional. There must have been a couple thousand people there. The streets were lined as the hearse took Jack's casket through the center of town and out to the cemetery."

"Sorry you had to go through that, honey. You know I would have been there with you if I could have but I had a deposition. So what's the news?" said Shelly.

"Tommy has been asked to take over from Jack to head up the cold case unit. I have been given the role as his deputy. Tommy will be promoted to detective sergeant and I'll get a pay increase for being his right-hand gal."

"Woo hoo! Congratulations, Marie!" But as Shelly went to give her life partner a huge hug and a kiss, Shelly could see that Marie was upset. "What is it, Marie, what's wrong?"

"Shell, you know I love Tommy, but I should have been the one to lead the unit," sobbed Marie.

Shelly put her arms around her and hugged her close.

"Look, we've been through a lot together and we'll get through this. You've fought hard to get where you are in the department and you're known as one of the best detectives in Travis County. We know it's still a man's world."

They hugged again and then Marie started crying uncontrollably. She let it all out. The department, Jack, Luther's gun to her temple, every stress from the Luther Fisher case poured out of her.

"I know I shouldn't feel this way, Shell. I really feel happy for Tommy," sobbed Marie. "I'll give everything to the job to make sure that he succeeds and that we as a team succeed. But right now, I'm just feeling sorry for myself. Where's that bottle of wine?"

Marie hugged Shelly and they finished the wine. Marie felt a lot better after that.

~

Tommy was late getting to daycare to pick up Claire. She was sitting waiting in the lobby with Miss Sydney. Miss Sydney loved Claire and she would make sure each day that Claire was ready for Daddy to pick her up after his long day fighting the baddies.

"I love you!" he whispered in Claire's ear as he swept her up in his arms and gave her a huge hug.

"I love you too, Daddy! Can we get French fries on the way home?" No matter how much she missed her daddy, French fries and chicken nuggets could always cheer up Claire.

As they drove through the Austin traffic on their way home to Cedar Park, Claire was secure in her car seat and munching on her fries.

"Guess what we're going to do this weekend, my love?" said Tommy.

"What, Daddy? What are we going to do?"

"You know that big church we pass on our way home every day, the one with the big colored window on the front that you like? We're going to visit that church this weekend, go inside and see all the people," said Tommy, watching in the rearview mirror for Claire's reaction.

"Can we go for ice cream after we go to church, Daddy?"

"Yes, we can go for ice cream and it's going to be fun. Like a big new adventure!"

Tommy wasn't sure if he was saying this for Claire's benefit or for his own.

~

Bill Ross had a stomach full of mixed emotions as he drove home. He was very happy for Tommy and would do everything he could to help him succeed in his new role as head of the cold case team. He also thought about Marie.

Marie was almost ten years older than Tommy, in her late forties, and had been a detective for over ten years. Yet, they had chosen Tommy to lead the unit rather than Marie. He knew that she would be hurt but also knew that she would support Tommy in every way she could. Bill loved Marie as much as Tommy did.

"Hi, honey, I'm home!" said Bill, the words straight from the '90s TV sitcom.

"How was Jack's funeral?" asked Elaine as she laid the table for supper.

"It was spectacular! Yes, that's the only word to describe it, Elaine. There was nothing ever like this back home. Sure, I've attended elaborate funerals for very senior officers in Glasgow and London but Texans hold their law enforcement officers in such high regard. There were well over a thousand people there and the respect that they showed as the coffin passed sent shivers up my spine."

As Elaine smiled and sat down at the table, Bill announced, "And one more thing. Tommy is taking over from Jack. He is being promoted to detective sergeant."

"Oh, that is such great news, Bill. I'm so proud of him, he's worked so hard!" said Elaine.

"I agree but I also hope that Marie is okay with it. Marie has worked hard as well and she has many more years' experience than Tommy. I've been asked to carry on in my role and I'll do everything I can to help both of them." Bill sat down at the table to enjoy the pork tenderloin that Elaine had prepared for their supper.

After supper, Bill took himself off to his office. He sat down in his favorite leather chair, stared at the ceiling for a few minutes and then closed his eyes. He thought of Jack and offered a silent prayer.

"Thanks for everything, Jack. You gave me a new lease on life when you handed me the job in the department. I hope all is well in heaven. If there are fences needing mending up there, you'll be just the man for the job!"

Bill reached for his laptop and accessed his iTunes account on the cloud. He had a collection of over five thousand songs that he had downloaded from the web and uploaded from his library of CDs that were now stored in boxes in the garage.

He refilled his Edinburgh crystal glass with Glenmorangie, put on his headphones and chose a playlist. "Something smooth tonight," mumbled Bill.

Percy Sledge was first up with "When a Man Loves a Woman" and Rod Stewart with "Mandolin Wind" followed that. It was track three when the dam burst. Eric Clapton's "Tears in Heaven."

Eric Clapton had written the song after the death of his baby son and the words seemed appropriate that night.

Would you know my name?
If I saw you in Heaven
Would it be the same?
If I saw you in Heaven
I must be strong
And carry on
'Cause I know I don't belong
Here in Heaven

The tears rolled down his cheeks as he thought of Jack. He made a commitment right there and then that he would honor the memory of his dead friend and colleague by serving the good people of Travis County the only way he knew how. He would bring all his years of experience to bear in helping Tommy and Marie succeed in their new responsibilities. Together, the Three Musketeers would bring the baddies to justice.

He was just nodding off when Elaine demonstrated her immaculate timing honed over years of practice. She grabbed the Edinburgh crystal glass out of Bill's hand just as his fingers relaxed and the glass was about to fall and smash on the tile floor.

She turned off the laptop, gently removed the headphones from Bill's head and tucked his Kilmarnock FC blanket around him. It was Friday night in Texas and already Saturday in Scotland; the football games kicked off at 3 p.m. local time.

"Hope Killie wins tomorrow!" whispered Elaine as she kissed her husband and turned out the light.

A brief extract from *What's left is right,* the next book in the *Detective Bill Ross Crime Series,* planned for publication Christmas 2015. Sign up for updates at www.irvingmunro.com

What's left is right.

RAUL HERNANDEZ WALKED ACROSS THE parking lot adjacent to the Gold's Gym on Lamar Blvd in Austin, feeling exhausted. It had been a ninety-minute workout on the treadmill and then another twenty on the weights. This was his normal routine at least twice a week. He also ran twenty miles on the weekend. For a forty-two-year-old, he was in great shape, and he meant it to stay that way.

He had just pressed the remote for the BMW when they hit him from behind, and everything went black. When he came to, he realized that he was tied up, a hood over his head and in the trunk of a car.

I guess this is it! I missed them in the parking lot. How did I miss them?

It was stifling hot, the smell of gasoline was overpowering, and his sweat was soaking the sackcloth of the hood. His military training had taught him not to panic in these types of situations. He was not in any great pain, but he knew that he had been knocked unconscious. His weapons were in the BMW. He never took them into the gym; they must have known that.

He guessed it must have been an hour or so later when the car stopped and the trunk was opened. They hauled him out of the vehicle and dragged him across a dirt track and yanked the hood off. There were about a dozen of them, and several trucks and cars were parked off to the side of the road. They were all dressed the same, all in white and their hoods were immediately recognizable—the Klan!

"A bit elaborate, boys; if you're going to kill me just do it, but why don't you untie me and let's have a little rock and roll first, or are you not up for that?"

"Who the fuck do you think you are talking to us like that, you piece of shit!"

He recognized the accent. It was the Honduran with the scar. "You come over the border to take our jobs, we round you up and send you back. And what do you know, you're right back where we found you! Well, no more; this will be a lesson to all of your kind!"

Raul quickly processed what he had just heard. *So this was what the Honduran had told this bunch. That he was muscling in on their turf and going to steal their jobs!*

"I'm not here to steal your fucking jobs. And I'm not Mexican and not illegal. This lying Honduran has told you a pack of lies! Do I sound like a fucking Mexican?"

He could see Rodriguez off to the side, standing by his limo, watching all of this go down. *Just untie my hands, you fuckers,* he thought. *And if you do, before I eventually go down I'm going to rip your head off, Rodriguez.*

He thought the guy behind him was untying the rope around his wrists, but, in fact, he was securing a second rope. The engine of one of the trucks to his right roared to life, and as he was yanked off his feet, he felt his shoulder joints snap. The pain was excruciating as he was dragged across the gravel road, and the truck gained speed. His head slammed into a rock, and the pain was gone.

Raul Hernandez died there that cold evening in Texas.

He had tried to explain to his killers that he was not Mexican. In fact, his name wasn't even Raul Hernandez. But as the roar of engines faded into the distance, it didn't matter. Those who had taken his life wouldn't have cared about the details anyway.

CPSIA information can be obtained
at www.ICGtesting.com
Printed in the USA
LVHW081546040319
609417LV00045B/1573/P